MARGARET THOMSON
DAVIS

CLYDESIDERS
AT WAR

B&W PUBLISHING

First published 2002
by B&W Publishing Ltd
Edinburgh

ISBN 190326510X

Cover illustration:
Aletha Harcourt, Ambulance Driver, 1942
by George Harcourt.
Photograph courtesy of
The Imperial War Museum

Printed by Omnia Books Ltd, Bishopbriggs

1939

I

The only thing that hinted at what an ordeal it must be for Wincey was the way she kept nervously tucking her hair behind one ear. Dark, ruby red hair, it was. Her fringe seemed longer too, as if she was trying to hide behind it, yet her steady, determined stare was still the same.

She was sitting in the Gourlay kitchen. The table was pale and grooved by the many scrubbings Teresa Gourlay had given it over the years. Around it sat Teresa and Erchie, and their daughters, Florence—a slim girl with large dark eyes and a proud tilt to her head, and the plump, round faced twins, Euphemia and Bridget. Granny sat in her wheelchair at one side of the fire, her short grey hair fastened with a large kirby grip, her fawn crocheted shawl clutched round her shoulders. Doctor Robert Houston sat at the other side of the fire.

The oppressive silence was only broken by the sparking of the fire in the old fashioned, black grate.

Then Florence said, 'You're kidding! You must be.'

Wincey shook her head.

'But you said . . . I mean, that first time when I found you,

3

you said you were an orphan. Your mother and father had been killed and you had nobody else and you were going to be shut away in an institution.'

'No, Florence, *you* said that. You always had a very dramatic imagination.'

Wincey remembered every detail of the night Florence had found her and every word that had been said. 'So you're an orphan?' Florence had said.

Wincey had nodded.

'So you've run away so they won't put you into an orphanage, or into the workhouse?'

Forgetting her tears, Wincey had stared curiously at the girl. She managed to nod again.

'Och, never mind,' Florence had said. 'My Mammy'll take you in. She's always taking folk in.'

'Is she?' Wincey said in surprise.

'Och, aye, our place is like a doss house sometimes. Girls come down from the Highlands and stay at our place for a few days until they get fixed up with a nurse's job at one of the hospitals. My Mammy used to come from the Highlands. Come on.'

'Well, you didn't contradict me,' Florence said now. 'Did you?'

'I was just a wee girl and I was frightened. I thought I'd murdered my grandfather and everybody would be after me, including the police. I just wanted to hide away somewhere where I could feel safe. And you were so kind to me. I know this must be a shock for all of you, and I'm sorry, but I just couldn't tell you before.'

'Why couldn't you?' one of the twins asked. 'You've had plenty of time. You've lived with us for donkey's years. You owed it to us. You've taken our name. Our Mammy and Daddy have been your mammy and daddy. We've been like sisters.'

'I know, I'm sorry.'

Granny piped up then, 'Ah always knew she wis different

4

frae us. A bloody capitalist. We were quite content wi' oursels wi' oor Charlotte an' Teresa workin' one sewin' machine in that wee hoose in Springburn Road. Then, before we know whit had happened, she had Erchie fixin' up machines frae aw ower the place. Then it was that auld warehouse made into a factory—an' then we'd moved hoose a couple o' times.'

'Now, now, Granny. You know fine it wasn't just Wincey, it was Charlotte as well.' Teresa's eyes darkened with sadness at the thought of her eldest daughter, who'd died so tragically in a road accident. 'And this is a much better place than the wee house in Springburn Road. Think of our nice bathroom now, instead of the lavatory out on the landing. And it's been Wincey who's been paying for these two nurses to come in every day to see you.'

'Aye, well,' Granny muttered.

'I wanted to tell you,' Wincey said. 'I longed to tell somebody, but I felt so guilty and frightened. If it hadn't been for Robert, I expect I'd have taken the secret to my grave.' She glanced at Robert Houston who had taken over as family doctor after his father had died. He smiled his encouragement. But Wincey noticed that, as usual, his smile was not reflected in his eyes. He had very serious eyes.

'Robert persuaded me to write to my real parents and tell them everything, and also to confess to you. He gave me the courage. But please don't think I'm not grateful to all of you. I have felt that you, Teresa, have been more of a mother to me all these years than my real mother. And Erchie, you've been more of a father than my real father. And Florence and Bridget and Euphemia have been my only sisters.'

Erchie jerked the peak of his cap, or 'bunnet' as he called it, further down over his brow. He always wore a bunnet outdoors and indoors because he was bald and said he felt the cold in his head something terrible. He always wore his boots indoors too. Teresa, who had given him a nice pair of checked slippers for his birthday, had been forced to wear them herself.

'Well, hen, as ah've often said, ye've aye been like ma ain

flesh an' blood. Ah knew somethin' was worryin' ye, right enough. That was why me an' Teresa decided eventually to ask Doctor Houston's advice.'

'I'm glad you did now, though God knows what'll happen next. They'll get the letter tomorrow. It took me weeks to get it right but in the end, I just told the truth. I put it in the post earlier today.'

'It'll be a terrible shock to them after thinking you've been dead all these years.' Teresa's gentle face creased with worry.

'They'll probably wish I was after reading my letter. They'll maybe want nothing to do with me. They never actually had much to do with me when I lived with them.'

'You were only—what—twelve or thirteen when you came here,' Teresa continued, 'Now I can understand why you never told us your full name, and would hardly ever put your foot outside the close. But your parents must have been distracted with worry and grief, thinking their wee girl had been drowned in the Clyde. They'll surely be overjoyed to have you back.'

'That's what I keep telling her,' said Houston. 'I've had one hell of a job trying to make her see sense. She's about as difficult and thrawn as Granny here.'

'Well, wan thing's for sure—that auld rascal deserved tae die,' Granny said. 'An' if ah had the chance, ah'd huv murdered him masel. Him an' his munitions factory. He wisnae content in causin' the death o' folk in his slums, he had tae find a way tae kill a lot mair.'

Houston groaned. 'Wincey did *not* murder her grandfather.'

'She's just telt us she did. She's just telt us that wis the reason she was feart tae go back tae her real mammy an' daddy.'

'He died of a heart attack. He had a heart condition. He had been abusing her for years and she was in a state of shock. That was why she didn't run and get his heart tablets. I keep telling her. But it's quite common, unfortunately, for the victim in this sort of case to feel everything's their fault. It never is, but it's always a devil of a job to get them to believe that.'

Wincey detected the glint of impatience in his eyes. She had seen it before and knew that it wasn't caused only by her guilt. The hatred of her grandfather and the bitterness she felt towards her family were going to cause her to lose him.

Theirs was a strange, uneasy sort of relationship. She knew she loved him, but he insisted that she could not truly love anyone else until she could love herself. And also forgive her family, including her grandfather.

She'd been trying to follow his advice. According to Houston, writing the letter to her parents had been an enormous step in the right direction. But she felt far from sure, remembering how isolated she had always been as a child.

Her father was Nicholas Cartwright, the famous poet and novelist. Wincey remembered how he was usually shut away in his paper cluttered, book lined, writing room. And when he wasn't immersed in his writing, he was either in the downstairs sitting room or the upstairs drawing room talking with friends. Her mother, Virginia's interests were political. Her first husband, James Matheson, had been a disciple of the celebrated Red Clydesider and pacifist, John Maclean. Matheson had long since been crippled by a stroke and hirpled about with the help of sticks. He had a grotesquely twisted face and, as a young child, Wincey had been rather afraid of him. He had also become friends with her father, and he and his political friends regularly filled the tall, terraced house, with lively discussion and heated debate.

Her older brother, Richard, sometimes took part in these verbal confrontations but as often as not, he was out playing cricket or rugby, or getting into some sort of mischief. However, in the eyes of the family, he could do no wrong. Tall, dark and handsome like his father, he had, as Matheson said, 'the gift of the gab'. He could have been a politician but they all knew that if he had gone into politics, it would have been as a true blue Conservative, like his grandparents. He never made any secret of the fact that he had no truck with his parents' radical views, or with Matheson's fervent socialism.

Wincey had always felt like she was the cuckoo in the nest. She hadn't her father's glossy black hair and dark eyes, nor had she her mother's long golden hair. A shy child with red hair and freckles, she couldn't match her brother Richard's extrovert and daring personality. Always hovering on the fringes of life in Kirklee Terrace, she felt ignored and neglected. More often than not, she was sent out with a dismissive, 'Go and keep your grandfather company, there's a good girl.'

Her grandparents lived in a big grey villa on Great Western Road, not far from Kirklee Terrace. Her grandmother regularly went out to her bridge club and also the church Women's Guild. Her grandfather couldn't get out and about because of his heart condition and so she was often left alone with him to 'keep him company'. Much too often, she realised now.

Richard was her grandmother's favourite—he was everyone's favourite really. She was supposed to be her grandfather's. She didn't realise the truth at first. She felt confused and sick and miserable. She didn't understand what was going on, or why.

A wave of rage swept over her as she sat at the table in the tenement kitchen, with its recessed, cream curtained bed. Opposite was the window with the sink underneath, or jaw box as it was called. The view outside was of the back yard, with its midden and wash house. This kitchen, this house, was the only real home she had ever known. The Gourlays had come to mean so much more to her than her 'real' family. How much better they had treated her than the wealthy Cartwrights ever had! For years she had been known as one of the Gourlay girls, and that's how she wanted it to stay.

'What saddens me,' Teresa's voice broke into Wincey's thoughts, 'is the idea of us losing you.'

'You won't be losing me,' Wincey protested. 'Nothing will change as far as I'm concerned. I've been a Gourlay for years, and I'll always be a Gourlay.'

'Wincey,' Houston groaned, 'you'll have to accept that your whole life will change. For a start your parents will want you to go and live with them.'

'My home is here with Teresa and Erchie and Granny.'

Florence rolled her eyes. 'I don't get this. Why would you want to go on living in a tenement flat in Springburn when you could live in a big posh house in the West End?' Florence, like the twins, had not long been married and she was especially proud of her new flat in Clydebank. She had acquired airs and graces since working in Copeland & Lye's in Sauchiehall Street.

Wincey knew that snobbish Grandmother Cartwright would have described Florence as having 'ideas above her station'. Grandmother Cartwright had never forgiven Wincey's mother—her former scullery maid—for having such ideas, and—much worse—for eventually marrying her son. Or, as she put it, 'trapping him into marriage'. Virginia had been pregnant with Richard, but in 1914, war had intervened and it wasn't until Richard was six that the marriage finally took place. Mrs Cartwright had taken the child away from Virginia at birth because she had been wrongly informed that her son had been killed in action in the trenches. She believed that the baby was all she had left of him. She hated Virginia for taking her grandson back after Nicholas had been found in a military hospital, and reunited with Virginia.

To keep in touch with young Richard was the main reason she visited the house in Kirklee Terrace, and was at least frostily polite to her daughter in law.

'I've been happy here,' Wincey insisted. 'I was never happy in Kirklee Terrace.'

'Things will be different now,' Houston said.

'Yes, worse!'

Houston rolled his eyes. 'Will you stop being so pessimistic.'

'Well,' Erchie said, 'at least you didnae turn up on her doorstep without a word o' warnin'. Yer mammy would probably huv died o' shock.'

'Of aw the families in Glasgow,' Granny shook her head, 'she had tae come frae that bloody lot.'

'Granny,' Teresa said, 'watch your language. Wincey didn't choose her family.' With a meaningful look at the old woman, she added, 'Whether we like it or not, we've all to make do with what we've got.'

Wincey smiled. 'I didn't choose the Cartwrights, right enough, but I did choose the Gourlays, and I still do.'

'Well, that's nice o' ye, hen,' Erchie gave her hand a pat, 'but ye cannae ignore yer ain flesh an' blood. An' after aw, it wisnae yer mammy an' daddy that hurt ye. It was yer auld villain o' a grandfather. Everybody hated him. Good riddance tae him, that's what ah say, but yer mammy an' daddy huvnae done anybody any harm. Quite the opposite, hen. Ah've read some o' yer daddy's books. An' yer mammy's been active at many a socialist meetin'. Ah've even been tae a meetin' that she spoke at, along wi' that friend o' Johnny Maclean, James Matheson.'

'Yes, he was my mother's first husband. My mother knew Maclean as well. I vaguely remember him. I was very young, but I even have a memory of being at his funeral. I remember my father carrying me on his shoulders. I was a bit frightened to see such a big crowd.'

'Fancy! Ah wis there as well,' Erchie cried out. 'Whit a turn out, wisn't it. Over ten thousand crowdin' the streets. Aye, James Matheson, that wis his pal's name. He went tae jail along wi' oor Johnny. Mair than once. It wis what Johnny suffered in jail that killed him in the end. Ah bet it wis the same thing that nearly killed Matheson. It wis a miracle he survived that stroke.'

Granny spoke up then. 'An' a man like him friendly wi' yer daddy? Whit's the world comin' tae?'

'Now, now, Granny,' Teresa said. 'It's a very civilised way to behave. What good would it do him to be bitter against his ex-wife's new husband?'

'Naebody got divorced an' had auld an' new husbands in ma day. They've nae sense o' shame nowadays.'

'Anyway,' Teresa smiled at Wincey, but her eyes remained dark pools of anxiety, 'if your mother and father arrive here tomorrow, or any day, they'll be made welcome. And . . . ' she hesitated, then continued with some difficulty, 'and if you leave with them, we'll understand.'

Houston said, 'You'd better stay off work tomorrow, Wincey, to be here when they arrive. As I'm sure they will.'

Wincey nodded, tucking her hair behind her ear and seeming to shrink beneath her fringe. She wanted to say that she wished she had never agreed to write that damned letter. No good would come of it, she was sure of that.

2

Virginia was on her way to do early shift in the Royal Infirmary, dressed in her Red Cross uniform of navy blue skirt and jacket, white shirt and peaked cap. She'd managed to get her Red Cross certificate, but was finding the experience in the Royal like being thrown to the sharks. The Outpatients Emergency department was especially fraught. At weekends it was like a battlefield, peopled mostly by wounded drunks with a lot of aggression to get rid of. There were other, more distressing cases of women who had been beaten by drunken husbands. Some of them were half dead, with broken bones and unrecognisable, bloody faces. It made Virginia sick, but at the same time she counted herself lucky that neither of her two husbands had ever physically abused her.

Her first husband, James Matheson, had been—and still was—obsessed with politics. His obsession had developed to such a degree that, although she'd tried her best to help him, most of the time he was hardly aware of her existence. They got on a lot better now as friends than they'd ever done as man and wife.

She'd repeated the pattern by marrying Nicholas Cartwright. Writing was his obsession. There had been a time when she'd hated Nicholas for isolating her, shutting her off from his life, leaving her to grieve alone for Wincey and to face the terrible trauma of not knowing what had happened to her. There was the awful guilt too. Round and round in her mind went the terrible question: had she and Nicholas neglected the child? They hadn't meant to, but the house had always been filled with either her friends or Nicholas's friends. Perhaps they had not always been as attentive to Wincey as they might have been. But she'd always been a difficult child, so quiet and shy. Richard had been a complete contrast to his sister—outgoing, full of energy, always wanting to join in with everything. Secretly, Virginia knew that all their love and attention had been lavished on Richard—and what had that done to Wincey?

Virginia's heart contracted in pain. How could they have been so thoughtless and insensitive? She had asked herself and Nicholas that question a thousand or more times over the years. It was easier for him. He could—and always did—escape into the seclusion of his writing room.

She'd challenged him about this eventually and they'd talked things out as much as they were able. Life had become more bearable after that, although secret little pinpricks of resentment still bothered her. Making love had helped. Nicholas had always been a very passionate man. All right, a great deal of his passion went into his writing, but he could still make love with great enthusiasm and virility.

Virginia also tried to get on with her life by joining the Red Cross and becoming a VAD nurse. To some degree she had Matheson to thank for that. He had lectured her on how she was allowing guilt, bitterness and hatred to ruin her life. He said taking her feelings out on Nicholas was helping nobody. Nicholas had suffered and grieved over Wincey's disappearance too. He'd done all he could. What more did she expect him to do? Matheson always seemed to be making allowances for Nicholas. But perhaps that was only natural—they'd been friends ever since he'd been in hospital unable to talk, and hardly able to move after his stroke. When Nicholas returned to Glasgow, he had gone to visit Matheson every day. He read the newspapers to him, and spoke to him about how he too had been hospitalised, with his memory gone, after being blown up in the trenches during the war.

Virginia had been shocked at Nicholas visiting Matheson. She had lied to Nicholas, who was her lover then, about her marriage to Matheson being over. She feared what would happen if and when Matheson recovered, imagining him trying to kill Nicholas. But instead the two men had become firm friends in that hospital. She supposed that Matheson had been grateful for Nicholas's conscientious attempts to help him. Admittedly, she'd not been much use. She'd even stopped going to the hospital, unable to look at Matheson in the dreadful state he was in, believing that he wasn't able to even recognise her, far less understand anything she said to him. Obviously she'd been wrong in this.

It turned out Matheson was perfectly able to understand every word, and he'd got to know Nicholas, it seemed, far better than she'd ever known him.

Matheson told her it was time she stopped feeling sorry for herself and started thinking of someone else for a change. And the best way to do that was to help other people with their problems. So she'd turned to nursing in the huge, soot blackened Royal Infirmary.

Now, despite the difficulties of the blackout, she was managing to make her way to the bus stop. The blackout order had gone out earlier that summer, before war had even been declared. As the threat posed by enemy bombers became a reality, all external lights and street lighting had to be totally extinguished. No lighting in houses was to be visible from the outside. Advice had been given about using close fitting blinds and curtains of dark cloth. Skylights, glass doors and fan lights had to have sufficient coats of dark distemper or paint. Roads were completely unlit and private vehicles had no lights. Travelling by public transport meant moving about in your own dimly lit world. Train compartments were now filled with the ghostly glow of a single blue bulb. Windows were painted out, except for a small circle. Even if you raised the blind and peered out through this circle, you couldn't read the station's name because it had been painted over.

Already, only weeks into the war, there had been a three hundred percent increase in fatalities in Glasgow due to road accidents. Virginia felt safer walking and then catching a bus. At least pedestrians were now allowed to carry torches, providing they were covered with a double layer of tissue paper. But it was becoming increasingly difficult to get hold of number eight batteries.

She was kept busy in the Royal every day of the week with casualties who'd fallen down steps, off railway platforms, had bumped into lamp posts and walls, or stepped into canals or rivers. It was even more dangerous trying to drive a vehicle in the pitch blackness.

Virginia certainly hadn't the nerve to drive her car. Now, as she slowly shuffled forward, she felt alone in the darkness that mirrored the black hopelessness inside her. Her hand edged along walls and railings, and slid across the icy glass of shop windows. Once at the bus stop, despite the regulation that told civilians not to wave torches at the bus driver, she felt it necessary to make the driver see her and stop. On the bus, she sat lost in thought as the vehicle crawled along through the gloom.

Matheson had been very supportive about her nursing. As long as she had nothing to do with the war effort, he was satisfied. He was a pacifist, as well as a socialist—her mother in law insisted that he was 'an out and out communist'. Maybe she was right. He had certainly remained steadfast in his beliefs, like his mentor, John Maclean, before him.

'I'd rather die in prison than have anything to do with this war,' he insisted.

She knew this to be true. He had nearly died in prison

during the 1914-18 war, but her feelings on the subject had never been as extreme as his. Her position was between that of Matheson and Nicholas. Although she regarded herself as a pacifist, she saw no reason for refusing to take a nurse's post—in the forces, if necessary. She had also volunteered to be an ambulance driver, and Matheson had no objections to her becoming involved in a humanitarian service that was now more vital than ever. It was something that many Quakers did. They were well known as pacifists, but that didn't stop them organising a 'Friends Ambulance Service'.

Nicholas, however, was all things to all men. She blamed his writing for this. He was always so obsessed with understanding other people's point of view and motivation, 'what makes them tick,' as he said. He was proud of the fact that their son Richard had become a fighter pilot in the RAF. On his desk there was a photograph of Richard standing proudly beside his gleaming new Spitfire. Her own heart melted every time she looked at the photograph. He was very like his father—tall and handsome with his black hair ruffled in the breeze and the sheepskin collar of his leather flying jacket turned up. He had his father's dark eyes and winning smile. No doubt he'd already broken a few hearts.

She loved her son as much—perhaps more—than his father did. For that reason alone, she wished he'd never joined the RAF. She lived in constant fear now of him being shot down and killed. She couldn't understand Nicholas's attitude. He seemed so proud and happy when he spoke of Richard in the RAF. She had always hated war, and she hated it all the more now. The last war had robbed so many mothers of their sons. The flower of British manhood had been thrown away in a brutal, pointless struggle over a few pitiful miles of French and Flemish wasteland. A land fit for heroes was what they had been promised, but many of the survivors who had returned were nervous wrecks, suffering from shell shock. Thousands of others came back badly wounded, mutilated or enduring the terrible after effects of poison gas. And all they got in the land they'd fought for and returned to were homelessness and unemployment.

Now, hardly twenty years later, there was another war to suffer. A war that would no doubt consume another generation of young men. Men like Richard.

'But this time it's different,' Nicholas insisted.

'Why is it different?' she'd wanted to know.

His tall, regal looking and infuriatingly snobbish mother had been there at the time. Mrs Cartwright had always been a regular and very active churchgoer, sailing to the church every Sunday morning in her musquash coat, or fox furs and an old fashioned cloche type hat. She had been president of the Women's Guild and God knows what all else in the church. It was enough to make anyone an atheist, Virginia thought bitterly.

'Do you not even know what that dreadful little house painter once said?' Mrs Cartwright peered through her lorgnettes at her daughter in law in disgust. ' "One is either a German or a Christian. You cannot be both." That is all he was, you know. An ordinary house painter.' She repeated the words in disgust. 'A house painter'. 'This has always been the danger. My late husband always maintained—give the workers an inch and they'll take a mile. Oh, how right he was!'

She glared at Virginia as if accusing her of proving the point. Virginia did not rise to the bait although she fumed in secret. She could remember a time when she would have argued with Mrs Cartwright. Now she didn't see the point. Her mother in law was too old and too set in her ways. No good would come of arguing with her. All it did was to turn Nicholas against her.

'She's an elderly lady and she's grieving for her husband. For goodness sake, Virginia, try to have a bit of patience and understanding.'

So now, for the most part, Virginia kept silent or tried to avoid Mrs Cartwright altogether. But it was very difficult trying to maintain this pretence of civility. The woman was such a snob, and she never missed a chance of running down the working class, or of reminding her daughter in law of her lowly origins and how she could never be 'one of them', meaning the upper class. All of which infuriated Virginia, who remembered only too vividly the suffering endured by her hard working mother, father, and brothers. Her mother and father were worth ten of Mr and Mrs Cartwright, and there was no comparison between her brothers and some of the wealthy chinless wonders who used to visit the Cartwright house.

Nicholas said, 'We tried our best for peace. We had to do something about Poland.'

'We?'

'Don't quibble, Virginia. You know perfectly well what I mean.'

Mrs Cartwright drew herself up, back stiff, bosom held high. 'Nicholas and I are proud of Richard fighting for his country, even if you are not.'

As far as Virginia knew, Richard had not as yet been involved in any fighting. She prayed every night that this situation would continue. It seemed as if nothing much had happened since war had been declared. To many people it had been a bit of an anti-climax, and some people were beginning to call it the 'phoney war'. Anxiety and expectation of the worst had been at fever pitch at first. Everyone had been issued with gas masks, Anderson shelters had been dug in almost every back garden, and brick shelters had sprung up in tenement back yards. New walls—known as baffle walls— had been erected in front of the shelter entrances and on pavements in front of closes. These brick walls were supposed to save lives by lessening the effects of blast, but already hospital emergency departments were inundated with cases of people having run or walked into them in the blackout. Virginia had seen some horrific facial injuries that had been caused in this way.

At least Mrs Cartwright was against Hitler, although for the wrong reasons in Virginia's opinion. However, at least up until the declaration of war, many aristocrats had been openly sympathetic to the Nazis. She remembered not so long ago at a dinner party she had been to with Nicholas, a woman at the table had said, 'Personally I like the Germans and I admire their leader. They are the best organised people in Europe.'

Nicholas ignored the remark but Virginia had said icily, 'Well, I certainly don't admire Hitler.'

Sir Oswald Mosley and his blackshirts were still marching in the streets of Britain, although not in Glasgow. He'd visited Glasgow Green and had to make a quick exit in his van with a howling mob of Glaswegians chasing him. Mosley's Fascists preached simplistic philosophies and easy answers. They just blamed the Jews for everything—from mass poverty to the war itself, but according to Matheson, there were other people in Britain who were far more helpful to Hitler than Mosley. There were at least nine other organisations supporting Hitler, Matheson said. One of these organisations had over four thousand members. They included two dukes and the chairman of Morris Motors. Another of the organisations, the Anglo-German Fellowship, boasted that its membership included sixteen peers, the governor and a director of the Bank of England, the chairman of ICI and the chief political advisor to the Foreign Office.

'They're all hoping Hitler's Storm-troopers will be a buffer between them and a communist revolution. Their greatest fear is something like the Russian Revolution happening here, and they'll do anything to avoid losing their privileges and their wealth.' It was the sort of thing that made Matheson so furious that Virginia feared he would have another stroke. 'These people don't care about the ordinary working man,' he told her bitterly, 'or woman. Remember how you were treated when you were in service, slaving in some of their houses. And in the munitions work that killed your brother.

They know, as well as I do, that trade unionists are being arrested and jailed by Hitler and his henchmen and they're all for it. They don't care about anything or anybody but their own selfish, greedy . . . '

'I know, I know,' Virginia soothed, 'but you're not going to change anything by making yourself ill. Calm down, for pity's sake.'

He always did calm down but his anger left him trembling. She felt sorry for him. She despaired of the whole complicated mess. But most of all, she worried about her son and the fact that, whatever happened, he and his fellow pilots would soon be in the front line.

3

Florence still couldn't quite take it in. Nor could the twins. While Wineey was saying goodnight to Dr Houston at the front door, they whispered together in the kitchen. 'There she was,' Florence hissed as if she was an actress in a melodrama, 'admiring my new house as if it was a palace. She even said it was like a palace, and all the time she knew her place in the posh West End was ten times the size of my wee house in Clydebank.'

'Now, now,' Teresa said, 'her place was here in Springburn. She still thinks it is. You heard her just now.'

'There was me so proud because my new house had a bathroom,' Florence continued. 'Not like most of my friends who start off with a toilet out on the landing. But I bet she was used to bathrooms en suite. Here,' her eyes became enormous, 'remember how she used to clean that outside toilet when we lived in the room and kitchen. She must be mad. I even thought so at the time.'

'Stop that, Florence. She was always a good, hard working wee girl. I won't have you, or anyone else, saying a word against her.'

Just then Wincey returned to the room. She was clutching her bottle green cardigan around her as if she was freezing. 'I didn't say to Robert, but I honestly wish I'd never sent that letter now. I feel terrible. I won't be able to get a wink of sleep tonight. We were perfectly all right the way we were. I was perfectly all right.'

Erchie shook his head. 'Naw, ye wernae, hen. Ye were awfae awkward wi' men, for a start. Even wi' Robert, an' ye couldnae meet a nicer fella.'

'Well, I suppose . . . But writing that letter isn't going to help that.' She sank onto a chair at the table. 'It's only going to make everything worse. What's my father going to think about what I've said about his father? It doesn't bear thinking about.'

'The chances are he'll wish his father wis still alive so as he could tell him whit an auld bastard he wis. Ah mean, ye were only a wee lassie, hen. It wis terrible whit he did tae ye.'

'The thing that worries me,' Teresa nursed her cup between her hands, 'is you letting your parents think you were dead all this time. I can understand how you felt, of course,' she added hastily. 'You were frightened, dear. Your grandfather dying like that and everything.'

'Well, I just hope they'll understand, but I doubt it.'

'Well never mind, it's not as if you'll have to face them on your own. Granny and Erchie and I will be right there beside you.'

Wincey went over to Teresa and hugged her. 'Oh thank you, Teresa.'

'Goodness me, you're an awful wee girl.' Teresa patted her straight, grey speckled hair and smoothed down her floral apron. 'I'll pour you a fresh cup of tea.'

Florence and the twins cried out, 'Can we stay overnight, Mammy? Then we can be here too.'

Wincey felt a bit overwhelmed but grateful at the same time. She knew she'd feel safer with all the family around her.

She still felt the Gourlays to be her family—far more so than the Cartwrights.

'But what about your man, Florence?' Teresa asked.

'Eddie's coming here after his work.' Eddie worked in Singer's factory and had escaped conscription because of mild epilepsy. Nobody outside of the family knew he had it, and at first the mere idea had frightened Florence, but she'd discovered that he only very occasionally took a 'wee turn' in which he just seemed to lose the place for a few minutes. Then he 'came back' and was all right again. Anyway he was a lovely man with brown curly hair and laughing eyes, and she loved him. They just didn't mention the epilepsy to anyone and he took his pills on the quiet.

The twins' husbands, Joe and Pete, had been conscripted but both had ended up in the Highland Light Infantry in Maryhill Barracks, which they regarded as a right bit of luck. Maryhill wasn't all that far from their homes in Dumbarton Road in Clydebank. Apart from bayonet practice, which meant them charging about thirty yards to plunge fixed bayonets at four foot sacks hanging on a line, they had never been involved in any action. Some men talked about the 'phoney war' and the 'bore war' and were restless for a fight, but Joe and Pete were very content with the way things were. They could see their wives regularly and Euphemia and Bridget were proud to walk along Dumbarton Road arm in arm with their men in their smart new HLI uniforms.

'Oh well, if Eddie's all right about staying . . . ' Teresa turned to the twins. 'What about Joe and Pete?'

Euphemia helped herself to another biscuit. Both she and Bridget enjoyed eating and didn't care how fat they got. The twins never used the word 'fat', they always proudly maintained that they were 'generously moulded'. Florence, on the other hand, was very careful of her figure.

Euphemia said, 'Joe isn't off until the weekend.'

'Pete's the same,' Bridget added, 'so I can stay the night as well.'

Teresa made a fresh pot of tea and put some more digestive biscuits onto a plate.

Granny said, 'This is gonnae be a right circus, if ye ask me.'

'Now, now, Granny, nobody's asking you. Have another digestive and drink your tea.'

Granny's gums chomped over the biscuit. Her arthritis was so bad that these days she couldn't even cope with wearing her teeth. 'Aye well, ah'll soon tell them whit ah think o' the Cartwrights.'

'You'll do no such thing, Granny. You'll be nice and polite to them.'

'Or jist keep yer gob shut, Ma,' Erchie said. 'It's gonnae be hard enough without you stirrin' things up.'

'Nice an' polite tae the Cartwrights?' Granny spluttered biscuit crumbs onto her shawl. 'Johnny Maclean'll be birlin' in his grave at the very idea!'

Florence lit up a cigarette, her eyes dreamy. 'Maybe they'll invite us over to their place. Fancy visiting in the West End! Wait till I tell the other girls about this.' Florence was now in the glove department of Copeland & Lye's. Ladies came in and, with hands stuck up, rested an elbow on the velvet cushion Florence placed on the counter. Then Florence would gently, expertly, smooth down over the hand a beautiful and very expensive leather glove. Maybe Mrs Cartwright senior and junior had been among her ladies.

'Aren't you girls supposed to be at work tomorrow?' Teresa asked as she went over to dust the crumbs off Granny and tidy her kirby grip further into her hair.

'For pity's sake, Mammy,' Florence said, 'I wouldn't be able to do a stroke. I'll get Eddie to phone in and say I'm sick or something.'

'And I'll phone Pettigrews,' Euphemia added. Both she and Bridget worked in the millinery department of Pettigrew & Stephen's in Sauchiehall Street, just along from the equally high class Copeland & Lye's. Florence always insisted that

Copeland's was *the* place, far more high class than Pettigrews, or anywhere else.

'Don't be silly, dear. They won't believe both you and Bridget are sick at the same time.'

Euphemia giggled. 'Yes they will. We're twins. We're supposed to do everything together.'

'That's right,' Bridget agreed. She looked exactly like her sister, they both had the same chubby faces, brown hair tucked behind their ears in a bunch of curls held firmly in place with kirby grips. A smaller, shorter but equally tight bunch of curls decorated each forehead, and they both had mouths slashed with the same scarlet lipstick.

'A right circus,' Granny repeated, stretching a shaky hand out for another biscuit.

'Well now,' Teresa said, 'if you're staying, you can make yourselves useful. This place will have to have a good clean. And that rug will have to have a good shake out in the back yard.'

Granny had made the multi-coloured rag rug many years ago, before her arthritis was so bad.

'For pity's sake, Mammy!' Florence cast her eyes upwards. 'Haven't you any modern equipment?'

'What do you mean, modern equipment?'

'I have a special mop for my kitchen floor. Nobody goes down on their knees with a scrubbing brush nowadays.'

'What nonsense. You're getting too stuck up for your own good, Florence. Ever since you've been in that Copeland & Lye's.'

'The kitchen's fine the way it is,' Wincey interrupted.

'Anyway,' Euphemia said, 'you should show them into the front room, not the kitchen.'

Bridget eagerly nodded her agreement. 'Yes, that's definitely the done thing.'

'A right bloody circus. Ye're no' gonnae wheel me through tae that cold room. Ah'm stayin' here by the fire. Far better tae bring them in here anyway. More natural in the kitchen.

They won't thank ye for puttin' on airs an' graces, an' tryin' tae impress them. They'll no' be comin' here tae admire oor front room. They'll no' be seein' anythin' or anybody but Wincey.'

'Yes,' Teresa nodded. 'You're quite right, Granny. It's best if we all just try to relax and be natural. After all, when anyone else drops in, especially in the morning, it's the kitchen we welcome them into. The kitchen's the heart of the house, I always say.'

Florence heaved a sigh. Her mother had no idea. She had never mixed with ladies. And she was so old fashioned. She had too many grey hairs for a woman not yet fifty. She refused to get it coloured and just had it cut short and held on one side by a large kirby grip, just like Granny's. Florence's own hair was long and glossy and smoothly curled in behind her ears and down onto her shoulders. Outside she always wore a smart brimmed hat, tipped well forward over her brow. Fancy entertaining the gentry in the kitchen!

'Yes, I'll feel much better if there isn't any fuss,' Wincey said.

'For pity's sake, Mammy! You've a four room and kitchen house here. Anybody would think you'd never moved up the Balgrayhill and were still in that horrible wee room and kitchen in Springburn Road. What's the point in having four rooms if you're always stuck in this wee kitchen?'

'It's not a wee kitchen, Florence. It's a lovely big kitchen.'

'She's worse than Wincey,' Granny said. 'Stuck up wee madam. Ah'll say that fur Wincey—she wis never stuck up. She wis different frae us—ah always knew that. There was aye a bit o' capitalist aboot her, wi' aw her money makin' ploys, but she wis never stuck up.'

'Thank you, Granny.' Wincey laughed and went over to plant a kiss on the old woman's loose skinned cheek.

'Get aff!' Granny roughly shoved her away. 'Ah cannae stand folk droolin' ower me.'

'That's settled then,' Wincey said. 'We're all just going to be ourselves. I still wish I'd never sent the letter though. It's all very well for Robert. He's not going to be here.'

'He has his patients to see to, dear,' Teresa reminded her. 'He's a very hard working doctor. You can't expect him to be always at your beck and call.'

'I know, I know, it's just . . . I'll be so glad once tomorrow's over. Of course,' she suddenly added, 'they might not come. That'll be worse in a way—the suspense!'

'Oh, they'll come all right, hen,' Erchie assured her. 'Ah'd bet ma life on it. As soon as their postie's been, they'll be over here like a shot.'

'We'd better all be up really early then,' Florence said. 'By the time I have a bath and do my hair and make up . . . '

'Ye selfish wee madam!' Granny shouted. 'Ye're no' gonnae keep us aw oot that bathroom. Forget yer bloody bath. It's no' you the Cartwrights are comin' tae see.'

'For pity's sake, Mammy, can you not do something about her language? What if she swears tomorrow. She's liable to give us all a right showing up.'

'Who's *her*?' Granny bawled. 'Ah'll *her* ye. An' ye dinnae need me tae gie ye a showin' up. Ye can dae that yersel'— ye're aye daein' it.'

'Have your bath tonight, dear,' Teresa soothed. 'That'll give you more time for your hair and make up tomorrow.'

'Oh, all right.'

'Now on you go through—the pair of you as well,' she added to the twins, 'and make up a couple of beds for yourselves. There's plenty clean sheets in the room press.'

'Oh very well.' The girls bounced up. Florence rose with more dignity and, despite her bored tone of voice, there was an air of eagerness and excitement clinging to the three of them. They were in fact dying to get on their own to discuss all that Wincey had told them, not to mention the potential drama of the next day.

4

It was lunchtime before Virginia returned from her shift. Usually she just relaxed with a sandwich and a cup of tea beside the Aga in the kitchen with the fragrant herbs hanging down from one of the oak beams. Gone were the days when her housekeeper, Mrs Rogers, would prepare a big pot of soup and perhaps a steak pie and vegetables and leave them just to be heated up. Mrs Rogers had been evacuated with her children to some safe haven in the country. Thousands of children, some accompanied by mothers, teachers and helpers, had already been evacuated. Walter Elliott, the Minister of Health, had described it as an exodus bigger than that of Moses. 'It's the movement of ten armies,' he'd said, 'each of which is as big as the whole expeditionary force.'

At least Mrs Rogers would be with her children to make sure that all was well with them. Virginia had heard that not every child had been welcomed or was having a happy time. She knew of one country host who'd written to a friend saying that there were six evacuated children in their house and he and his wife hated them so much, they'd decided to take away something from them at Christmas.

There hadn't been any evacuees during the First World War. Even the songs were different in this war. There were no rousing marching songs as there had been in August 1914. Instead there were now songs of longing for wives and sweethearts. And there was no talk of heroism or glory or adventure. Just a dull sense of foreboding and uncertainty about what the future might hold.

As often as not, while Virginia was eating her sandwich and drinking her cup of tea, she listened to the wireless. She always seemed to be on her own. Now, as her heels clacked across the marble floor of the hall, she remembered how, when she'd first heard about this house and been told about the marble floor, she'd imagined a huge palatial building. In fact it was quite a modest sized hall.

She pushed open the kitchen door and was suddenly taken aback to find Nicholas sitting waiting for her in the kitchen. He looked very strange—white faced, agitated, yet eager and shining eyed.

'What on earth's wrong?' Virginia asked. It had to be something really cataclysmic to bring him out of his room at such an early hour.

'Virginia, you'll never guess—never in a million years.'

'Guess what?'

'Sit down.'

Obediently she sank onto a chair.

'A letter came this morning.'

'Good news about your book?'

'No. Even better.'

What could be better than that to Nicholas? For a moment she thought he must have gone mad. She'd often wondered if his intense concentration on so many fictitious people and situations might one day tip him over the edge.

'You'd never guess,' he repeated. 'Never in a million years.'

'For goodness sake, Nicholas.'

'A letter came this morning from Wincey.'

29

Virginia stared at him. Now she *knew* he had gone mad. He repeated the words, 'From Wincey. She's alive and well, Virginia.'

'Wincey?' Virginia felt faint.

'Yes, Wincey. Read the letter. It's beside you on the table.'

She stared at it. Then, at last, with a trembling hand, she picked it up and began to read. As she did so, tears welled up and trickled down her cheeks. 'Forgive me,' the letter said.

'Forgive me?' Virginia said out loud. 'Oh Nicholas, it's us who need to be forgiven. If only we'd known.'

Nicholas dazedly shook his head, making a lock of black hair flop down. 'When I think of us—time after time—sending her over there and all the time, her being so frightened and not able to tell us. And for all these years, she's felt—she obviously still feels—guilty and afraid. Oh Virginia! We must go to her right away.'

'Yes, right now. It's an address in Springburn—the Balgrayhill. That's up near Springburn Park. We've been there. To think we went there once to hear that brass band recital. Remember? In the park. She might have been in the crowd.'

'I know. Are you ready?'

'I'm not sure if I can even stand up, Nicholas. I feel shattered, don't you?'

'Yes, but I've had a little more time to recover. Come on, I'll help you out to the car.'

'I'm still in my uniform.'

'Does that matter?'

'I suppose not.' It still hadn't sunk in. Virginia felt utterly drained. She wanted to believe that Wincey was alive and well and that they were about to be reunited, but she wasn't able to get used to the idea. She didn't believe it. Perhaps it was some sort of cruel joke that somebody was playing on her and Nicholas. It was too cruel. She couldn't bear it. She allowed Nicholas to support her, half carry her, outside. She sat very still beside him in the car.

'I wonder what she'll look like,' Nicholas was saying. 'She'll be what, twenty, now. Remember her red hair with the fringe and her freckles and her lovely long lashes? I expect she'll still look the same. I wonder if she'll be as quiet and shy.' His voice tightened. 'Maybe she was so quiet because she was afraid. That never occurred to us, did it? But then how could it?'

A silence held between them until Nicholas began speaking again.

'I wonder what this Gourlay family are like. They've obviously been good to her. Thank God they took her in and looked after her. God knows what might have happened to the child if she'd been left to wander the streets in the dark.'

'I think I must be in shock, Nicholas. I can't believe this is happening.' Virginia stared at his long-fingered hands clutching at the steering wheel and shook her head. 'I just can't.'

He laughed. 'It's happening all right, darling. And isn't it wonderful? A miracle. She's come back from the dead. That's what it feels like. We've believed for so long that she was dead.'

The car was slowed down by tram cars trundling along the dusty Springburn Road with its lines of shops at either side and the windows of tenement flats glimmering above them. Virginia noticed a long queue of women outside the Co-op grocers. Food rationing had just started, with butter, sugar, bacon and ham the first to be rationed. Rationing had been introduced partly because, in the first few weeks of the war, people in poorer districts were infuriated by the sight of well heeled middle class matrons motoring into working class areas, stopping at one grocer's shop after another, and buying up large amounts of essential foods like sugar. Obviously to hoard. Now when something extra would arrive in a shop, the word would spread like a hallelujah and bring local women running to the shop to form a queue. Virginia had done it herself for a packet of raisins. Bananas were one of the things

31

that had completely disappeared.

Virginia couldn't stop her mind from wandering. She realised this was partly due to fatigue. Never in all her life had she worked so hard—or felt so tired. On top of her work for the Ambulance Service, she had just finished a long and harrowing shift at the Royal Infirmary. She hadn't even had time for a cup of tea before receiving the shock of the letter. Not only her mind, but every nerve and sinew in her body, was absolutely exhausted.

She could see the Balgrayhill now, along at the far end of Springburn Road. Balgrayhill looked much wider and airier. She could see a church steeple at one side and at the top, a block of respectable looking red sandstone tenements. Her heart pounded and she felt faint again. One of these houses, in that block of red sandstone tenements, was where Wincey lived.

The tram rails stopped at the foot of the steep hill and the car was able to increase its speed until it reached the top.

'There's the number,' Nicholas said, stopping the car outside a close. 'The bottom flat, the letter said. Look, that must be it. There's somebody at the window.'

Virginia couldn't look.

'Is it . . . ?'

'No, an older woman. She's gone now, probably to open the door. Come on, Virginia. Don't just sit there, darling.'

Somehow her legs carried her across the pavement and into the close. The door of the house on the left was open and a woman with a slight stoop and speckled grey hair held neatly on one side by a kirby grip stood waiting. Beside her was a small, skinny, beaky-nosed man wearing a peaked cap pulled well down over his forehead. Both the man and the woman put out a welcoming hand.

'I'm Teresa Gourlay, and this is my husband, Erchie.'

They shook hands and followed the couple into a windowless lobby.

'Wincey's waiting in the kitchen with Granny and our

other girls, Florence, Euphemia and Bridget. Poor Wincey is so nervous, she couldn't come to the door. She's in a right state, poor soul. We've all been up and waiting since early morning.'

'I've only just seen the letter,' Virginia managed. 'We came right away.'

And there she was. Just the same as ever. The same dark red hair fringed over her forehead, the same rich, dark sweep of lashes, the same sprinkle of freckles, the same tense, apprehensive looking Wincey.

Virginia and Nicholas rushed towards her with arms outstretched. The three of them locked together in a wild embrace.

'Oh, Wincey. Oh, darling, we can't believe it. It's so wonderful, wonderful . . . '

Eventually Virginia had to sit down.

'Are you all right,' Teresa asked. 'You've gone awfully pale, dear. Would you like a nice cup of tea? The kettle's on the boil.'

'Oh yes please. I've just come off duty at the Royal and we dashed straight over.'

Nicholas kept a grip of Wincey's hand as they too sat down, but he had to release it as introductions were made and he politely shook hands with Granny and the three Gourlay sisters who kept staring at him in obvious admiration. He wasn't young like them but nevertheless they thought him breathtakingly handsome.

'First of all, my wife and I must express our deep appreciation to you for taking Wincey in and for looking after her so well for all this time. It was truly wonderful of you and we cannot thank you enough.'

'Och,' Erchie grinned, 'she's a grand wee worker. She's been the makin' o' this family. She an' my eldest daughter Charlotte, God rest her soul, built up a great business. Now Wincey runs it on her own.'

'Not on my own, Erchie. I couldn't do it without you, and

33

such a good team of managers, and a marvellous workforce.'

'What line of business is it?' Nicholas asked, not taking his eyes off Wincey's face.

Erchie said, 'We started in the dressmakin' but now we've a great contract for shirts for the forces.'

'Whit?' Granny suddenly roared. 'Ah never knew that. Ye sly, traitorous devils.'

Erchie laughed. 'Granny wis a disciple o' John Maclean an' she's against aw wars, includin' this one.' He turned to the outraged old woman. 'It's no' as if we're makin' guns an' bullets, Ma. Just shirts for the boys.'

'It's helpin' the bloody war effort.'

'Have a biscuit, do.' Florence leapt up from the table which was, as a concession to the momentous significance of the day, covered with a pristine cream lace table cloth. She offered the plate of biscuits first to Virginia and then to Nicholas.

Teresa passed around the teacups. 'You'll have to forgive Granny. She's . . . '

'Ah'm no' wantin' or needin' anybody's forgiveness. It's them two faced, lying warmongering villains that need forgiveness—an' that's somethin' they'll no' be gettin' frae me.'

'We never lied to you, Granny,' Wincey protested. 'When did I ever lie to you?'

'You let me think ye were still sewin' clothes.'

'Well, so we are.'

'Ye've jumped on the bandwagon tae make yer fortune durin' this war.'

'No, no, we were making the shirts before the war.'

'See her,' Granny addressed Nicholas, 'she's a Cartwright, right enough. A bloody capitalist. But,' she added with a grudging mutter, 'no' a bad wee lassie for aw that. Ah huv tae admit she's been a good wee lassie tae me. But ah want none o' yer stupid carry on,' she suddenly bawled at Wincey, stopping her en route to deliver a kiss. 'Ah've telt you before,

34

ah cannae dae wi' folk droolin' ower me.' She turned to Nicholas and Virginia. 'Are you two dumb or whit? Dinnae think we're gonnae let that lassie go away wi' you until we know somethin' about ye. So ye'd better tell us what the pair o' you huv been up tae.'

5

It was agreed eventually that Wincey would continue to live with the Gourlays in Springburn during the week. At weekends she would stay with Nicholas and Virginia in the West End.

'It's so handy for the factory here, you see,' Wincey explained. 'I can walk to work and all my friends are here.'

Erchie laughed. 'She means her fella, Dr Houston. He's got a local practice. Ye'll like him. He's been a good friend tae all o' us, especially tae Granny. Isn't that right, Ma?'

'Aye, well, at least he's a bit better than his auld man wis. Aw he ever did was stick a thermometer in yer mooth an' ask if ye were constipated.'

'He was the one who persuaded you to write to us, wasn't he?' Nicholas said to Wincey.

'Yes.'

'Well, God bless the man. I can't wait to meet him and thank him.'

'You'll stay for a bite to eat?' Teresa said. 'It's just stovies but there's plenty. I always make a big potful.'

'Gosh,' Virginia sighed, 'that brings back memories. My

mother used to make stovies. I don't think I've ever tasted them since she died.'

'Where did your folks live, dear? Were they from the West End too?'

'Oh no, I was brought up in Cumberland Street in the Gorbals.'

Florence gasped. 'Cumberland Street? The Gorbals? Then how did you . . . ? I mean . . . '

'I originally worked as a scullery maid for Nicholas's mother.'

'A scullery maid?' Florence echoed, making Granny bawl, 'Dae you think ye're a bloody budgie? Stop repeatin' everythin' the woman says.'

'Then Nicholas and I fell in love and eventually got married and moved to Kirklee Terrace.'

Teresa sighed with pleasure. 'That's so romantic. Just like in a book.'

'That's what I do,' Nicholas said, 'write books.'

'Aye, ah know, son,' Erchie said. 'Ah've read a few o' them. Good stuff. Ah like yer style an' the way ye work yer poems in.'

'That's how I began—by writing poetry. Virginia was the only one who encouraged me in my writing. I didn't dare confess to my parents that I wanted to be writer.'

'De ye no' make a livin' at it, son? Is that why yer wife has tae go out tae work?'

Nicholas laughed. 'Oh, I make a living at it all right.'

'I joined the Red Cross because . . . well, because I was bored at home,' Virginia said. 'I suppose. I'm glad I did now because I believe nursing is a worthwhile job.'

'Aye, well,' Granny nodded her agreement, 'ah suppose ah cannae say anythin' against the Red Cross. They help everybody an' anybody. It disnae matter whit side ye're on.'

Florence and the twins had set the table with all the best rose patterned china from the display cabinet in the front room. Teresa began dishing the stovies.

'Come on now, pull in your chairs. Make yourselves at

home. It's a wee bit of a crush but never mind. I'll sit over beside Granny and help her. Usually she feeds herself but her hands are swollen today so she needs a wee bit help, don't you, Granny.'

'Aw, get on wi' it. They're no' wantin' tae hear about ma problems.'

As they were enjoying their steaming plates of stovies, Virginia said to Wincey, 'Are you sure you can't come home with us today, darling?' It was Thursday, and Friday evening seemed a lifetime away.

Wincey shook her head. 'I've already taken today off work. I must go in tomorrow to make up for it and get a few things organised. I've also an important meeting tomorrow afternoon but I'll come over on Friday straight from work and stay until I leave for work on Monday morning. I'll do that every weekend, I promise.'

Virginia tried to feel content with this arrangement but she hoped that soon, she'd be able to persuade Wincey to come back home to Kirklee Terrace for good, to live there all the time—weekdays and weekends. She felt sure that this is what would happen sooner or later. Hopefully it would be sooner.

Eventually Teresa said, 'You're welcome to stay as long as you like, Mrs Cartwright.'

'Virginia.'

'You're welcome to stay as long as you like, Virginia. But you look so tired, dear. I think you should go home and have a rest.'

'Yes, Mother,' Wincey said. 'You'll be collapsing if you don't. I'll see you tomorrow night.'

'You'll come home in time to have dinner with us?'

'Yes, I promise.'

Reluctantly Virginia and Nicholas rose and took their leave of the cosy crowded kitchen, but not before they'd shaken hands with everyone again and thanked them again and warmly embraced Wincey.

'Oh Wincey,' Virginia said, 'we're so glad we found you.'

Nicholas kissed Wincey and said, 'Let's make this day a new start in all of our lives. Let's put the past behind us and make the most of our second chance. All right?'

Wincey smiled and nodded. 'Yes, all right.'

In the car on the way home, Nicholas was almost bouncing with happiness and delight. Virginia could hardly keep her eyes open. She managed to say though, 'We must get word to Richard. He'll be so pleased.'

'I'll send a telegram the moment I get home. I'll try to phone as well. In the circumstances, I'm sure his C.O. will give him compassionate leave, even if it's only for this weekend.'

'He's already been off quite a few weekends visiting your mother. I shouldn't think there'll be much difficulty.'

Richard and Mrs Cartwright were very close. The old woman adored her grandson and, Virginia suspected, she was far too generous with financial gifts to the boy. She'd even arranged for a regular allowance to be paid to his bank account. Nicholas had told his mother, 'You're spoiling him, Mother. He gets paid by the RAF. He doesn't need all that extra money.' But Mrs Cartwright had always been a strong minded woman and would not be diverted from 'helping the dear boy'.

At that moment, her 'dear boy' was in a local pub not far from the airfield. He needed to talk. So did the others. There had been a scramble earlier in the day. He remembered first of all the feeling of relief. The suspense of waiting for something to happen had ended at last, and he was on his way, running, with his parachute bumping awkwardly against his legs. He felt keyed up, trigger happy, ready for anything, as he jumped on to the wing of his Spitfire and clambered in. The engine started up and the whole airframe seemed to come to life, roaring and shaking. Never before had he felt so fully alive. He was strapped in. The trolley accumulator was pulled away, he was given the thumbs up, the chocks were pulled away. Then it was tail up, ease back the stick, and he was off.

The ground dropped away beneath him, until it was just

39

a vague patchwork of greens and greys. Breaking through the clouds and emerging into the searing brilliance of the sunlight above, he suddenly found himself directly above a formation of Heinkel bombers. Without hesitation, Richard threw the Spitfire into a shallow dive, switched on his gunsight and opened fire on the leading bomber. A moment later the Heinkel burst into flame and spiralled out of sight. Now his own aircraft was rattling, shaking, and screaming as his dive took him back down through the clouds. Just as he levelled out, he checked his rear view mirror. His heart raced as he saw a German fighter—probably an Me 109, he thought—appear right on his tail. Throwing the Spit into a violent climbing turn, he prayed that the German pilot's reactions weren't as swift as his own. As he scanned the sky all around, he breathed a sigh of relief. The 109 was nowhere to be seen. He decided to get out while the going was good.

'All our chaps OK?' He asked the airframe mechanic as soon as he landed.

'Yes, they're all back.'

It was a relief. He felt good as he sauntered away from his Spitfire, dangling his flying helmet in one hand. The next stop, as ever, was the local pub. Somebody said they'd downed a few 'kites'. The squadron had been lucky today. Nobody had been killed—although the word 'killed' was never used. 'Bought it' was a much better phrase. The RAF had a slang language all of its own. It was known for its understatement, its throwaway lines. Pilots flew a 'kite', and put it away in a 'shed'. They often slept in an 'iron lung' (a Nissen hut), bombing was referred to as 'leaving visiting cards' or 'laying eggs'. When they talked about going on operations 'over the ditch', they hoped they would not 'go for a burton', 'write themselves off' or 'have had it'.

That night, he'd had something to eat and was relaxed and laughing at one of Knocker White's jokes when a WAAF rushed in in great excitement. They all knew this girl. She was always getting into a flap about something. They couldn't see her lasting long in the service. Most of the WAAFs were pretty cool and capable types.

'A telegram.' She was almost shouting at him. 'And a phone call. She's been found alive.'

'Silly bitch,' he thought.

'Who's been found alive?'

'Here, read it.' She pushed the buff coloured piece of paper at him.

'Well, what do you know?' he said eventually. 'That's a turn up for the book. What the hell has she been up to all these years?'

The others were intrigued and wanted to know what it was all about.

'My young sister, Wincey. She disappeared donkey's years ago. We all thought she was dead. Now, apparently, she's turned up out of the blue. I'd better have a word with the C.O.'

And so he found himself next day on a train bound for Glasgow. First he called on his grandmother at her great hulking villa crammed with Victoriana. He loved his grandmother, but could not honestly say he even liked her house. He said that he wanted to accompany her over to Kirklee Terrace. He knew it would please the old girl.

'Can't have my favourite person wandering about on her own?' he joked with her. She was so happy and proud, as he knew she would be, to hang on to his arm as they walked along Great Western Road. She had been invited to join the family for a special celebratory dinner to welcome Wincey back into the fold. He knew of course that Wincey had never counted for much with his grandmother and so he wasn't surprised at the lack of enthusiasm the old woman had for the event.

'Wicked, selfish girl,' she said. 'Disappearing for so long, and then just turning up as if nothing was amiss. Nicholas is delighted. She's his daughter after all, and so I suppose it's understandable. But nothing that girl could do would surprise me. She takes after her mother, you see.'

Richard felt amused. It was as if he had had a different mother from Wincey. He knew he could do no wrong in his grandmother's eyes. He had come to the conclusion that she saw him as a reincarnation of her son as a young man, and somehow she'd completely shut her mind to any blood connection he had to his mother. True, he had never felt he had much in common with his mother—or his father for that matter. They could be such bores, his father with his constant talk of books and writers and his mother with all her Commy friends. Her first husband, for instance, was the absolute dregs, and a pacifist to boot. He hoped to God Matheson hadn't been invited to the dinner. He found himself saying the words out loud to his grandmother as they made their way along Kirklee Terrace.

'Oh, I do hope not, Richard. What a dreadful man he is, and it's just not decent that he should keep visiting Nicholas's house. Apart from being a Communist, he is her ex-husband.' She gave shocked emphasis to the words 'ex-husband'.

'I know,' Richard agreed. 'I can't imagine what Mother's thinking of, allowing him to hang around. I think he's mad. He certainly looks mad.'

'If he's there, I'm just going to ignore him. You should do the same, Richard. Oh, I couldn't have faced this ghastly dinner party on my own.'

He patted her hand. 'I'll hope I'll always be here when you need me, Grandmother.' He smiled down at her and she thought what a handsome boy he was and how good to her he'd always been. She was glad she had made a new will, cutting everyone out—even Nicholas. Everything, everything down to the last halfpenny and the last teaspoon, was to go to Richard. Her 'dear boy'.

6

Wincey went home for lunch, and also to collect an overnight bag. She could have had a sandwich and coffee in the factory, as she often did. She could have taken an overnight bag with her when she left the house in the morning, but she had developed a sudden need to spend as much time as possible with Granny and Teresa and Erchie. Erchie worked in the factory, but he was usually so busy that they seldom saw each other during the day, and he never went home for lunch. Every day, regular as clockwork, he and a couple of the other men went to a local pub and had a pint or two. She at least could sit down with Granny and Teresa, enjoy a bowl of Teresa's home made soup and just appreciate being with them.

The reunion of the day before with her mother and father had been heart warming, and such a relief, that she was glad she had written the letter. The burden of worry and guilt had been lifted from her shoulders. At the same time, she felt a need to cling to the Gourlays. No way could she risk losing them.

'I'll feed Granny,' she told Teresa.

'You've your work to get back to, dear. I've plenty of time to see to Granny.'

'I've plenty of time as well. I don't mind.'

'Will the pair o' ye stop talkin' about me as if ah'm no' here,' Granny said irritably. 'Whit's got intae you?' she asked Wincey. 'Away ye go out the road an' no' annoy us.'

'Granny. Wincey's just trying to be kind.'

'I'm not looking forward to this dinner tonight. Mrs Cartwright's going to be there. I wish I could keep out of *her* road. She never liked me.'

'I'm sure she'll be so relieved to know you're all right, dear, she'll welcome you with open arms.'

'I can't imagine it. I *will* be glad to see my brother, though. I always secretly admired him. He was so handsome and clever and daring. I'm not surprised he's a fighter pilot now. I can just imagine him being wonderfully brave in the face of danger.'

'A fighter pilot?' Granny said in disgust. 'Whit next? Whit a family! Ah'm no' surprised ye're no' lookin' forward tae goin' there the night.'

'I'll wash up the dishes,' Wincey said in desperation, but Granny raised her voice,

'Will you get away tae yer work. We're no' wantin' ye here.'

'Granny,' Teresa gasped, shocked.

'Ah just mean the now,' Granny muttered. 'We want ye tae come back on Monday. Ye ken fine whit ah mean.'

Wincey nodded and reached for her camelhair coat, belted it, then pulled on her fawn beret. 'Yes, I know. It's all right, Granny. I'll see you on Monday. I'm meeting Robert for lunch but I'll be home at tea time. OK?'

The evening meal was still known to the Gourlays as tea.

'Aye, OK.'

'I'm going to kiss you now whether you like it or not.' She kissed the old woman's hollow cheek. 'You behave yourself while I'm away, do you hear me, Granny.'

'There's nothin' wrong wi' ma ears.'

Wincey kissed Teresa before picking up her overnight bag and leaving the house. All afternoon she struggled to concentrate on business but at the back of her mind, the return to Kirklee Terrace hovered like a sword of Damocles. She tried to tell herself that she was being foolish. After all, meeting her mother and father had been a happy occasion. She should be looking forward to her visit to her old home, seeing her grandmother Cartwright again, and her brother Richard. She should be remembering with pleasure sitting in the elegant dining room, sleeping in her old bed. Yet all she felt about the visit was apprehension.

The first person she saw after her mother embraced her and ushered her across the hall and into the sitting room was Richard. He looked taller and even more handsome than she remembered. He suited his moustache. He suited his RAF officer's uniform too. Its tailored lines accentuated his broad shoulders and the way his body tapered to a slim waist and hips. The grey blue colour of the uniform matched his eyes.

'Wincey!' He came towards her with outstretched arms. 'You little devil. Why on earth did you disappear like that? Where have you been all this time and what have you been up to?'

Nicholas cut in before she could say anything. 'We've agreed to put the past behind us, Richard. We don't want any third degrees. We're just glad she's back and it's a happy future together now that matters.'

Wincey returned Richard's hug. 'I've been living in Springburn and running a small factory. I was in partnership with one of the Gourlay sisters that I lived with—Charlotte, her name was. Then when she was killed in an accident, I took over the factory. We probably made that shirt you're wearing.'

'Good for you,' Richard said.

All the time Wincey had been trying to suppress feelings

of panic at seeing her grandmother Cartwright again. Not that she was afraid of her. But somehow the old woman catapulted her back into her grandfather's presence. She felt afraid of him again, and guilty again, and dirty.

Mrs Cartwright sat on a silk covered chair, shoulders back, spine stiff and straight. 'I fail to see,' she said coldly, 'what is good about disappearing without one word of warning or explanation. Apart from anything else, you cost the tax payer a great deal of money. The police search was very extensive, I remember. There were even divers.'

'Yes, we know all that, Mother, but as I said, it's in the past. Wincey has explained everything to her mother and myself and we understand, and totally accept the reason for her action. We just think it's best if we don't say any more about it. What happened, happened. There's nothing anybody can do now except look to the future and build a new life together.'

He poured champagne into glasses and passed them around. 'Let's drink to that.'

They all raised their glasses high, except Mrs Cartwright, who only raised hers as far as her thin lips. The champagne helped Wincey to suppress her panic, or at least to hide it. She concentrated on talking to Richard and listening to his stories about his 'Spit', as he called his Spitfire, and how he loved flying.

'It's the feeling of power and exaltation it gives you,' he said, his eyes glowing. 'It's being up there above the world, alone, and entirely responsible for one's own return to earth. Marvellously exciting. We haven't seen much real action yet, but it'll come and we'll be ready.'

Wincey spoke about Charlotte and what a marvellous person she'd been and how she'd been killed in a road accident. She'd dashed across a road in an effort to save someone she saw being attacked and hadn't seen the car speeding towards her. What Wincey didn't say was that the person being attacked was Charlotte's husband, big Malcy McArthur. He was a

46

reckless gambler who owed a huge amount of cash to a local money lender. It had been the money lender's hard men who had been attacking Malcy. Charlotte's tragic death seemed at least to have cured Malcy of his gambling, or so he said. Shortly after the funeral he had joined the Army. The last she'd heard he was somewhere in France.

She still missed Charlotte. Charlotte had always been closer to her and felt more like a sister than Florence or the twins ever had. Charlotte had been kind and loving, but clever too, with a really good business head on her shoulders. Right from the beginning, she'd recognised Wincey's business capabilities, despite her youth. She'd coached her and encouraged her. The only thing that ever come between them or caused any friction was Charlotte's love for Malcy.

Everybody except Charlotte, it seemed, knew exactly what Malcy was like. He had been well on his way to ruining the business, in Wincey's opinion. Not content with wheedling money out of Charlotte, he'd even resorted to stealing the petty cash from the office. Charlotte's death, however, had shaken him badly. Even Wincey had to come to the conclusion that his tears of grief were genuine.

Richard announced that he would be spending the night at his grandmother's house. 'I'm walking Grandmother home so I might as well stay. I'll see you again tomorrow, Wincey, and we can talk some more. We could have a walk through the Botanic Gardens and then go for a coffee down Byres Road.'

'Yes, fine,' Wincey agreed.

'Well, you see that she's back in time for lunch,' Virginia said. 'You mustn't keep her all to yourself all weekend, Richard.'

Wincey kissed her brother goodnight, then she forced herself to kiss Grandmother Cartwright, but only when she was free of the old woman's presence could she completely relax. Indeed it surprised her how peaceful she felt as she stood at the tall windows of the sitting room and looked out towards the quiet terrace and the elegant Great Western Road beyond, faintly lit by the moon. She watched her brother and grandmother leave arm in arm from the front door. Their torches casting faint grey fingers of light.

'Would you like another glass of champagne?' Nicholas asked behind her.

'Or a milky drink?' Virginia suggested.

'Champagne'll be lovely, thanks,' Wincey said, despite knowing she'd already drunk too much.

'You'd better come away from the window, dear, and shut the curtains,' Virginia said, 'or we'll be having an ARP man shouting, "Put that light out!".'

'Oh, sorry, I was forgetting.' Wincey tidied the heavy curtains shut. 'I bet the ARP men would turn the moon off if they could, but I'm always glad of it. Aren't you?'

'Yes, but even so, I never drive now. Except during daylight hours.' Virginia passed Wincey a glass of champagne. 'Nicholas manages somehow though.'

Nicholas shrugged. 'Not that either of us venture out much at night. There's nowhere to go, now that they've closed all the cinemas and theatres.'

'That won't last, surely. People are already getting far too bored and depressed.'

The three of them settled round the fire and Nicholas added another piece of coal and used the poker to bring the flames warming out.

'I've put a hot water bottle in your bed,' Virginia said. 'It's such a cold night. Perhaps we should have lit a fire in the bedroom, Nicholas.'

'I could do it now. I could take a shovelful from here ...'

'No, no,' Wincey protested. 'Please, I'll be fine. I've never had a fire at home—I mean, in Springburn. You mustn't spoil me.' Although in fact it felt very nice to be spoiled.

'Why not?' Nicholas said. 'We ought to have paid so much more attention to you when you lived here before.'

'The past has gone. Remember what we agreed—the future is all that matters now.'

'I must remember that myself,' Wincey thought. 'The past has gone,' she told herself. 'I'm all right now. Everything's all right.'

Nicholas nodded, then said, 'I'm looking forward to meeting your Dr Houston. When can we see him? How about bringing him for dinner next Friday?'

'He usually has a surgery on a Friday evening but he's got a partner now. I'm sure he'll be able to arrange something.'

'Good.'

Virginia said, 'I would suggest this Sunday but we just want to keep you to ourselves this weekend. We can still hardly believe it, you see. That you're actually here, beside us. It's so wonderful.'

The champagne was swimming around in Wincey's head, making her feel warm and relaxed. Later she lay in her old bedroom, with its blue and silver wallpaper and its looped blue curtains and silver blinds. How beautiful it was. She could hardly believe that nothing had changed. Even her old teddy was still there. She took it into bed with her and cuddled it close, just as she used to. She became aware of her mother tip-toeing in and heard her whispered 'Goodnight, darling'.

She heard her father's whisper too. She knew now that they loved her. Now she realised they always had, and felt hugely grateful and relieved. Snuggling down under the crisp sheets, warm blankets and satin quilt, she drifted happily into peaceful sleep.

1940

7

At the end of January 1940, Malcy McArthur was stationed in France in a village called Bondue. On pay day, which was usually on a Friday, he and some of his mates would take a bus into Lille where they had a few drinks and a meal. In a street there they called ABC Street, every house was a brothel and at each one, there were long queues of soldiers waiting their turn. Malcy stood in one of the queues. Sex had become almost as strong an addiction as gambling had once been. He'd conquered the latter urge, even though he now had money in the bank. He resisted the temptation because his weakness had led to Charlotte's death and he'd never forgiven himself for that.

The best he could do now was to avoid any form of gambling. It could be said though that the sex with prostitutes was taking a chance. He was well aware of the risk of venereal disease, but like everyone else he took precautions and hoped that he would be all right. He missed Charlotte for sex as well as for everything else. Not that they had had a very active sex life. For most of the time she was too exhausted with working so hard in factory. But she did love him. She was always telling him she loved everything about him.

'I especially love your laughing eyes and your dimpled chin,' she said. Sex wasn't the only way to be close to someone and to show them that you cared about them. Tired or not, he bet her fiery haired partner wouldn't say no to sex. Even before he'd started going out with Charlotte, he'd had his eye on Wincey. She'd been a bit young then, nevertheless he'd seen that quiet, smouldering quality about her that spelled sex to him. Unfortunately she'd also been greedy and suspicious. Making money and the factory had been everything to her.

Charlotte would have given it all up for him if he'd let her. But not Wincey. She'd hang on in there come what may. He was sure of it. The factory and making money was her life. He'd one thing to thank Wincey for though—or two, to be exact. She'd paid off his last debt to the money lender. It was what Charlotte would have wanted, she'd told him.

Then she'd said, 'Rest assured, for all your faults, Malcy, and no matter what you did, Charlotte always loved you.'

He would be forever grateful to Wincey for that. He had been feeling so grief stricken after Charlotte's death, and so guilty. Wincey's words had comforted and reassured him, although at the same time they had made him weep. One thing he could say in his favour—he had never been unfaithful to his wife. Despite often feeling sexually frustrated, he never turned to anyone else for sex.

It was different now. He had no one to consider but himself. No one to be faithful to.

As he was shuffling forward in the brothel queue, his mind strayed back to Wincey. He wondered if she'd made any time yet for a man in her life. He doubted it. Unless just for sex. She wouldn't want any serious distraction from her journey to the top. She'd get another, bigger factory, or she'd extend the one she had. She'd buy up half Springburn if necessary, if she decided on the latter course. You had to admire her in a way. She was a right little devil. Looked it too, with her red

54

hair and eyes like grey-green glass. He'd had a few spats with her, and even though he had never done her a moment's harm she obviously hated his guts. He'd come to the conclusion eventually that money was behind it—her fear of losing it. She had found out about Charlotte keeping him going with cash handouts.

Now, without poor, generous hearted, loving Charlotte and without him, Wincey would be coining it. The factory was already going full blast making clothes for the forces before he'd left to join the army. Probably the shirt on his back at this very moment had been made at Wincey's factory.

His part of the queue moved into the first brothel. Down the stairs came a young girl wearing only a pair of knickers. She looked no more than sixteen and her face was completely blank. It made him feel sad. A huge wave of depression engulfed him. What was he doing here in this god-forsaken country? He could see no point in the whole business. He had been perfectly willing to fight the Germans in order to defend Britain but since joining up, the worst thing they'd had to fight was boredom. The 'Bore War', they called it. Sex with prostitutes depressed him even further, yet the next week he was back, hopefully trying a more expensive, supposedly higher class brothel.

He spent some time in a room lined all round with red plush seats. On one side of the room, on some of the seats, sat five girls in underwear. They were quite attractive and he tried to believe that they wanted him and enjoyed having intimacy with him. But all the time he knew he was conning himself.

He had acquired what could only be described as an ache to be back in Glasgow. He'd been born and brought up in the city but he'd never bothered or thought much about it while he lived there. Now he thought about little else. He remembered with real longing the ornate Victorian buildings. It was always said that to appreciate Glasgow, you had to go about looking up all the time and that was certainly true if it was architecture you were interested in. And what other city had so many parks? The dear green place was supposed to be what the word Glasgow meant. And it certainly could boast many green places. Even the East End had its Glasgow Green and the People's Palace. Many a time he and Charlotte had enjoyed walking arm in arm on the Green and then exploring the history of the city in the People's Palace.

Glasgow was a hilly place. Streets reared up everywhere until, within half an hour's journey from the centre of the city, you were among the green hills of the Campsies. Or you were away in the glorious scenery of Loch Lomond.

But it was the heart of the city that he loved and longed for most. The tenements, warm and welcoming—especially at night—with the street lamps and the close lights beckoning. And busy family life lighting up every window.

He had never had a family. Often he made one up. Sometimes he almost believed his stories to be true. The truth was he'd been an orphan and the only home he'd known was a children's home. He seldom allowed himself to think about his life there. He had certainly never experienced any love as a child. Plenty of punishments, though. He had been branded a liar because of the stories he used to tell about imaginary parents. He had a card hung round his neck with LIAR written on it in big capital letters. On other occasions he'd been forced into cold baths.

He'd wanted so much to prove himself worthy of Charlotte. He told himself that's why he gambled. He had this dream of winning a fortune and spending it all on her. Impressing her with expensive presents. Showing her what a big man he was.

Sometimes his horse, or dog, or whatever he'd bet on, did win. Then he would give Charlotte a great time. He'd take her to the best restaurant in Glasgow and order champagne. They had lots of laughs, despite her protests. He'd enjoyed being good to her, although he could see now he had been showing off as well, acting the big man, showing her—and

56

Wincey—that he could be just as clever as them, or even more so, at making money.

Then of course he began losing and in trying to rectify the situation, he'd made it worse by getting into the money lender's crooked hands. He kept believing that he'd win again. Next time he'd win and he'd be able to pay everything back. But the interest the money lender heaped on made paying back impossible.

What a bloody fool he'd been! He realised that now. He'd no Charlotte to go back to but still he longed for their native city. The bustle and noise of the Barras and Paddy's Market, the discussions and arguments in pubs about everything from football to politics and the state of the world. He thought about Springburn with its proud history of engineering. He remembered seeing steam locomotives being towed through the streets en route to the River Clyde. There they were hauled aboard a ship destined for India or some other far off land.

He remembered the concerts in Springburn public park. All the works had their own band and took turns playing in the bandstand in the park. The best known and loved, by all the children at least, was the Salvation Army Silver Band. They marched from Flemington Street to the Citadel in Wellfield Street every Sunday with a whole ragged army of children dancing after them. He remembered the noisy shuffling of hobnail boots of the workmen on their way to clock on at the various workshops. Then the housewives trailing zinc baths, or pushing prams laden with clothes to catch their turn at the steamie.

After five o'clock, the place would be black with workers dashing home for their tea. Later, young folk would be turning out for entertainment at the pictures, or the theatres, or the dancing.

Oh, how he longed for it all. Even just to hear a Glasgow voice on the street. He hated the yattering sound of the French. He couldn't understand a word of it and felt completely

57

alienated. Again and again he asked himself, 'What the hell am I doing here?'

He remembered the Gourlays. Good old Erchie. And Granny—what a character! And Teresa who reminded him so much of gentle Charlotte. Snobby Florence and the fat twins, who thought they were a cut above everybody else. The last he'd heard, they'd all got their own houses. Florence was as proud as punch of her place in Clydebank in the area known as the Holy City because, from a distance, the flat roofed houses looked so much like Jerusalem. The twins were living just a few closes apart from each other in Dumbarton Road and were equally carried away with themselves—even though they had only one room and kitchens. He could imagine Florence believing she had really made it to the big time with her two room and kitchen and bathroom flat.

He had once been as proud as punch himself of the house he shared with Charlotte in Broomfield Road, facing the park. Now that *had* been a house to be proud of. But it was gone now and meant nothing. Nothing was of any value, or had any meaning, without Charlotte. Still, he would dearly love to be back in Glasgow and in Springburn and walk again where they had once walked together.

He'd even begun to think nostalgically about Wincey. He wished he could see her again and talk to her. There had been a lot of bad feeling between them, but before he'd left, that had evaporated. They had their grief at losing Charlotte in common and for once Wincey had been sympathetic to him. And Wincey had loved Charlotte like a sister.

To everyone else they were sisters. Wincey was just Wincey Gourlay—one of the Gourlay girls. Charlotte had confided in him, however, that in fact there was a mystery surrounding Wincey. Years before, they had found her in the street and taken her in and she'd become one of the family. He wondered who she really was. Even Charlotte hadn't known. As soon as he got back to Glasgow, he'd make a point of finding out.

Oh, it would be so good to see them all again. The thought kept him going through the weeks and months of the Phoney War. But it wasn't long before everything changed for Malcy, and pleasant thoughts of the Gourlay girls and the dear green place were the last thing on his mind.

8

'But you're needed here,' Wincey protested to Robert Houston. 'What about all your patients in Springburn?'

Houston's eyes narrowed and hardened with impatience. 'They'll still have Doctor McLeod. It's my duty to do something for the war effort, Wincey. After all, you're doing your bit by keeping our forces supplied with uniforms.'

'But you might be sent overseas.'

Houston shrugged. 'I might be at some point, I suppose.'

She could hardly believe the coolness of him. Had he never loved her after all?

'I don't suppose you've ever given me a thought,' she said bitterly.

'Now don't be like that, Wincey.'

'Like what?'

'All twisted and bitter. I thought you were beginning to come to terms with that.'

'Don't you dare accuse me of being bitter and twisted. How am I supposed to feel? I thought we cared about one another. Yet you suddenly announce, cool as a cucumber and without any previous discussion, that you've joined the Navy.'

'When do you take enough time to discuss anything, Wincey? You're a workaholic. I see less and less of you these days, especially since you've been spending every weekend over at Kirklee Terrace.'

'You've been there too—for lunch, every Sunday.'

'I hardly get to speak to you, Wincey. They do all the talking. The three of you talk together. I don't blame them, or you. They've a lot to catch up with. So have you.'

'We usually manage to go for a walk together.'

'Yes, for a few minutes in the Botanic Gardens, with your parents waving and eagerly watching our every move from their side windows.'

'Well, Robert, it was you who started all this,' she reminded him. 'I was perfectly all right before—just being a Gourlay girl.'

'No, you weren't.'

She shrugged. 'I thought I was. Now I don't know what to think.'

'I'll probably still be able to see you most weekends. I've been posted to the hospital at Port Edgar. That's at South Queensferry. I'll let you know when I can get off duty.'

They were having a drink in the bar of a small country hotel near the Campsie hills. They'd been here before—on their very first date, in fact. The hotel was an old coaching house and the restaurant and bar had once been the stables. It still had the original flagstones under foot, whitewashed stone walls and dark oak beams. It had been a beautiful spring day but now in the evening, it had turned cold. Icy winds were whipping the trees outside, but inside there was a huge log fire crackling cheerily in the ancient hearth. It was cosy where they were sitting. It was only when the door opened and someone came in that an icy blast flurried about their ankles, chilling them for a second or two.

'It's not just at weekends,' she said. 'We see each other during the week—like now.'

'Only occasionally, when you're not working late at some urgent order, or when I haven't got an evening surgery.'

'What are you trying to tell me, Robert?'

'What do you mean?'

'Are you trying to tell me that you don't want to see me again?'

'Wincey, for goodness sake.' He put his hand over hers. 'Of course I want to see you again, darling. I love you. I'm just telling you that I feel my duty lies as a medical officer in the Navy at the moment. They're crying out for doctors. There's a war on, remember, and it's not a phoney war any more. Fighting has started in earnest.'

She tried to be reasonable. After all, he'd always been a man who'd been in charge of himself and didn't give way to any display of strong emotion. He wouldn't have been as good and as reassuring as a doctor if he'd been any other way.

'How about . . . ' he said quietly and still holding her hand, 'if we book in here for the night and I show you how much I love you.'

She was about to say that she couldn't possibly do that because she had a thousand and one urgent things to attend to at the factory first thing in the morning. She had planned to go into work an hour early.

Just in time she controlled her tongue. She smiled and nodded her agreement. They'd never made love before. He knew how she shrank with distaste at any thought of sex. Not because of him. It was something inside herself. He knew it and she knew it. It didn't matter how often he explained that she was not to blame for what her grandfather had done to her. She ought *not* to feel guilty or dirty. But she did.

As an adult, she knew perfectly well that she was being illogical and unfair to Robert Houston. She admitted to him that she knew he was right. What she did not admit to him was that deep inside her, she remained that frightened, sickened, guilty child.

Tonight, however, she was determined to ignore her foolish,

infantile emotions. Robert was going away and this was her chance—maybe her last chance—to show him not only that she loved him, but that she trusted him and because of that, she could express her love in the most intimate, physical way.

Upstairs in the low ceilinged bedroom, however, she began to feel claustrophobic. Panic skittered about in her stomach. Determinedly she fought to quell it.

'Darling,' Robert sighed, 'you look as if you're about to face your execution. I thought that maybe tonight . . . But I see I was wrong.' His face drained of expression. Suddenly he was the polite doctor that his patients saw sitting behind a desk in his surgery.

'Don't worry,' he said. 'I'm not going to force myself on you. So just relax. We'll have another drink and then I'll take you home.'

'No, Robert, I'll be all right. I'll have to get over this. I must.'

He shook his head. 'Not this way. Not when you're so tense and anguished. It's as bad—if not worse—than it would be for me to force you. Come on,' he said brusquely, 'get your coat on. I'm taking you home right now.'

She could have wept. Instead she sat beside him in the car, silent and white faced. She felt suicidal. She hated herself. She despaired of herself. What a fool she was, what an idiot. No sane woman could treat the man she loved like this. The awful thing was she wanted him, she wanted to belong to him, she desperately wanted to. The car stopped outside the close in Balgrayhill and she managed to say, 'Oh Robert, I'm so sorry.'

He put an arm around her shoulders. 'It's all right, I understand. I'm sorry for rushing you tonight. Originally I'd planned to give you much more time to get over this—for both of us to work through the problem—but because I'm leaving, I'm afraid I allowed my feelings to get the better of me.'

'Robert, I love you. You do know that, don't you?'

'Yes.' He dropped a gentle kiss on her lips. 'And I love you, Wincey. Don't worry, darling.' He grinned at her. 'I'll cure you if it's the last thing I do. I wouldn't be worth my salt as a doctor if I don't.'

She clung round his neck. 'You'll write to me?'

'Yes, of course. You look after yourself now. Don't be working too hard and getting even more anxious than you are at the moment.'

'It's just . . . I never dreamt the factory would be so successful. We can hardly keep up with all the huge orders. I'm trying to buy up some adjoining property . . .'

'Never mind all that now. Just let me know how you get on.'

'Yes, I will.'

They kissed again and he opened the car door. 'On you go before my feelings get the better of me again.'

Her smile hid a secret twitch of fear, followed by relief once she was safely out of the car.

Later she lay in the blackness of the recessed bed listening to the occasional bout of coughing from Teresa through in the kitchen. She felt deeply worried and depressed. She wondered if she ought to see a psychiatrist. It was so illogical to keep the man she loved at arm's length the way she did. Of all men, he was the one she should be able to trust and feel at ease with. He was a highly thought of and respectable doctor. She'd even known his father, who had been equally loved and respected by the people of Springburn. If she couldn't trust Robert Houston, she'd never be able to trust anyone. But it had really nothing to do with him, she reminded herself. Something had gone wrong deep inside her. Maybe only a psychiatrist could root it out, heal the sickness in her mind.

In an effort to make up for the night before, she took time off work, despite the urgency of the workload, and she went to see Robert off at the railway station. His face lit up with surprise and pleasure when he saw her.

'Darling, I never expected . . . '

'I know, but believe it or not, Robert, you're more important to me than my work. How handsome you look in your uniform. You know what they say—all the nice girls love a sailor. I'm jealous already of all the nice girls who'll fall for you.'

She'd bought some newspapers and magazines for him to read on the train.

'Here, just concentrate on these for a start.'

He laughed as he accepted the reading material. 'I promise I'll not look at any other woman. Well, maybe a nurse or two . . . '

She gave him a playful punch on the arm. 'Don't you dare!'

The guard was blowing his whistle and Robert had to board the train. Wincey blew him a kiss and he waved to her as the train steamed away. It disappeared from view, leaving her drained and empty. If she'd never felt lonely before, she felt it now. She forced herself to walk from the station and into her car. Work was what she needed now. She mustn't give herself time to think about anything else.

She had a meeting with a government official in the afternoon and she was wearing a chic spring dress and jacket in soft green boucle wool with a cinnamon coloured belt for the occasion. A brimmed cinnamon coloured hat pulled down over her brow topped the outfit, and she wore good brown leather gloves, especially fitted by Florence in Copeland & Lye. It was there she'd also purchased her matching and very expensive leather handbag. She could see the government official was impressed by her and the hard working girls in the factory, all beavering away at line after line of sewing machines.

He did however express some doubt at her capacity to take on another, bigger order. She assured him that she was extending her premises and installing more modern machinery. He had no need to worry about her capabilities to deal with any size of order, she assured him. Her self confidence was infectious. She had no problem in business—never had.

There had been the problem of Malcy McArthur, but there was nothing she could do about that. Big Malcy, as he was known, had been Charlotte's responsibility. Poor Charlotte. It had been understandable how she'd adored Malcy, despite his obvious weaknesses. He was an attractive devil, with his laughing eyes and his swaggering, muscly body. She wondered how he was getting on in the army. Erchie said Malcy would be in the thick of the fighting now.

'Poor auld Malcy,' Erchie had said. 'He hasnae had much luck in his life, wi' one thing an' another. Now he'll be lucky if he gets out o' this lot in one piece.'

Teresa sighed. 'Such a nice big man. He was always good and kind to Charlotte. She always said so. I hope he'll be all right.'

'Aye, but ye can never trust a gambler,' Granny said.

'Now, now, Granny. He's given up gambling. It was a wee weakness he had for a time. None of us are perfect.' She turned to Wincey. 'I know you never liked him, dear, but I always had a soft spot for him. He wasn't a bad man.'

Wincey shrugged. 'I got over that in the end. I could see he really did love Charlotte. I don't feel any dislike for him now.'

'Oh, I'm so glad, dear. We can all welcome him back when the time comes, God willing.'

9

'Believe you me,' Mrs McGregor said with grim satisfaction, 'ah gave her what for.'

Mrs McGregor was one of the Gourlays' old neighbours from Springburn Road. She had fourteen children, the youngest of whom had been evacuated to a supposedly safe haven in the country. 'She'll no' torment another wean. The police are gonnae keep an eye on her, for a start. I telt them, an' ah showed them ma weans, aw bleedin'. Aw bleedin', they were. Their clothes were soaked wi' blood. That monster had been beatin' them wi' a horse whip. Put her in jail, ah telt them. Lock her up an' throw away the key. Fancy doin' that tae weans.'

'Is that not terrible!' Teresa's eyes widened. 'And her supposed to be a respectable farmer's wife. Isn't it a mercy, Mrs McGregor, that you decided to pay a surprise visit?'

'Aye,' Granny said, 'an' good for you, givin' her a good punchin'. Ah jist wish ah'd been there as well, tae get ma fists in along wi' ye.'

'Thank goodness they're not all like that, Mrs McGregor.

The Donaldsons are being very well treated, I've heard.'

'Ah widnae trust anybody wi' helpless wee weans,' Granny said. 'There's far too many bad bastards goin' about. Rich or poor, it's aw the same wi' bastards like that. They're no' right in the heid.'

'Granny, watch your language.'

'Granny's quite right, Teresa. That's what they are. Do you know, ah'm that upset. It's gonnae take me ages tae get over seein' ma weans aw bleedin' like that.'

'Have another cup of tea, dear. The children are all right now. It's amazing how resilient children can be.'

'Aye, the doctor sorted them an' they're out playin' as happy as larry now.'

'No' always, they're no',' Granny said, chomping her gums on a piece of Teresa's home made shortbread. It was a special wartime butterless recipe but quite tasty all the same.

'What do you mean, dear?'

'Weans. They're no' aye able tae bounce back as right as rain. Look at oor Wincey. Ah always knew there was somethin' far wrong wi' her.'

Mrs McGregor perked up with interest. 'Was Wincey beaten when she was wee?'

'Granny, you know what we promised.' Teresa turned to Mrs McGregor. 'It happened a long time ago, before she came to us. We promised—swore on the Bible—we'd never talk about it to a living soul. All I can say is that poor Wincey has never quite got over what she suffered as a child. Now please, dear, promise me you'll never mention a word of this to anybody. Wincey would never forgive us. She's really a very private kind of person.'

'Ma lips are sealed, hen. Ah'm no' a stair heid gossip, Teresa. Never have been. But is that no' terrible. Poor wee Wincey. Ah'm glad she's got pally wi' Doctor Houston. A nice man, that.'

'Yes, I know. I was hoping for wedding bells but nothing's happened so far. An' now he's away to the Navy.'

'Aye, so ah heard. They were needin' doctors. Now they're cryin' out for women tae join up. My eldest's goin' tae the WAAFs and she's goin' tae work on somethin' awfy secret. She's aw excited. "It's a lovely uniform, Mammy," she says, as if that was aw there was tae it. It's the same wi' ma next one. It's the WRENs wi' her. "The WRENs have the smartest uniform, Mammy," she said. See weans!'

Just then the front door bell rang.

'That'll be Florence.' Teresa got up to answer it. 'This is her half day off. She usually does a bit of shopping and then pops in for a cup of tea.'

In a minute Florence was in the kitchen looking very smart in a Dorita wool coat, topped with the fox fur her husband Eddie had bought her for Christmas. Her hat was from Pettigrews, a fashionable little number decorated with two bird's wings and some veiling draped around the brim and down the back. She peeled off her gloves, finger by finger.

'Hello, everybody. Oh, tea, good. I find shopping so exhausting.'

'What are ye bletherin' about,' Granny wanted to know. 'You work in a shop. Ye spend aw yer days in a shop.'

Florence rolled her eyes. 'It's different trailing about, Granny. Anyway, in Copeland & Lye's, we're treated as ladies. That's what we're known as.'

She took off her coat and draped it carefully over the back of the chair, before checking that her hat was perched at the right angle. Then she sat down.

'Sales ladies. The ladies from the glove department, or the millinery, or whatever. It's all very high class.'

'High class?' Granny snorted. 'We're aw workin' class here, an' don't you forget it. Ah'm proud o' that fact. Always have been. Ah remember . . . '

'Have another piece of shortbread, Granny,' Teresa interrupted. Then to Florence, 'What have you been buying today, dear? Anything nice? Help yourself to shortbread.'

'Oh, just a half dozen table napkins, but they're very good

quality linen.'

'Table napkins?' Granny hooted. 'What next? Here, Mrs McGregor, ah hope ye've stocked up wi' enough table napkins for your crowd.'

Mrs McGregor's chest bounced up and down with laughter. 'Ah dinnae think ma crowd would know what a table napkin was, tae be honest.'

Florence nibbled daintily at a piece of shortbread. 'Yes, I could believe that, Mrs McGregor.'

'Florence, there's no call to be cheeky to Mrs McGregor.'

'I wasn't being cheeky. I was just agreeing with her.'

'It's OK, hen. Ah'm no' that thin skinned,' she assured Teresa. Then to Florence, 'How's yer hoose daein', hen. Ah hear it's like a wee palace.'

Florence preened with pleasure. 'Well, it is rather nice, though I say it myself. You must come for afternoon tea one Sunday with Mother.' She was calling Teresa Mother instead of Mammy as often as she could remember.

'Well thanks, hen, ah'd love tae come. Just you say the word.'

'I'll study my diary and let you and Mother know what Sunday.'

Granny spluttered out some tea and crumbs. 'Study her diary? Could ye beat it? Honest tae god, our Florence is a better turn than anythin' in the Pavilion.'

'Granny, everybody has diaries nowadays,' Teresa said.

'Ah huvnae, an' neither huv you. Ah bet Mrs McGregor hasnae such a thing either, huv ye, hen?'

'No' me, but ma eldest has, right enough. Her that's goin' tae be in the WAAFs.'

Florence held up a pinky as she sipped from her tea cup. 'Joe and Pete have been posted to France, Mother. Did you know?'

'Yes, dear, the twins told me.'

'Of course my Eddie wanted to volunteer but I said, "No Eddie, you're doing important war work at Singer's. That's

70

where you're most needed."' Everybody knew the secret of Eddie's epilepsy but out of consideration for Florence, as well as for Eddie, no one referred to it.

Mrs McGregor nodded wisely. 'Aye, ye're quite right, hen.'

'Poor Euphemia and Bridget are really worried now,' Teresa said. 'They were quite happy while the boys were at Maryhill but now, when they're so far away in a foreign country . . . Oh, I do hope they'll be all right. They're good boys, both of them.'

'Well,' Granny said, 'that's war for ye. The chances are they'll be blown tae smithereens.'

'Granny!' Florence and Teresa cried out in unison.

'Ah always said . . . '

'We know what you always said, Granny.'

'Aye, but naebody wid listen tae me, wid they? Or tae yer daddy. Ah've been a Socialist and a pacifist aw ma life, an' so has ma Erchie. Ah mind the first war. The war tae end aw wars, they said, an' look at us now. Ah always said . . . '

'Yes, all right, all right, Granny,' Teresa interrupted desperately. 'Mrs McGregor, can I pour you another cup of tea.'

'No thanks, hen, it's time ah wis back down the road. They'll aw be in soon wantin' their tea. Ah've still the tatties tae peel.' She rose. 'Nice tae see ye, Florence. Ye look lovely, hen, but ye'd better watch that hat disnae fly off yer heid.' She left the kitchen with a howl of laughter, followed by a smiling Teresa.

When Teresa returned to the room, she said, 'Fancy! Mr McGregor's been called up.'

'He'll be glad to escape that mob of his,' Florence sniffed. 'I mean, fourteen, Mother. It's not decent.'

'Oh well, at least it'll give Mrs McGregor a rest. She's the one I'm sorry for. Poor soul. She's been pregnant nearly every year since I've known her.'

'It's sheer ignorance, Mother. There's ways and means

after all.'

'Oh aye!' Granny cast a sarcastic look in Florence's direction. 'Miss know all. See if your man wisnae . . . '

'Granny,' Teresa almost shouted, 'have another piece of shortbread. I made it specially for you.'

'First ah heard o' it.'

Nevertheless Granny couldn't resist another piece and chomped away quite happily for a few minutes while Teresa admired Florence's purchase of linen napkins.

'Are you going to keep them for special occasions, dear?'

'No, no, Eddie and I like to do everything properly. We'll use them all the time. He's the same as me. He likes to see a nice table, so I always set it nice. We always use fish knives and forks.'

'All the time?'

Florence rolled her eyes. 'No, of course not, Mother. When we have fish for dinner, I meant. By the way, has there been no invitation to the West End yet?'

'To the Cartwrights'?'

'Can't you at least drop a hint to Wincey, Mother? After all, they've been here and they know how good we've all been to Wincey. One would think the least they could do . . . '

'Doctor Houston has been for lunch a few Sundays but that's different. I don't see the need for all of us to go over there, Florence.'

'Well, I do, Mother. Does Wincey suddenly think she's better than us, or what?'

Teresa sighed. 'Don't be silly, dear. Wincey's still the same as she's always been. She only goes over there to the West End at weekends anyway.'

'Well, I think we're entitled to an invitation. And if you don't say anything to Wincey, I will. If you and Father don't want to go, that's fine. And of course Granny wouldn't be able. But I think me and the twins are entitled. After all, we've been like sisters to Wincey all these years.'

'Oh, all right, Florence. I'll have a word with Wincey.'

Florence brightened. 'Thank you, Mother. I'll get a new dress. I saw a really smart one in Pettigrews today. A ginger crepe trimmed with black cord and a gorgeous hat that was really a huge bow attached to a tiny cap.'

'Sounds ridiculous,' Granny said. 'Ah can see you makin' an ass o' yersel, as usual. She enjoyed a good laugh that revealed her pink gums. 'Aye, as ah said before, hen, ye're a better turn than anythin' in the Pavilion.'

10

'That awful old man,' Florence said, 'was sitting in the close smoking a pipe when I came in.'

'Oh here, Teresa.' Granny became anxious. 'Get me oot there, hen. Mr McCluskey likes me keep him company. Poor auld soul. That daughter o' his should be shot for the way she treats him! What harm would he dae havin' his pipe in the house?'

'He'd make it all stinky and horrible,' Florence said. 'I perfectly understand why Miss McCluskey won't allow that filthy old pipe in her house.'

'*His* house,' Granny corrected. 'Come on, Teresa, hurl me oot.'

'All right, I was just getting your tartan rug and your hat. There's a cold draught whistling through that close.' Granny was already clutching a shawl around her shoulders. Now Teresa tucked the tartan rug over the old woman's waist and legs and pulled a felt hat over her wiry grey hair. Then she pushed the wheelchair from the kitchen, along the lobby and out to the close. Mr McCluskey's wrinkled face, with its bushy moustache and eyebrows, lit up with pleasure.

'There you are, hen.'

Granny pushed Teresa's hands off her shawl. 'Stop fussin' about me. Away ye go an' listen tae Florence talkin' a whole lot o' rubbish.'

After Teresa had retreated back into the house, she added to her companion, who was well wrapped up in jacket, muffler and bunnet, 'See oor Florence! She's a younger version o' your lassie. Mad about her house! She wid shoot ye rather than let ye smoke in her place. Ma Erchie—that's her daddy —wisnae allowed tae enjoy a Woodbine when we visited her. We were frightened tae move. Ah've never gone back. Ah dropped a scone on her front room floor. Ye know how ah suffer wi' ma hands. My God, ye widnae believe what a carry on Florence had. She was runnin' about like a headless chicken. Ah telt her, "See you an' yer stupid house, it'll no' see me again." An' ah've kept ma word. Ah've never gone back there.'

Mr McCluskey sucked at his pipe. 'Awfu' hard tae thole lassies like that.'

'At least ah'm no' stuck wi' oor Florence aw the time. Or the twins. They're about as bad. Ah don't know what's got intae the three o' them. Wincey's no' like that. Ah telt ye about oor Wincey, didn't ah?'

'Aye, fancy the Cartwrights, of aw folks! Ah mind him. Bad auld bastard!'

'The son—that's Wincey's daddy—isnae like his auld man. Ma Erchie says as far as he can judge by his books, he's maybe no' a pacifist but he does seem tae be a bit o' a Socialist.'

'Auld Cartwright'll be birlin' in his grave if that's true.'

Granny nodded. 'Aye, mind that munitions factory he had? He made a fortune out the last war. He'd be doin' that same wi' this one, if he wis alive.'

'An awfu' business. Ah saw ye had Mrs McGregor in. She said her man had been called up.'

'Aye, they're aw gettin' shoved over tae France, ready tae

75

stop the Germans in case they turn up there. But it's no' now that Adolf Hitler should have been stopped, it's at the time o' the Spanish Civil War when he was flexin' his muscles that he should've been told tae get off. But did ye hear a peep out o' the high heid yins then? Naw. They were aw for him. So of course he thought he wis ontae a good thing.'

'Aye, an' now it's ordinary lads like your grandweans' men and Mrs McGregor's man left tae clean up the mess. An' if they dinnae manage it, he'll be over here.'

'Hitler, ye mean?'

'Aye, wait till you see. If he gets intae France, it's only a hop, skip and a jump from there tae here.'

'What a carry on, eh?'

'Aye,' Mr McCluskey sucked contentedly at his pipe. 'Ah mind Johnny Maclean prophesyin' that there would be another war.'

Granny sighed. 'We'll no' see the likes o' him again. Our Johnny had the courage o' his convictions an' he suffered an' died for them.'

It was Mr McCluskey's turn to sigh. 'He wis a good man, our Johnny.'

Suddenly Miss McCluskey's lean, aproned frame appeared in the doorway of the house. As usual, she was gripping a duster in one hand.

'You're tea's ready, Father,' she announced. 'Put that filthy thing out.'

She began flapping her duster around in an effort to dispel the sight and smell of tobacco smoke. 'That filthy thing will be the death of you yet.'

Granny let out a sarcastic 'Mair like *you* will! Always naggin' at the poor auld soul. Ye'll be auld yersel wan day.'

Miss McCluskey's face tightened with anger but she turned back into the house without another word.

'Ah'm sorry, Mr McCluskey,' Granny said. 'Ah should have kept ma mouth shut. But she makes that angry, the way she treats you.'

'Och, she's no' a bad lassie. It's just she's that house proud. She'll have a nice tea waitin' for me an' she aye puts a hot water bottle in ma bed at night. She knows ah feel the cold somethin' terrible.'

In that case, Granny felt like saying, she shouldn't force you to sit in this cold draughty close every day. However, for once, she controlled her tongue.

'Ah'd better away in,' Mr McCluskey said, extinguishing his pipe and fixing a wee metal lid on it before stuffing it into his pocket.

'Nice talkin' tae ye, Granny.'

'See ye tomorrow, Mr McCluskey.'

'Aye, fine.' He staggered up and struggled to lift his chair.

'Leave that. Ye'll do yersel a mischief. Teresa,' she suddenly bawled.

Slippers scuffing on the linoleum, Teresa came hurrying along the lobby, shouting, 'What's the matter, Granny?'

'Help Mr McCluskey in wi' that chair, will ye, hen. He's no' very steady on his feet.'

'Yes, of course.'

Teresa took the chair from the old man. 'On you go, Mr McCluskey. I'll follow you in.'

In a couple of minutes, Teresa had returned and was pushing Granny's wheelchair back into her house.

'You gave me a fright there, Granny,' she said, shutting the door behind her. 'I thought you'd taken a wee turn.'

'When have ah ever taken wee turns? Ah'm no' like Florence's man. It's arthritis ah've got, no' . . . '

'Yes, all right, Granny.' Teresa raised her voice as they entered the kitchen. 'Oh, is that you ready to go, Florence? Are you not waiting until your daddy comes home. He'll be sorry to have missed you.'

'I know,' Florence said, smoothing on her gloves, 'but I like to be home in time to set the table properly for Eddie's dinner and have a nice meal ready to dish up.'

'Wi' yer fish knives an' forks?' Granny said.

'No, it's not fish this evening, Granny. It's spaghetti bolognaise.'

'Oh!' Granny pretended to sound impressed. 'Isn't Eddie the lucky one.'

'Yes, but he's very appreciative,' Florence said. 'I believe this Sunday would be all right for afternoon tea, Mother. You can bring Mrs McGregor and I'll invite the twins as well.'

'Oh that'll be nice, dear.'

'About two thirty, then?'

'Yes, I'll look forward to it. Maybe Granny will be able to come this time.'

'Naw.' Granny sadly shook her head. 'It's funny but ma arthritis is aye worse on Sunday afternoons. But maybe ye can keep a wee bit cake for me, Florence hen.'

'Yes, of course, Granny. I'll give Mother something nice for you. Now I'd better go.'

'Cheerio, hen.' One of Granny's arthritic hands raised in a feeble effort to wave.

'You could have gone. You know fine,' Teresa said, after she'd returned from seeing Florence to the door. 'It would have been a nice wee outing for you.'

'A nice wee outin', ma erse!'

'Granny!' Teresa scolded as she removed Granny's hat and eased a comb through her hair to neaten it again and secure it with the oversized kirby grip.

Granny said, 'Well, ah cannae be doin' wi' aw this fuss she makes an' that house o' hers. An' dinnae kid yersel'. She disnae want me clutterin' up the place.'

'She doesn't mean any harm, Granny. She's really very fond of you.'

'Och, ah know. What's for oor tea the night?'

'Shepherd's pie. And there's some apples and custard for pudding.'

'Great.' Granny's eyes brightened. 'That's Erchie's favourite as well. Is Wincey goin' tae be here.'

'Yes, it's just Tuesday, Granny. You know fine well she

doesn't go to the West End until Fridays.'

'Aye, but she sometimes goes out wi' Doctor Houston straight from her work.'

'He's gone away to the Navy, Granny.'

'Och aye, ah forgot. Ah hope that's no' the end o' it.'

'Oh, I don't think so. I certainly hope not—for Wincey's sake. He's just going to be in the naval hospital at Port Edgar. He says he'll probably get home for the occasional weekend.'

'What dae ye bet he'll end up in France wi' the rest o' them.'

'Oh, I don't think so, Granny. It's just the army that goes over there. Anyway, don't say anything like that to Wincey. You'll just upset her.'

'Maybe. Maybe no'.'

'What do you mean?'

'She's a funny lassie. Ye widnae know how she's feelin' about him goin' away. She could be feelin' relief for aw we know.'

'Now, now, don't be silly, Granny. She loves the man. That's always been obvious enough to me.'

'Aye well,' Granny muttered. 'Aw ah say is, she's a funny wee lassie. No' that ah blame her, mind, after aw that she's been though. It's no' surprisin' that she's no' normal.'

'For goodness sake, Granny, don't exaggerate, and don't you dare let Wincey hear you saying anything like that.'

'She'll work night an' day until she forgets aw aboot him, if ye ask me.'

'Nobody's asking you, Granny, so just hold your tongue.'

'Aye, well,' Granny humphed, 'ye'll be auld yersel' one day.'

II

'Have you read this?' Virginia asked, showing Nicholas the newspaper. He nodded gravely. The doom-laden message confirmed that this was no longer a 'phoney war':

LOCAL INVASION COMMITTEE

A local invasion committee has been set up in order to deal with invasion conditions. During the present period, the committee is engaged in making preparations to deal with the local problems which will arise in invasion, such as:

1   *Organisation of civilian labour to assist the military in preparing defence works, digging trenches, clearing roads etc.*

2   *Care of wounded.*

3   *Housing and sheltering the homeless.*

4   *Emergency cooking and feeding.*

5   *Emergency water supplies.*

6   *Messenger service.*

If invasion comes, the committee will direct its action:

a   *To meet the requirements of the military.*
b   *To attend to the needs of the civilian population.*

'It'll never come to invasion, surely?' Virginia said.

'Didn't you hear what's just been announced?'

They had finished supper and Virginia had read the newspaper while Nicholas listened to the wireless. The announcer had said, 'Here is the BBC Home Service. The German Army invaded Holland and Belgium early this morning, by land and by landing from parachutes. The BEF are fighting a desperate battle in the northern zone of the Western Front . . . '

'But never here, surely, Nicholas?'

'Why not? If the BEF can't hold them back, they'll be into France. Then what's to stop them crossing the Channel? Except . . . ' A look of pride registered on his face. 'the RAF. Boys like our Richard.'

'You really think it'll come to that?'

'I hope not, but it doesn't look too promising at the moment. I was thinking of joining the local defence volunteers. Anthony Eden was on the radio earlier appealing for volunteers.'

'Local defence volunteers?' Virginia echoed—so he couldn't take time off from his writing to have lunch with her or to go for a walk in the gardens in the afternoons but he could join the army without a second thought. 'Aren't you too old?'

'No, it's men aged sixteen to sixty five, and I'm sure my experience in the last war will come in handy,' he said. 'It's an important job—guarding railways, factories and canals and opposing enemy paratroops.'

'What about your writing?'

'The LDVs will only be part time. I'll still be able to write.'

'Oh great,' she thought, 'you'll write every morning and most of the afternoon, as usual. Then for the rest of the day and evening you'll be playing at soldiers.' But she managed to control her feelings. She had come to face the fact that she had a deep seated jealousy of his writing—or at least the time and priority he gave to it. She was ashamed of these feelings and, as often as possible, affected an interest in Nicholas's work. But secretly she wished she had never encouraged him to develop his talent in the first place. It seemed so long ago now that he'd needed her praise and encouragement to boost his self confidence. Now he didn't need her for anything. As far as she could see he was perfectly content. And why not? He was a fine poet and novelist, respected by critics and admired by his many loyal readers.

She loved him and was proud of him. If only he was not so obsessive about his work. He never seemed to be free of it. If only he would just work in the mornings, and then switch off at lunchtime as soon as he left his desk. According to Nicholas, however, it was impossible for writers to switch off like that. She tried to be fair. After all, she had her nursing duties now. One week she worked mornings and another week she was on late shift. He could complain about how often she was immersed in her work. But he never did.

She suspected he was quite glad of the opportunity to put in extra hours at this writing when she was out of the house. For the first few weekends that Wincey had been staying, he had not worked his usual Saturday and Sunday morning stints. He had devoted all his attention to his daughter.

Last weekend, however, he'd explained to Wincey that he needed continuity at his writing and had to work Saturday and Sunday mornings. But, he assured her, he'd finish in time to have lunch with her, which he did. Nevertheless, Virginia thought it was terrible of him—in the circumstances—to shut himself away even for half an hour while Wincey was in the house.

Wincey assured both her parents that she didn't mind. 'After all,' she said to Virginia, 'it gives *us* a chance to do lots of things together and to talk on our own.'

Wincey appeared perfectly content with the arrangement. But Virginia was secretly furious. It was so typical of him. After all, she'd got herself into trouble by refusing to work in the Royal at weekends. Her work was surely every bit as important as Nicholas's work. After all, she was dealing with real people.

Now Wincey was talking about just coming on Saturdays in time for lunch, instead of on Friday evenings in time for dinner.

'That gives you the chance to work Friday evenings and Saturday mornings, if need be, Mother,' Wincey said. 'We shouldn't forget there's a war on. We've all got a duty to give our best for the war effort. I often have to work late on Fridays as well.'

It had been Nicholas's fault that they were going to see less of Wincey. He had started the rot with his selfishness. She hadn't minded the time he'd spent digging the hole in which he'd built the Anderson shelter in the back garden. She'd even helped him fill the sandbags. She'd carried chairs and cushions and blankets down to try to make the awful damp, fousty smelling place with its ugly corrugated steel roof as comfortable as possible. She hadn't minded that they'd got sweaty and dirty, and she'd had to pin her long hair up because it had worked loose from her normally tidy chignon. None of this mattered to her—because they were doing something together. And all the time she prayed that they'd never need to use the Anderson shelter.

But she'd enjoyed working with him. It was different when he chose to shut himself away from her—even from Wincey now—to concentrate on his precious writing. Sometimes she longed to burst into his room and tear up every piece of paper in sight. Tear up and destroy whole manuscripts. Yet she managed to remain in control and act in a civilised, even caring manner. She'd put on kindly enquiring looks and ask how his current book was progressing.

He was so pleased when she did that. His face would light

up with eagerness and gratitude and he'd launch into a news bulletin of what stage he was at and what problems he was having. She strained every nerve in her body to appear interested and she believed she succeeded, when in actual fact his writing bored her. He was dealing with a make-believe world and make-believe people. She had to live in the real world and nowhere was more real than Glasgow Royal Infirmary. Recently she'd driven an ambulance ferrying servicemen with venereal disease to the military hospital in Cowglen. Most of them had been over in France. As far as she could see, the disease was reaching epidemic proportions over there.

Had the men over there nothing better to do? She was perfectly aware at the same time that the soldiers abroad had been having plenty to do. It was just that her frustration and irritation with Nicholas was spilling over into the other areas of her life. She was having a continuous struggle with herself to be fair and reasonable.

She could hardly contain her anger at him, however, when Wincey began coming half way through Saturdays, instead of on Fridays when they'd enjoyed dinner together and a pleasant evening of talking and relaxing over a glass or two of wine. As for Sunday mornings, surely no one in their right mind would work on Sunday mornings unless they had to. But now he was joining the Local Defence Volunteers. He would work all day Saturday and Sunday if they asked him.

That didn't happen, but he did work as an LDV weekdays and Saturday afternoons, digging secret bunkers, helping remove all sign posts which might help enemy invaders, manning roadblocks and practising fighting.

James Matheson shook his head when she told him. 'I'm disappointed in Nicholas. If he'd done something like you, Virginia—medical work, driving ambulances or whatever—I could have understood it. But he has in effect joined the army.'

'I know, and the other day he had bayonet practice, he told

me. Can you imagine it? He insists that it's a case of defending one's country. That's what it comes down to now, he says. He feels he has no choice.'

Matheson sighed. 'He showed me a pamphlet he was issued with. It's called *Shooting to Kill*. Real gung-ho stuff written by an army colonel. I took a copy of it and used it as a subject for discussion in one of my classes. Have you seen it?'

'No.'

'Here, read it.'

She took the piece of paper and allowed her eyes to skim over it.

> *'In the invasion of Britain, there will be no quarter given. It will be you or the other fellow. The taking of prisoners will probably be out of the question for both sides . . . Make sure that everyone hides his week's supply of food. Burying it in the vegetable garden is probably the safest place until the enemy has passed   A service rifle will kill anything from a Nazi to an elephant . . . The experienced and practised shot should have no difficulty in bagging five Nazis, in a charge as short as fifty yards. Pick out your enemy and shoot him . . .'*

Matheson said, 'They're in their element now, these army men. I bet that colonel really enjoyed writing that.'

'I keep having difficulty in believing all this is happening, James. Despite the blackout, the rationing and these monstrous barrage balloons hanging above us, it all seems like a dream somehow.'

'Oh, it's no dream, Virginia. I only wish it was. Although I can't see it coming to invasion, but that's just my opinion —or gut feeling, if you like.'

'Everything seems to be happening so quickly now.'

It was always a comfort to speak to Matheson. She had more in common with him now, it seemed, than with Nicholas, or even with Richard. Richard was so naively enthusiastic about the war and the part the RAF were going to play in it.

'One minute you're nipping along the deck,' he had told her excitedly, 'and then with just a gentle pull on the stick, you're soaring up and up. What power you feel at your fingertips. The Spitfire was designed by a genius, Mother. It's too beautiful to be a fighting machine, yet what better weapon of war could anyone want.'

The way he talked and his obvious eagerness for the fight made her tremble with anxiety and fear. It made her hate war all the more. Oh, how desperately she prayed for his safety and how she hated Nicholas for apparently encouraging his son to talk so proudly about his life as a fighter pilot. Nicholas loved to listen to Richard and lit up with pride every time he set eyes on the boy.

It would all be grist to his novelist's mill. That was all that mattered to him. Him and his stupid, unreal world in which, no doubt, everything would end happily. 'Oh, wake up,' she wanted to shout at him. 'Can't you see what terrible danger our son is in?'

It was getting more and more difficult to put on a show of sweet reasonableness in the face of everything Nicholas said and did. Emotion kept building up inside her, ticking away remorselessly like an unexploded bomb.

12

They could see by Florence's flushed face and shining eyes that she was excited. She had obviously gone to a great deal of trouble preparing for the visit. As she showed them around, the pungent smell of Mansion polish was heavy in the air in every room.

'This is our bedroom,' she announced, her chin tipped up with pride as she led Teresa and Mrs McGregor into the room. 'Just put your coats on the bed. I bought that gold satin bedspread in Daly's.'

'It's lovely, dear,' Teresa said.

'Aye, just lovely, so it is, hen,' Mrs McGregor agreed.

'This other room we use as both sitting room and dining room. See, we've made a dining alcove where the set-in bed used to be.'

'Oh, here, is that no' a great idea, Teresa?'

'Yes, it must be really handy, dear.'

'Do you like the HMV portable gramophone. It's got a rather unusual leather cover, don't you think?'

'It's lovely, so it is, hen.'

'We've done the same with the set-in bed in the kitchen.'

'Fancy!'

'Our kitchen is so big and roomy that we eat there most of the time. That's where we'll have our afternoon tea, if you don't mind.'

'That'll do us fine, hen.' Mrs McGregor looked relieved. She'd heard the story of Granny's scone. It had been spread liberally with jam and it had stuck to Florence's carpet. The linoleum in the kitchen was highly polished, the range sparkled. Even the swan-necked tap at the sink under the window glistened with cleanliness. As Mrs McGregor said afterwards, 'Ah could see ma face in that tap.'

'We're going to get the range taken out soon,' Florence announced. 'I've got my eye on a modern gas cooker.'

'Fancy!'

The table in what had been a bed recess was a picture with its crisp white table cover and napkins held by chrome napkin rings. A three tier cake stand graced the middle of the table, surrounded by plates of sandwiches without crusts, scones and pancakes. Florence's finest china tea cups, saucers, plates and little white handled tea knives completed the meticulous arrangement.

'Oh here!' Mrs McGregor was quite overcome. 'Isn't that just lovely.'

Florence could hardly contain her joy and delight. 'The tea service is genuine art deco.'

'Fancy!' Then after a pause, 'Whit's art deco when it's at home?'

Florence gave a long suffering sigh. 'Just sit in at the table, Mrs McGregor. And you too, Mother. Do you recognise this apron, Mother?' Florence patted the little frilled apron tied in a large bow at her waist.

'Isn't that the one I gave you for Christmas, dear?'

'It is.'

'I thought you'd like it.'

'I knew you got it in Copeland's, Mother. They have such

high quality goods. Nothing but the best, I always say.'

'Yes, I know you always say that, dear.'

Florence perched herself on a chair at the head of the table and with great dignity lifted the tea pot.

'Where's yer man, hen? He disnae work on a Sunday, dis he?' Mrs McGregor scratched one side of her loose, sagging breasts.

'He does now, Mrs McGregor. The war effort, you know. Everyone must do their bit.'

'Aye, right enough. Ma man's away doin' his bit for the army. The HLI. The same as Joe an' Pete. Ah'm that worried about him. They aye shove oor boys in first in any fight. Scots soldiers are aye on the front line, so they are. He'll go an' get himself killed, so he will.'

'Let's hope not,' Florence said kindly. 'Have a sandwich, Mrs McGregor. Egg or meat paste?'

'Thanks, hen. Egg. What a treat.'

'I made the scones and pancakes myself, by the way.'

'Did ye, hen. My word, Teresa, ye've got a clever wee lassie here, so ye have.'

'I know, and I'm very proud of her.'

'Eddie's a lucky boy, so he is.'

Florence smiled and said modestly, 'I'm lucky to have such a good husband, Mrs McGregor. Every penny Eddie earns goes into his home. Not like some men who spend all their earnings on gambling and cigarettes and drink.'

Teresa said, 'Joe and Pete are good boys. I hope they don't get shoved to the front of any fight. The twins are missing them terribly.'

'Mind for a time they used to go wi' brothers,' Mrs McGregor said, treating herself to another scratch.

'Yes, that seems ages ago now, doesn't it?'

'I invited the twins round today,' Florence said, 'but they'd already promised to visit one of the ladies they work with in Pettigrew's.'

'Ah'll see them some other time then,' Mrs McGregor

said, in between enjoying her sandwich. 'Yer mammy says they've got real nice houses as well.'

'They only have one room and kitchens, but they certainly have made them very nice,' Florence conceded. 'They copied my idea of making a dining alcove in their kitchen. They've had their range taken out and got a modern gas cooker instead, as I think I mentioned Eddie and I are going to do. By the way, Mother, did you have a word with Wincey. I can't wait to see her mother's posh house in Kirklee Terrace. Fancy, a big house in Kirklee Terrace!'

'Fancy!' Mrs McGregor echoed.

'Yes, dear, and she's promised to arrange something very soon.'

'Thank you, Mother. I can't wait. I'm so excited.'

'Nae wonder, hen,' Mrs McGregor said, helping herself to another sandwich. 'Whit did ye dae wi' all the crusts? Did ye feed them tae the birds?'

'Oh no, I made breadcrumbs. Breadcrumbs are very handy. Will the twins be included in the invitation, Mother? You know what they're like. They'll go into such a huff if it's just me.'

'No, the twins as well.'

Florence clapped her hands in excitement. 'I can't wait, and of course I'll return their hospitality. This house won't be as big as theirs and Clydebank isn't exactly Glasgow's West End, but I'm not ashamed of my home. Quite the reverse.'

'Quite right, hen. It's lovely. A credit tae you an' Eddie, so it is.'

After the visit was over and Teresa and Mrs McGregor were on their way to Springburn, Mrs McGregor said, 'Ah enjoyed masel', an' tae be honest wi' you, Teresa, ah didnae expect tae. Florence isnae a bad wee lassie . . . '

'I know, she just gets a bit carried away at times.'

'Och well, good luck tae her. She might as well enjoy her house the now. Once she has a few weans, she'll have more tae bother her.'

'Strictly between you and me, Mrs McGregor, I think Florence is frightened to have any children.' Teresa lowered her voice and moved her pale face quickly from side to side as if to make sure Florence wasn't anywhere near. 'You know, it's Eddie's problem. It could be passed on.'

'Och, the poor wee soul.'

'And poor Eddie. I'm sure he feels guilty but he tries to make it up to her. He's done a lot to that house. All the decorating and improvements and everything—he's done it all himself.'

'Fancy! It's no' the same as havin' weans though. Ah don't know what ah'd do without ma crowd. It disnae bear thinkin' about.'

'I know. I miss Wincey when she goes away at weekends. And she's not even my own flesh and blood. But somehow I've always felt she was a Gourlay. Right from the start she fitted in so well with us I couldn't bear the thought of losing her.'

'Well, ye're no' goin' tae lose her, are ye, hen?'

'No, and it's such a relief, especially now that Florence and the twins have left. It's only natural. I know that. They've their own lives to lead.'

'Aye, so has Wincey.'

'It would be different if she'd been getting married. Doctor Houston lives just round the corner from us in Broomfield Road. She wouldn't have been as far away as Clydebank or even the West End.'

'They were like two peas in a pod, the doctor an' her. What's wrong they're no' married yet?'

Teresa fixed her friend with an anxious stare. 'I don't know. But strictly between you and me, Mrs McGregor, I've a feeling it's Wincey to blame. She's funny about men.' Hastily she added, 'It's not her fault she's like that, you understand. It's because of what she suffered in the past.'

'Is that no' terrible. The poor wee soul.'

91

'I just hope and pray that Doctor Houston can help her and everything will work out eventually.'

'Aye, well, he's a good doctor. If anybody can sort that lassie out, it's him.'

They parted in Springburn Road and Teresa plodded on to the Balgray and then up the hill to her house.

Granny was sitting at the front room window. She shouted at Teresa as soon as the front door opened, 'Hurl me through, hen. Ma tongue's hangin' out for a cup o' tea.'

'Where's Erchie? He shouldn't have left you on your own, Granny.'

Shoulders hunched forward, Teresa pushed the wheelchair through and parked it in its usual place beside the kitchen fire. Then she tucked the crocheted shawl tighter around Granny's shoulders and up under her chin.

'Ah wis cravin' for a wafer,' Granny said, 'an' he said he'd try an' get one for me. But he hasnae much hope, noo that they've taken the Talies away an' locked them up. What harm did they Talies ever do anybody? All they ever did was sell us ice cream. Nice folk like that, it's a bloody disgrace.'

'Yes, I know. I'm sure everybody in Springburn felt terrible about that.'

'No' everybody, hen. Erchie telt me some ignorant rascals had broke their shop windows.'

'That's awful. As if the poor souls haven't enough to worry them.'

'Aye, ah know. An' them wi' a son in the army. Ah wonder how he'll feel when he finds out his mammy an' daddy have been interned.'

Teresa filled the kettle and put it on the fire. 'You'd think the authorities would have better things to do than arrest a decent Italian couple like that.'

'Aye, it's a bloody disgrace. Dear knows when ah'll get a decent ice cream wafer again.'

13

Belgium had been overrun. Now France was being battered into submission. The British army was retreating, trying to make for the sea, and it had been like walking through hell. Villages and towns were bombed. The terrible stench of death and smoke from burning lorries hung over everything. Injured horses struggling to stand up had to be finished off with rifles. For a time, in order to get past the slow moving civilians, soldiers took to the fields and so when the German aircraft attacked, it was mostly the refugees they hit. Horses, carts, and people were being blown to bits, pieces flying everywhere.

Now the army was trapped in a narrow strip of land that was choked with refugees. Malcy and many of his fellow soldiers, including Joe and Pete, kept taking cover in the nearest ditch but there was always somebody shouting, 'Get a move on. Get a move on. That way. Keep moving.'

German aircraft swooped and dived from the brilliant blue of the French sky. Machine guns chattered and plumes of earth made their deadly progress along the road until they met the churning mass of humanity. Men, women and children huddled together, while at the same time desperately trying to keep moving along. Some were pushing bicycles heaped with belongings, some shuffled along carrying loads on their backs, others were pushing hand carts. There were innumerable horses and carts all piled high with family possessions. Children plodded along at the side of the road, old people collapsed with exhaustion and others struggled to lift them on top of a cart.

Malcy felt sick as he watched machine gun bullets rake over the lines of helpless, terrified people. He didn't know where the refugees were going. He doubted if they knew themselves, but they were moving in the opposite direction from the army who were retreating to Dunkirk. Already Malcy, Joe, Pete and the others had trudged for miles across country until they were in a kind of trance, dazed with fatigue caused by lack of sleep. Their faces were taut with exhaustion and fear, the soles of their boots had completely worn through and their feet were bleeding. They could only hobble very slowly and painfully. The broken flesh absorbed the dust of the road, forming a skin that cracked and recracked as they trudged on, leaving tiny crimson flowers on the grey dust as they passed.

While they were in the ditch, Malcy said, 'By God, if I ever get back home to Glasgow, I'll count my blessings. Just to be back in that place'll be enough for me. I won't care about bloody money, or anything else. Just to get back to Glasgow in one piece, that's all I ask.'

'Me too,' Pete agreed, 'and see if Bridget starts wittering on about her precious china tea cups or stupid ornaments, I'll break them over her empty head.'

'Fuckin' right,' Joe fervently agreed. 'See Euphemia and her fuckin' floor polish! I'll tell her where to shove it.'

Malcy wanted to laugh but hadn't the energy. He kept fading into a hazy dream world. The only thing that saved him from floating into complete unconsciousness was the agonising pain in his feet. Once again, during a lull in the bombing and shooting, they struggled from the ditch onto the road and followed other ragged soldiers. As they got nearer to Dunkirk, they saw more and more discarded equipment cluttering either side of the road.

Eventually they were forced to walk in single file. They shambled painfully across two canal bridges and at last came out on the dunes.

'Christ!' Malcy said. 'What chance to you think we've got here?'

All the sea front buildings had been bombed and miles of white sand in both directions were littered with abandoned vehicles like huge, dead insects. The bodies of soldiers lay scattered around and vast numbers of troops were huddled in the dunes, while queues snaked over the sand. German fighters were strafing the beaches, seemingly unmolested by the RAF, and every now and again the queues of soldiers scattered as the Messerschmitts flew low over the top of them.

Malcy and the others joined the nearest queue. Despite British and French ships being sunk, the evacuation went on. The next day, more small boats appeared manned by fishermen, lifeboatmen and almost anybody else with any experience of handling boats. There were pleasure craft that without doubt had never ventured anywhere near as far from home. They had certainly never crossed the Channel before. Nor had many of the civilian volunteers who were manning them.

The next day the sea was flat calm with a dense sea fog and the bigger ships were hardly troubled by the Luftwaffe, while the smaller craft were busy trying to lift men off the beaches.

Malcy and the others were still in a long queue that stretched across the beach and into the sea. They had waited for endless hours, trying to ignore the floating corpses that gently nudged the waiting boats as if, even in death, they were trying to escape the beaches of Dunkirk. Ahead of him, Malcy saw a small boat coming in. A crowd of men all tried to clamber aboard on one side and tipped the boat over. It was a scene that Malcy had already witnessed many times that day. As these desperate, overladen soldiers sank beneath the waves, other small boats, all with soldiers cramming the decks, headed out to sea. After their terrible experiences on the beaches, the exhausted survivors were just glad to be moving out into deeper water and the relative safety of the bigger ships

Malcy, Joe and Pete eventually found themselves wading out neck deep into the sea, before being pulled on board one of the smaller craft. In no time they were being transferred onto a British destroyer and were on their way across the Channel.

As soon as they were safely on board, most of the men collapsed. Malcy lay on the deck, unable to cope with the enormous relief he felt. He was ashamed of the tears flooding down over his face and salting his lips, but he couldn't stop them.

He knew the ship could be bombed. Messerschmitt 110 fighter bombers and the dreaded Stuka dive bombers were still flashing about in the sky. Joe crawled alongside him. 'It's OK, mate. We're going to make it. Glasgow here we come.'

Malcy heard himself give a feeble laugh. 'Aye, right.' He could barely make out Joe's rugged, dirt streaked face topped with lank, black hair. A vague recollection came to him of Joe helping him, half dragging him, along the road towards Dunkirk. He remembered too a man lying by the side of the road. Both of his legs had been blown off. He had been blinded in one eye and he was slowly dying in agony. Joe had killed him—shot him through the back of the head. Nobody else could bring themselves to do it.

Pete joined them. He was dragging himself along the deck on his hands and knees. 'See when I get back. The first thing I'll have is a double Johnny Walker.'

'They'll maybe no' have any, Pete. It's England, no' Scotland, we're goin' to.'

'Och, every civilised country has Johnny Walker.'

'That's right, but as I said, it's England they're takin' us to.'

Malcy managed a weak laugh. 'Watch what you're saying, Joe. Some of these English sailors might chuck us overboard.'

'We'll surely get some leave after this,' Joe said. 'Then it's Glasgow here we come, eh?'

'Aye.' Malcy took a deep determined breath in an effort to stop another gush of tears. He had no one to go back to. Still, as long as he got back. There was always the Gourlays. They had never blamed him for Charlotte's death. On the contrary, they had shown him nothing but sympathy. Even Wincey had been all right in the end. He clung to the thought of Springburn and the Gourlays' house on the Balgrayhill.

'I'll get in touch with the Gourlays,' he said out loud.

Joe said, 'The very thing. And if you can't go there, Malcy, you can always come to my place.'

Pete joined in. 'You'll be welcome to stay with me and Bridget.'

'Great, thanks. But I expect the Gourlays will want to put me up for a wee while anyway.'

It was then that Joe shouted, 'My God, look at that.' The air to the east was seething with German aircraft—bombers, with their fighter escort high above them. They watched as dive bombers peeled off towards the evacuation fleet and the hundreds of smaller civilian boats. The destroyer they were on tore through the water at full speed, trying to evade the Stukas attacking it from different directions.

'Oh no,' Malcy thought, 'please God, no.'

The ear-splitting shriek of the Stuka filled their world. Then they saw the dark cruciform shape of the plane flash past the bridge. Everything now seemed to be happening in slow motion. A huge yellow bomb tumbled from its rack under the fuselage of the bomber. Another bomb scored a direct hit on the side of the ship. Water cascaded over the deck, the ship shuddered and slowly started to lean further and further, the deck canting over at a steep angle. Yet another bomb exploded with shattering force deep within the ship. On the signal deck, the coxswain bellowed,

'Abandon ship!'

Pete said, 'Oh Christ. Jesus Christ.'

Malcy tried to struggle up.

Joe said, 'There's a ship coming alongside. Come on, boys, we've still got a chance.'

Ships were sinking all around. They could see other destroyers going down. But they weren't quick enough to get onto the ship that had come alongside. Anyway, one of the sailors shouted that they were only taking wounded on board. As they watched the ship move away, they saw a bomb go straight down its funnel and blow the whole vessel sky high. When the smoke cleared, they saw the crew of that ship were now in the water, along with survivors from several other ships—men who only moments earlier they had been trying to save.

Everywhere, men were floundering around in the oil-covered water, screaming and yelling. A couple of sailors cut a life raft clear and Joe, Malcy and Pete were lowered into it. The sailors—who were wearing cork life jackets—jumped into the water, hung onto the sides of the raft and paddled slowly away from the sinking destroyer. Only a few minutes later, two Messerschmitts swooped down straight at them. Bullets and cannon shells tore through the water, killing the two sailors in an instant. As their bodies floated aimlessly away, the three soldiers huddled together in the bottom of the raft.

Malcy opened his eyes for a second, only to see the fighters turning once more, closing in for the kill. 'Oh no,' he thought. 'Oh please, God, no.'

14

Virginia had invited the Gourlays, more to please Wincey than anything else. She didn't mind Teresa, or Erchie, or Granny. But the girls were a bit tiresome. It was arranged they would come for afternoon tea on Sunday. As it turned out, Granny couldn't come and Erchie had to stay and look after her, so it was just Teresa, the Gourlay girls, and Wincey.

Florence and the twins looked as if they were wearing brand new outfits. Wincey looked very smart too, but business-like in her black suit and crisp white blouse. Florence's tip-tilted face was framed by an off-the-face halo hat. Her dark blue coat and paler blue dress had square padded shoulders. The twins each wore an ensemble of skirt, jacket and coat.

They were shown into the sitting room. It was a comfortable room with an Axminster carpet and gold covered chairs and sofas. Tasselled curtains draped the tall windows.

Florence and the twins gasped in undisguised admiration.

'Do sit down and make yourselves at home,' Virginia told everyone.

Nicholas appeared for a few minutes to say hello, then

excused himself. He had to go out to tend his vegetable garden. The back garden at Kirklee Terrace had become a blessing. Vegetables, like everything else, were scarce, some were unobtainable, and the government were telling people to grow their own wherever possible.

A tea trolley was set ready and Virginia began pouring the tea. 'It gets so irritating, doesn't it?' she said to Teresa. 'So many government posters and pamphlets telling us what we must or must not do. The other day, on my way to the hospital, I spotted forty eight posters telling people things like "Eat wholemeal bread", "Don't waste food", "Keep your children in the country".

'Well, I'd have second thoughts about that after what happened to Mrs McGregor's youngest. Thank you, dear,' Teresa said.

'Oh, I know. Wincey told me. Wasn't that awful?'

Florence said, neatly crossing her legs, 'I saw one poster which told you how to help build a plane and to fall in with the fire bomb fighters, whatever that meant.'

'And of course,' Virginia sighed, 'newspapers, magazines and the wireless are endless founts of wisdom. I keep thinking, when will it ever end? I sometimes feel quite worn out with it all—so many regulations and instructions.'

Wincey helped Virginia by passing round a plate of sandwiches.

'How do you manage this big house, dear,' Teresa asked, 'and you out working?'

'I miss my housekeeper but I'm lucky. At least I've got a cleaning lady. She's elderly and only comes in for two hours a week but she does manage to do the washing and ironing. And she runs the carpet sweeper over the carpets.'

'Your hall, of course, doesn't need a carpet. Marble,' Florence's voice dropped with awe, 'like a palace. I do admire this carpet, Mrs Cartwright. What a beautiful rich colour! And so soft under foot. I have a very nice carpet in my front room. Not as expensive as this one, no doubt, but very nice all the same. You must come and visit Eddie and me. Come one evening for supper so that Eddie would be in.'

'That would be very nice. Thank you, Florence, and please, just call me Virginia.'

'Virginia.' Florence put her cup and saucer back on the trolley and immediately fumbled in her handbag. 'Let's consult our diaries and make a date.'

Teresa looked embarrassed. 'For goodness sake, Florence,' Wincey said. 'At least give Mother time to finish her tea.'

'Oh.' Florence looked disappointed. 'Oh, all right then.'

Euphemia said, 'Bridget and I live in Dumbarton Road. Just room and kitchens, but I believe you once lived in a room and kitchen, so you'll know it's nothing to be ashamed of. We've got ours very nice. Our front room has a carpet as well.'

'That's right.' Bridget earnestly nodded. 'Hers is more reddish and mine is more bluey, although it does have some red in it.'

Virginia tried to look interested.

'And,' Bridget went on proudly, 'I've got a lovely china tea set.'

Florence said, 'I think you'll like my art deco table wear. Genuine art deco,' she repeated the phrase in order to make absolutely sure that Virginia understood the importance of it.

Virginia managed to appear suitably impressed.

'Have a fruit scone,' Wincey urged, knowing that Florence would be too lady-like to speak with her mouth full.

Teresa said, 'Did you bake the scones yourself, Virginia?'

'Oh no, I've barely enough time these days to cook dinner, far less bake anything. Especially after having to wait in endless queues. You know what it's like.'

'Oh, I do, I do, dear, but it's the shortage of cigarettes that's upsetting Erchie. He always enjoyed his Woodbine so much. I feel really sorry for him. He get so nervy without his smoke.'

'I'm quite friendly with our local newsagent. I'll try to get an occasional packet from him, and Erchie will be welcome to it.'

'Oh, that's awfully kind of you, Virginia, and I know it'll cheer Erchie up.'

Wincey said, 'Robert has started to smoke. He gets them issued from the Navy. He'll probably get rum as well—but I think that's only when they're at sea.'

'Does he like it?' Euphemia asked.

'What? The rum?'

'No, silly, the Navy.'

'I think so, but he doesn't talk much about it and we haven't been seeing so much of each other lately. He's been posted down south somewhere. Robert says things are going from bad to worse in France, and as many ships as possible are needed to go across the Channel. But he's not supposed to talk about it, or even say where he's going, so I don't know exactly what's happening.'

Virginia sighed. 'Nicholas says our troops are retreating and trying to make for the coast. It's turning into a very dangerous situation. If the Germans reach the coast, what's to prevent them coming over here?'

'Oh!' Bridget's plump face tightened with anxiety. 'I hope Pete's all right.'

'And my Joe,' Euphemia said.

'Oh, I'm sure they will be, dear,' Teresa comforted. 'As far as I understand it, the battle's over. Our lads can't hold the Germans back any longer—they're just trying to get away now. They'll be home soon. That's why extra ships are needed—to bring our boys safely back home.'

'Do you really think so, Mammy?' In her anxiety Euphemia forgot to use the more polite 'Mother'. 'They'll come back safe?'

'Of course, dear. Don't worry. Everything's going to be all right.'

Virginia felt guilty at upsetting the girls. At the same time, it seemed a bit foolish of them to be hiding their heads in the sand, or in their precious houses. The war news was not good. It didn't look as if everything was going to be all right at all. Richard had recently been moved to an RAF station down south, and she felt increasingly anxious about him. In a way, she was glad that she had such a lot to do. It kept her from thinking too much about Richard and the danger he was in. Eventually Teresa said, 'Let me help you with the washing up, Virginia.'

'No, I'll do it.' Wincey started gathering up the dishes and putting them onto the tea trolley.

Florence sprang to her feet. 'No, please. The twins and I will do it. We insist, don't we girls?'

'Oh yes, please. Let us do the dishes.' The twins bounced up like two rubber balls.

It was obvious to Virginia that they just wanted to see her kitchen and probably have a sneaky look into the other rooms of the house, but what did that matter? Thoughts of Richard had brought more important concerns to her mind. She nodded. 'Yes, if you want.' And she told them where to find the kitchen.

Off they hurried with the loaded trolley, their faces alert with excitement and expectancy. Wincey sat down, rolling her eyes in exasperation.

Teresa shook her head at the three retreating backs. 'They're not bad girls, you know. They just get a wee bit carried away at times.'

'That's all right. How's Granny?'

'Her arthritis comes and goes, and she's got one of her flare ups just now. When that happens, she suffers awful pain, poor soul. We're very grateful to Wincey for getting these two nurses. I don't know what Granny would do without them. Or me. I was beginning to get awful puffed trying to move her. The nurses are big strong girls, they get her up every morning, give her a bath and dress her, then every night they settle her down.'

'I could afford to have got Granny into a private nursing

home, but she doesn't want to leave the family. I can understand how she feels.'

Virginia's heart missed a beat. Was that a hint that Wincey didn't want, and would never leave the Gourlays? If only Wincey would settle properly in Kirklee Terrace, where she belonged. Not that Virginia felt any ill will towards the Gourlays. Far from it. She liked them, but her daughter belonged with her. She would have to have another talk with her, be firm with her.

Just then, Nicholas appeared, slim and tanned in rolled up shirt sleeves, his black hair rumpled. He was carrying a basket in which nestled a cabbage, some carrots, potatoes and a leek.

'I thought you might like these,' he said, handing the basket over to Teresa. 'They're jolly good, though I say it myself.'

'Oh, thank you, Nicholas. I'll be able to make a lovely pot of soup. What a treat!'

'You're welcome. I'd better go and have a wash. I've a meeting of the LDVs tonight.' He grinned. 'It's all go these days.'

Virginia immediately felt depressed. Another long night on her own. Wincey had an urgent order to fulfil, which meant she had to spend this Sunday evening in her factory office. Virginia tried to convince herself that Wincey couldn't help that. Both Wincey and Nicholas were doing their best in every way for the war effort.

'Don't forget there's a war on' had become the most used phrase in the country and after all, there were lots of things she could do. There were potatoes to peel for the next day's dinner. She also had to make a pot of soup. Although she tried to organise her time as efficiently as possible, being on day shift tomorrow meant she wouldn't have enough time to do the cooking . It would have to be done tonight. She could even set the table in readiness for the next day.

'Are you feeling all right, Mother?' Wincey asked.

'What, darling?'

'You look a bit pale and tired.'

'Oh, I'm fine. Don't worry.'

'I'm sorry I have to go to the factory tonight, but it is so important. There's so much paperwork to do these days.'

'Yes, yes, darling. I understand. Of course you must go.'

And it meant Wincey would go 'home' afterwards. She still referred to the Gourlays' place as home, which hurt Virginia more than she ever cared to admit. 'I'm fine,' she repeated.

When Florence and the twins returned, Florence immediately burst out, 'Gosh, what a lovely big kitchen. I love your Aga. And I hope you don't mind, but we popped into your bathroom. It was lovely too. Your whole house is lovely.'

'Just lovely,' the twins echoed.

Virginia felt like saying, 'Oh shut up, you silly, empty headed girls.' But instead she gave them a smile and said, 'Thank you.'

As if sensing her irritation, Teresa struggled to her feet and said firmly, 'Come on, girls. It's time we were away. Virginia has had us long enough.'

'Oh no,' Virginia said, feeling guilty now. 'You're all very welcome to stay as long as you like.'

'I know, Mother,' Wincey said, 'but I must get back to my office as soon as possible. And I'm giving everyone a lift home.'

The word 'home' wounded Virginia again.

And later, sitting at her dressing table gazing bleakly at herself as she undid her loop of long hair, she allowed tears to spill from her eyes and trickle helplessly down her face.

15

Richard was proud of the luxuriousness of his moustache. He combed it regularly, put on a discreet spot of wax and tweaked it up at each end. The local girls certainly seemed to like it. The uniform too. RAF pilots were very popular with the ladies. They weren't so popular with the local men. In the pub, after a few pints, angry words were often exchanged, along the lines of 'Why are you lads loafing down here drinking, instead of up there shooting the bastards down?'

The last time somebody said that to Richard, he'd been with a buxom upper class girl called Davina. She'd had to hold him back and hustle him out of the place. He was so angry and humiliated that he'd wanted to punch the ignorant fellow. Once outside with Davina, he'd gazed up at the searchlights criss-crossing in the dark sky and said, 'I would be up there now if it had been left to me. Even though our Spits aren't really any good as night fighters.'

'They were only teasing you,' Davina soothed. 'I expect they're jealous. They're just old men who aren't able to do anything to help with the war effort.'

Davina, he discovered, was a member of the Women's Land Army. A land girl, of all things. She explained that she had been used to horses and was familiar with everything that went on in 'Daddy's estate'. As a result, she thought working on the land would be her most suitable contribution to the war effort. Davina, just like most of Richard's fellow officers, had a very upper class English accent. But this didn't worry Richard. He hadn't gone to a private school for nothing, and no one could guess from his own accent that he came from Scotland, far less Glasgow. Glasgow had a very bad image down south. It was enough to put anyone off. Edinburgh, being the capital and known as a beautiful, historic city, was different.

Nowadays, if asked, he just said he had been brought up first of all in the country and then in Edinburgh. To an extent, this was true. He had lived with his grandmother and grandfather in their country house for the first few years of his life. Then he'd been sent to a boarding school in Edinburgh. That had been paid for by his grandparents. No doubt the idea had been to prevent him living under the same roof as his mother. His grandmother hated his mother. He didn't. Not at all. He got on well with her, and with his father. All the same, both his parents were a bit Bolshie.

His father had begun to see sense now that there was a war on, but his mother was still influenced by her first husband, the ghastly James Matheson. The man was not patriotic. But he'd always been the same, apparently. He'd been a damned conscientious objector in the last war. Richard could never understand his mother having anything to do with a chap like that. At least she was doing her bit as a VAD. He'd told Davina about that and she had been impressed.

'They work jolly hard. Good luck to her.'

'And my father's doing his bit in the LDVs. He served with distinction as an officer in the last war.'

'You must be very proud of them both.'

'Yes, I am.'

'I'd like to meet them some day.'

He smiled down at her tanned, unmade-up face. 'Remind me to arrange that. There doesn't seem to be much possibility of leave at the moment, though.'

'No, things don't look good, do they?'

'Don't worry, the Jerries won't set foot on British soil. Not once we get a real crack at them.'

Davina linked arms with him. She had a good firm grip. 'When I see any Spitfires going up now, I wonder if it's you and I hold my breath and keep my fingers crossed that you'll be all right.'

He felt touched. She really cared about him. Gently he turned her towards him and kissed her on the mouth. She responded warmly and he tightened his grip. They both opened their mouths, their tongues exploring. Eventually they were startled by the sound of a crowd of men approaching through the darkness, bawling and singing. The pub had shut and the drinkers were making for home. He and Davina drew apart and began walking along side by side. Too soon, they reached Davina's billet and she bade him a quick goodnight.

'Wait,' he called after her retreating back. 'When can I see you again?'

'Next Tuesday. Same time, same place.'

'Jolly good.'

He turned away quite happily then. It was something to look forward to, something to dream about. Life was suddenly even better than it had been before. He loved his Spitfire. He loved flying. He loved his life in the RAF. Now, this was a different kind of love. He savoured the experience. Yes, he was in love with the girl. All right, he hadn't known her for very long, but she was the girl for him. He was sure of it. He swaggered whistling cheerily all the way to the camp.

The only thing that would have increased his happiness at the moment was if he could be sure of being involved in more action. Almost every other fighter squadron had done a stint covering Dunkirk, but the evacuation had ended just before he'd got a turn. He had acted as 'Arse-End Charlie' a few times recently, weaving backwards and forwards above and behind the squadron, to protect them from attack from the rear. On the last occasion, he'd had reason to remember the truth of the warning, 'Beware of the Hun in the sun'. He had been peering into his mirror when out of the sun, and dead astern, he saw bullets peppering his port wing. It was a miracle he got home that day—but then, he'd always been lucky.

Once up in the air, they all believed they were immortal. No one accepted that they could be killed. And Richard was a born optimist. Even this business in France didn't depress him. He knew they'd sort it all out eventually. The only thing that really got to him these days was the growing chorus of undeserved criticism that the RAF was subjected to.

One evening, in the local pub, the regulars were treating a group of Dunkirk evacuees to round after round of free drinks. Before long, Richard and his RAF companions were involved in heated arguments with some of the soldiers.

'Where were the RAF when they were needed? They certainly weren't over Dunkirk,' someone said.

Richard found it very hard to keep his temper. He had known several pilots who had been killed over France, even before Dunkirk. Lysanders, for instance, had been flying across the Channel two or three times a day in an effort to drop supplies to the besieged garrison in Calais. Sometimes they had only a solitary fighter for support. And there had been British planes over Dunkirk.

Fortunately, a Frenchman spoke up to remind the others that there had been times when there was a heavy fog over the beaches and the planes were high above it. He also told of one fight he had seen between a lone Spitfire and four Junkers. He had watched it shoot down two Germans and cripple a third. The fourth made off.

Now the invasion scare was on. No one was allowed more than half an hour's call from the airfield. All leave had been cancelled, and all officers had been ordered to carry side arms. Richard was issued with an antiquated, short nosed .45 and six soft lead bullets. But he'd managed to get himself another twelve bullets. Now every newspaper had as its front page an appeal to every citizen to stay put. And people had come to believe that it could actually happen—that England's peaceful, pleasant land could at any moment be filled with the thundering noise of German tanks. At any moment, an army could drop from the skies.

But they were reckoning without the RAF, Richard told himself. He and his fellow pilots were ready for anything the Luftwaffe could throw at them. Far from being apprehensive or afraid, Richard was keyed up, and raring to go. They had learned a lot about the Germans, and their aircraft. The Germans had a mass psychology that they applied even to their planes, which were so constructed that their crews were always bunched together. This gave them confidence and a false sense of security. And the RAF had soon learned how to shatter that. The crews of the Heinkel bombers soon came to feel intensely vulnerable, hunched inside their greenhouse-like, perspex cockpits, with precious little protection against the white-hot tracer from the Spitfires eight machine guns.

Richard and the other fighter pilots could almost sense the bomber crews wincing as the Spits dived in for the kill. But some of the German gunners stuck to their task to the bitter end, and there were always one or two of Richard's squadron who didn't get back. But that was how it was. Kill or be killed. And he was always lucky.

16

'It's called the Home Guard now,' Erchie told Wincey. 'The LDVs that yer father's in.'

Granny glared suspiciously over at her son. 'Whit are ye suddenly so interested in them for? Ye're no' thinkin' o' joinin' them, ah hope.'

'Och, don't worry, Ma. Ah'm quite happy doin' ma bit keepin' a shirt on their backs. That's essential enough work for me. Anyway, wi' ma flat feet, they wouldnae huv me, especially now ah've caught yer ruddy arthritis.'

'It's no' infectious, so don't you go blamin' me. Anyway, aw ye've got is a few twinges in yer knees. Think yersel' lucky ye've no' got ma arthritis. Ye'd know aw about it if ye had.'

'Aye, OK, OK, Ma.' He turned his thin face towards Wincey. 'How's yer father doin', hen? Does he still get enough time tae write his books. Ah suppose he'll have tae make the time. It's his livin', isn't it?'

'Yes. I don't think he gets paid for being in the Home Guard and I shouldn't think Mother'll make much in the VADs. I offered to pay for my keep at weekends but they wouldn't hear of it.'

Teresa was busy at the kitchen table, her hands and arms floury with making a batch of scones. 'I'm sure they appreciated the offer though, dear. You're a very generous girl.'

'I can well afford to be generous, Teresa. The factory's making a lot of money.'

Erchie laughed. 'She's made me take another raise, wid ye believe.'

Teresa stopped kneading the scones for a few seconds. 'Oh, now Erchie, do you think you should?'

'He works for everything he gets, Teresa. I don't know what I'd do without Erchie. He's worth his weight in gold to me.'

'Oh well, dear, if you're sure . . . Have you heard any more from Doctor Houston, by the way?'

Wincey tucked her hair behind her ear. 'No, not since that last letter and a quick phone call to the office. To be honest with you, Teresa, I'm very worried about him. There were so many ships lost at Dunkirk.'

'They would have let you know, dear. No, I'm sure he'll be all right. He'll turn up unexpectedly at that door any day now.'

'If we'd been married, they would have let me know as next of kin, but he has nobody.' Much to her own embarrassment, and to everyone else's surprise and distress, she suddenly burst in to tears. It wasn't like Wincey to indulge in any outward displays of emotion.

Teresa rushed over and despite her floury hands, pulled Wincey close to her. 'Och now, now, don't be upsetting yourself. We'll hear these wedding bells yet. He'll be back safe and sound—just you wait and see.'

Desperately, Wincey took deep calming breaths and rubbed at her eyes with the sleeve of her cardigan. 'I held him at arm's length, Teresa. He said he understood but oh, I wish I could have been different.'

Erchie said, 'Of course he understood, hen. Anybody would,

once they knew what ye'd been through as a wean. It's no' so easy to get over things like that, but ye will. Just give yersel' time.'

She gazed at him with tragic eyes. 'Oh but Erchie, have I got time? I'm so worried about Robert.'

'He'll be back, hen, an' ye'll be all right.'

Granny said, 'There's surely ways tae find things out. Just sittin' bubbling' isnae any use. Write or phone to the Navy. Somebody's bound to be able to tell ye whit's happened.'

'I never thought of that.' Wincey fished for her hankie and rubbed it over her face. 'I know the name of his ship. He couldn't tell me in his letters because they were censored, but that last time he phoned, he let it slip.'

'Well then . . . '

'Thanks, Granny.'

Wincey lost no time in taking Granny's advice. As soon as she was back in her office, she wrote to the Admiralty. Several days passed before she received a reply. It was to inform her that Robert's ship had gone down during the evacuation of Dunkirk. There were no survivors.

The letter had arrived by the second post and Wincey had been sitting at lunch in the Gourlays' kitchen when she opened it. It was strange, she thought, that now no tears would come. She just sat, staring at the letter.

'Whit's up?' Granny hunched forward, pushing her spectacles closer to her eyes.

'The ship was bombed. There were no survivors.'

'See bloody war!' Granny bawled. 'What a bloody waste! Rabbie Burns was right aw these years ago, an' he's still right —Man's inhumanity to man makes thousands mourn.'

'Oh dear,' Teresa said, not knowing what to do or say for the best.

'A decent fella like that,' Granny raged on. 'Aw he ever did —or wanted to do—was tae help folk. See these bloody high heid yins an' politicians, ah know whit ah wid do wi' them. Ah'd . . . '

All right, all right,' Teresa interrupted. 'Oh Wincey, I'm
so sorry. If there's anything we can do to help, you know
you've only to ask.'

'I know. Thanks, Teresa. I think I'd better get off to work
now.'

'Oh no,' Teresa protested. 'I don't think you should,
Wincey. You've had a terrible shock. Why don't you take at
least the rest of today and tomorrow off.'

'I'm always better if I keep busy. I must keep busy.' She
rose, automatically collected her bottle green coat and matching
hat, and called back from the front door, in a parody of her
normal cheerful sing-song, 'Bye, see you later.'

Just before she left the door to go through the close, she
heard Granny's outraged bawl, 'See bloody war!'

Wincey escaped out to the street and began walking smartly
down the Balgrayhill. She was concentrating on what she had
to do in the factory that afternoon. She had to keep her mind
safely on ordinary, routine problems. Such a lot of paperwork
nowadays, it was getting worse all the time. Inside the office
there was one kind, and outside there was another. Everywhere
paper was stuck up on walls. Everybody was being bombarded
with it. Even cigarette packets contained cards which gave
instructions for everything, including air raid precautions,
how to deal with incendiary bombs, how to use a stirrup
pump, how to protect your house from the danger of flying
glass.

There were instructions on how to black out your home.
They were contained in *Public Information Leaflet Number 2*.
There were other instructions on how to make your home
safe against gas and anti-bomb blast measures. 'Women of
Britain,' yet another urged, 'give us your aluminium. We
want it and we want it now. We will turn your pots and pans
into Spitfires . . . '

'Women of Britain,' was the rallying cry on some posters,
'come into the factories.' So many posters, leaflets, pamphlets,
forms to fill in. She had so much to do in the office. Her feet

quickened towards it. She wanted to run but instinctively knew running would let loose the panic that she was desperately trying to control.

Another poster caught her eye. 'Be like Dad—keep mum. Careless talk costs lives.' And yet another: 'Your courage, your cheerfulness, your resolution WILL BRING US VICTORY'.

Victory? What did victory mean to her? What did anything mean any more? So many so-called helpful instructions but who could instruct her? Who could help her now?

Suddenly she was at the factory door. She went inside to her office. Her secretary, Mrs Allan, who should have retired long ago but refused to give up, appeared in the doorway. 'Are you all right, Miss Gourlay? Would you like me to fetch you a cup of tea?'

A cup of tea—the panacea for all ills. What a bloody joke!

'Yes thank you, Mrs Allan,' she said, picking up the nearest pen and beginning to write.

17

In July Adolf Hitler ordered preparations to be made for the invasion of Britain. Previously however, in a speech to the Reichstag, he had made it clear that he hoped for peace with Britain. It was, he said in his speech, his 'Final Appeal to Reason.'

> *'A great empire will be destroyed, an empire which it was never my intention to destroy or even to harm . . . I consider myself in a position to make this appeal since I am not the vanquished begging favours but the victor speaking in the name of reason.'*

A *Daily Express* journalist was quick to respond on BBC Radio. The tone was suitably uncompromising and full of defiance,

> *'Let me tell you what we here in Britain think of this appeal of yours to what you are pleased to call our reason and common sense. Herr Fuhrer, and Reichskanzler, we hurl it right back at you, right in your evil smelling teeth . . .'*

The German High Command made no secret of how they felt after hearing their Fuhrer's words being ridiculed on the BBC. They thought the British were crazy, and after the rejection of the Fuhrer's terms, the Luftwaffe began to attack in force. They planned to wipe out RAF Fighter Command and so clear the way for the invasion. But their first targets were the slow-moving convoys. The RAF tried to defend the convoys, and for the first time, radar equipment was used. But often things didn't work out. Sometimes radar contacts proved to be friendly aircraft, sometimes delicate equipment malfunctioned in wet weather.

But the main problem was timing. Often by the time the Spitfires and Hurricanes were scrambled, the convoys had already been attacked and the German planes were returning home. Coastal convoy losses became alarming, and as a result squadrons had to be sent further south to smaller stations much nearer the coast. There, in small tents, pilots slept, or wrote letters, or played cards—ready to scramble at a moments notice.

Richard's squadron was not among those that had been moved and he was disappointed. However, he made the most of his time by getting to know Davina better. They met at every opportunity now and more than once, they'd spent some memorable hours in a room at a local hotel. He'd asked her to marry him and she'd said yes. She'd phoned her parents and they lost no time in motoring down to meet him, knowing that he couldn't get any leave at present, or travel any distance from the airfield.

They had turned out to be a charming upper-class couple. Lord Clayton-Smythe was tall and lean, with slightly protruding eyes. His wife was almost as tall as him, with grey hair and an aura of dignity and elegance. They knew the estate his grandparents had once had in the Highlands. They had been guests on a neighbouring estate before the war. Lady Clayton-Smythe knew of his father's reputation as a talented writer. Both Lord and Lady Clayton-Smythe were impressed when

Richard told them of his father's distinguished record in the last war. They were extremely patriotic, and great admirers of the RAF. They also understood that nothing was normal during wartime, and that long courtships were out of the question. They believed, although Richard certainly did not, that he could be killed at any moment while defending his country. He basked in their warmth and admiration.

Recklessly he suggested a wedding while they were there so that Lord Clayton-Smythe could give his daughter away. It was a registry office affair with only Lord and Lady Clayton-Smythe present. But they had a good meal afterwards and it had all been very jolly. He had phoned his parents but neither his father nor his mother could get away at such short notice. But they spoke to Davina and her parents on the phone and sent their best wishes. His grandmother was too old to make the long journey from Scotland but when he phoned her with the news, she said she was immensely proud of him and it was so typical of him to make such a good match. They all looked forward to meeting his new wife, and her family, as soon as possible.

He was in seventh heaven. Davina was a super girl—well bred, courageous, generous hearted, beautiful and she loved him. How lucky he was. On their honeymoon night, he watched as she sat at the dressing table in her white satin nightdress brushing her short brown hair, and he experienced a wave of deep tenderness. She had full breasts, a flat stomach and rounded hips. Her face had a glow of health about it. So had her shining grey-green eyes. He imagined the beautiful, sturdy children they would have. His love and happiness encompassed everyone, including his parents and his sister, Wincey. His parents weren't so bad. Very decent, actually. He didn't quite know what to make of Wincey choosing to live for years in a slum in Springburn, instead of with her family. Still, she was his sister and he couldn't think badly of her.

After the war was over and done with, and the Germans

sent packing, he must make a point of seeing more of his parents and his sister. He felt a pang of guilt when he thought of how much more of his time and attention he had devoted to his grandmother.

Davina smiled at him in the mirror and he went over and gathered her gratefully into his arms. Later in bed, he made love to her with a hungry passion that was almost a desperation. It was as if he was suddenly afraid it might be his last chance of loving her—the very last time.

The next day he saw her back to her billet and stayed with her until she changed out of her moss green wedding dress with its fashionable padded shoulders and into her Land Army Uniform. It consisted of a wide brimmed, khaki coloured felt hat, a green pullover over a shirt and tie, belted breeches with thick wool socks that reached to below her knees and sensible laced up shoes. Around her upper arm was a band showing the letters WLA. Even in this somewhat masculine and unflattering uniform, Davina looked lovely. He was so proud of her.

They kissed goodbye and he made his way back to his airfield. He had only been back for a few minutes when he heard the controller's voice: 'Large enemy bombing formation approaching . . . Take cover immediately.'

At first Richard didn't see anything. Then he saw them— about a dozen Heinkel bombers, their wings glinting in the sun. He heard the rising scream of the first bomb. Then his feet shot from under him and his mouth filled with dirt. He scrambled up and sped like a rocket for the shelter. He shot through the entrance before falling on his face again in its gloomy interior. One of his ground crew spoke to him. He could discern the man's mouth moving but the scream and crump of falling bombs made it impossible to hear him. The shelter filled with dust and shuddered with every explosion. Bedlam reigned outside for about four minutes, and then ceased.

The sudden silence was as much of a shock as the noise

at first. For a long minute, neither Richard nor his companions moved. Then they all rushed outside to view the damage. The Germans were clearly attempting to destroy the RAF on the ground. The runways had been left in a real mess. Deep, smoking, craters were everywhere. A bomb had landed near Richard's own Spitfire and covered it with earth and rubble.

The first thing he did was have it cleaned up and checked over. All the other machines, he knew, would be landing at the reserve landing field. The station commander immediately ordered every man and woman onto the job of repairing the runways and in a few hours, they were back in service. Casualties had been relatively light—there had been four men killed in a lorry, another got a bullet through his foot and three pilots had suffered a few scratches. It had been a lucky escape because, apart from the bombing, the entire station had been repeatedly strafed.

Before long the pilots were back in the mess, relaxing, or playing poker, until the voice of the controller ordered them to scramble. They raced for their Spits. Soon they were getting instructions to intercept about twenty enemy fighters. They climbed until they reached twenty eight thousand feet. Then with a yell of 'Tally ho', Richard led his section in a shallow dive to intercept the approaching German planes.

They were about two thousand feet below him. The Germans had spotted them, however, and began to take evasive action. One after the other, the Spitfires peeled off in a power dive. Richard picked out one of the enemy aircraft and switched his gun button to 'Fire'. Immediately he got the leading enemy plane in his sights, he opened up in sharp, four-second bursts. Then he pulled up so hard, it felt as if his eyes were dropping down through his neck. The sky had become a mass of individual dogfights. Then, in an instant it seemed, the sky changed from a bedlam of machines to a silent emptiness with not a plane to be seen.

Back at the airfield, Richard discovered that a couple of his fellow pilots had not returned. All he could hope was that things wouldn't get any worse. As things stood, he reckoned they'd just about have enough pilots and aircraft to stop the German onslaught.

Morale was high, despite the loss of friends, and all the pilots shared a burning desire to live life to the full. For Richard, there was the unique excitement of combat flying, and the joy of seeing Davina at every possible moment. Even though he was often shattered by the lack of sleep, in the air he could still maintain the intense concentration every fighter pilot needed simply to stay alive. He still felt a wild, leaping of his heart when he saw the enemy. Switch on sights, range and wingspan indicators checked, gun button on 'Fire', then into action—his body stiff against the straps, his teeth clenched, thumb ready on the gun button, his eyes narrowed intent on getting the enemy in his sights, and holding him there. Then the kill, the moment of victory, and the savage, primitive exaltation.

He hadn't told Davina about how he felt when flying. Only another fighter pilot would understand. Nevertheless, he and Davina talked a lot together. They planned what they would do after the war, where they would live, how many children they would have, whether they would have sons or daughters. Two of each sex, they eventually decided, would be perfect. They even thought of suitable names. She told him of her happy childhood roaming around her father's estate.

She had been a difficult child, she said, but he refused to believe it. 'Darling, of course I was,' she laughed. 'I nearly drove my nanny to despair. Then after I was packed off to boarding school, I hated being cooped up and having so many rules and regulations to conform to, so I rebelled and failed everything. Eventually I was expelled and sent home in disgrace. At least that's what the school thought. I was overjoyed at living at home again. Oh, the glorious freedom of it.'

He could understand what she meant. Often now he felt that glorious surge of freedom. But boarding school had never bothered him. There were all sorts of sports on the curriculum and he'd been good at that sort of thing. He'd also enjoyed the company of his fellow pupils and indeed, practically everything else at the school. He'd never felt he'd been denied any freedom.

'Maybe it's different with boys,' Davina said. 'With so many rough games like rugby. Hill climbing and rock climbing sounded super as well. We were mainly taught to be sedate and ladylike.' She made a face. 'What a bore it was.'

He had to laugh at her. They laughed a lot together. He thought of her a lot too. But never while flying. Especially when things began to hot up.

18

'Talk about lucky?' one of the sailors told them. Malcy and the others had been rescued a second time, hauled once more onto the heaving deck of a destroyer. But this time they were wounded. Malcy had copped it down one side—his face, his shoulder and his arm. Joe and Pete had taken some shrapnel in the legs. Now they were in Dover, all bandaged up and grateful to be alive. Women were handing out sandwiches and big mugs of steaming hot tea. They'd never tasted tea or sandwiches like it.

Afterwards, they were led onto a train, with no idea where they were going. All was confusion, around them a teeming mass of unshaven, oil-streaked, filthy, humanity. The news that greeted them was worse than they had expected. Hitler was winning the war. Most of western Europe had fallen to his storm-troopers. Churchill's marvellous rhetoric didn't change the fact that they were getting beaten.

Now Churchill was saying that the RAF was going to blow the Luftwaffe out of the sky and save Britain. Knights of the air, he'd called the pilots. Well, Malcy and his pals agreed, they hadn't seen much of them so far. Certainly not at Dunkirk.

Malcy, Joe and Pete found themselves delivered to a hospital. There they had various pieces of metal cut out of shoulders, face and legs. Malcy had trouble sleeping—he suspected it was much the same for Joe and Pete and the rest of the survivors, although none of them admitted it. When he did eventually fall asleep, Malcy had nightmares. He was always back in the life raft with Joe and Pete, with the fighters diving down on them and the bullets tearing across the water towards them. He remembered becoming sleepy then as he bled into the sea. In his mind, everything became mixed up. Planes shooting at ships, ships shooting at planes, the endless queues of men on the beaches, dead bodies floating, machine gun bullets spluttering and boiling the water. He couldn't clear his head of it all. He suspected that he'd never again enjoy a peaceful, dream-free sleep. Not like he used to—it seemed so long ago now. In another life. And what a fool he'd been in that life, how he'd wasted it.

Malcy, Pete and Joe were eventually transferred to the nearest barracks, en route to a short survival leave. It wasn't even long enough for them to make the journey home to Scotland and back. Nor did they feel fit enough. They wrote home, however, and told their families that they were all right. Malcy wrote to Erchie and Teresa Gourlay. In the local pub where they spent most of their few days of freedom, they found LDVs masterminding the defence of the country. They seemed to have a wonderful faith in the Navy. The Navy and Winston Churchill.

The three survivors weren't all that sure of either, but they kept their thoughts to themselves. During the day, they often lay on the grass outside the pub and watched the vapour trails criss-crossing the sky, as RAF fighters struggled to defend their airfields.

'Right enough,' Malcy said, 'if the Germans knock out the RAF, what's left to stop them landing here and taking over the whole place. I mean, I'm more than willing to make a stand. I'm sure we all are. But look at us. What good would we be against thousands of Hitler's bloody storm-troopers?'

'Aye, ye're right,' Joe agreed. 'The battle's up there, and no mistake.'

It made them feel even more depressed. They had fought the best they could and been defeated. What did these LDVs know about it? Damn all. They didn't enjoy their leave. They felt distanced from the local population. Oh, they were kind enough—plying them with drinks and talking as if Dunkirk had been some sort of wonderful victory. It was well seen they hadn't been there.

'Victory my arse,' Joe said, but only once they were out of the pub and walking together through the solid blackness of the night outside. There was no point in getting into arguments or fights with the locals. Some of them were often drunk enough to be blind to the state the soldiers were in, and start a fight. Joe for one was still unsteady on his feet and unable to venture far without the help of his crutches, but he had great spunk and determination.

'Fuck them.' He was meaning the crutches. 'I'm going to get rid of them any day now if it's the last thing I do.'

'That's the spirit, Joe,' Malcy laughed. 'You've got to be a hundred per cent by the time Jerries arrive. Britain's depending on you.'

'You can laugh if you like,' Pete said, 'but soon enough we'll all have to be fit and ready to have another go at them.'

'Aye,' a more serious Malcy agreed, 'and this time we'll have to make a better job of it.' Secretly Malcy thought it would be stretching their luck too far to believe that they'd survive another onslaught.

Then one night, as Joe and Pete were writing to their wives, he began to think of Wincey, and to remember her red hair, her pale, freckled face and unblinking stare. He felt curious about her more than anything. She'd always been a bit of an enigma. He had already written to Teresa and Erchie to let them know that he was all right. Now he wondered if he should write to Wincey. At least it was something to do. He never took part in any of the card games that went on because they played for money. Not that it amounted to much—just coppers mostly. Even so, he rigidly avoided anything that involved gambling.

So he settled down and began writing a letter to Wincey. He told her about Dunkirk, going into more graphic detail than he'd been able to do in his hasty note to Teresa and Erchie. He poured out his thoughts on the course of the war, and the bravado of the locals. Then he asked about life in Glasgow, and if the factory was still doing well. It was a long letter—so long that he wondered if he should send it at all. In the end it went off to the post with the other envelope that contained Joe and Pete's letters home.

Immediately afterwards, he felt strangely anxious and agitated. He put it down to the state of his health. Very few of the survivors had fully recovered from the trauma they had suffered. Malcy had come to believe that most of them never would. His own experiences continued to haunt him, although on the surface he appeared quite normal. Or at least he thought he did. He never cried out in his sleep like some, or gave in to the humiliation of weeping. Nor did Joe or Pete. But a few others he knew had been reduced to pitiful wrecks of humanity.

He wished he was back home in Glasgow. He talked about Glasgow a lot with Joe and Pete—the football matches they'd gone to and the teams they'd cheered on, their favourite pubs. Joe had been born and brought up in the East End and Pete had come from Springburn. Both Joe and Pete confessed that they'd rather have stayed in the East End and Springburn than move to their new homes in Clydebank. But at least the twins were happy, that was the main thing.

'So once I'm home in the dear green place,' Joe said, 'I'll never step out of it again. At least never out of Scotland. You can keep your foreign countries. You can stuff England as well.'

126

'Me too,' Pete fervently agreed.

'The dear green place,' Malcy echoed dreamily.

Pete shook his head. 'The English seem to think we all go about with razors up our sleeves and do nothing but fight each other. I was talking to one of the locals and when I mentioned I came from Glasgow and asked if he'd ever visited the place, he actually said, "Oh, I'd be too frightened to go up there." '

Joe laughed. 'Never mind, it's bad enough worrying about being invaded by Jerries, without having to think about hordes of Englishmen coming up north.'

'I mean . . . ' Pete was still feeling insulted, 'it's such a good place to live, and damn it, it's a friendly place as well. It's a damned sight friendlier than London.'

'Aye, well,' Joe said, 'they're no' so bad around here. They've treated us to a few good drinks, you have to admit.'

Pete shrugged then said, 'I still wish I was in Glasgow. I'd give anything to be enjoying a drink in the Boundary Bar right now.'

Malcy nodded in agreement and his mind wandered far away.

19

It was strange how Malcy, who had once come between Wincey and the rest of the Gourlays, now had the opposite effect. They had all liked and defended Big Malcy while she had despised him. She would have got rid of him from the factory if she had her way. But it was always Charlotte who had the last say, and he had been Charlotte's husband.

Now, however, Wincey was glad to share Malcy's letter with the family and Teresa and Erchie and Granny were glad and grateful.

After poring over the first long letter that Wincey received, Granny said, 'Och, it's just wicked what that poor fella had to suffer.'

Teresa sighed. 'I remember him in my prayers every night. I pray that one day soon he'll be back safe and sound.'

'He's no' out o' the woods yet, hen,' Erchie said.' Aw the soldiers down there'll have to pitch in an' fight the Germans if they start invadin'.'

'But,' Wincey looked worried, 'Churchill said the RAF would . . . '

'See him,' Granny interrupted, 'he's got the gift o' the gab, I'll gie him that, but aw this grand talk is no' goin' to be any comfort to aw the mothers that's lost their sons. An' aw the mothers that's gonnae lose theirs. An' he'll no' be any help to oor Malcy, will he? Just the opposite, if ye ask me. See him an' his finest hour—ah'd finest hour him if ah got ma hands on him.'

Teresa's voice came out sharper than she intended. 'I wish you'd just keep your opinions to yourself, Granny. You're always such a pessimist. We're all worried enough without you making us feel worse.'

It was true that they were all worried and depressed. Life in general had become more and more difficult. It was a struggle now even just to get a few lumps of coal for the fire. Teresa had to trundle a home-made barrow to the nearest coal yard and stand for ages in a queue—even though she wasn't really fit enough for such heavy and exhausting tasks. As she said herself, she was 'a wee bit chesty'. More often than not, a few coal briquettes made with dross was all she got after her long wait in the pouring rain. Now in August coal wasn't so urgently needed as it had been in the winter months, but Granny still felt the cold and with her arthritis, she had to be kept warm. Teresa couldn't even find the wool now to darn Granny's stockings.

Autumn would soon be here, and winter creeping in, and food getting scarcer. Teresa had always believed it was important to eat plenty of good nourishing food to generate heat inside you, and energy. Food—or rather the lack of it— was now a real worry. A lot of folk had to have their pets put down because they weren't able to feed them. Only warehouse cats were entitled to a dried milk ration. Queues, queues— there were queues everywhere for everything. It was beginning to get them all down, although everyone tried their best to keep their spirits up. Or at least to make an outward show of doing so.

There was the black market, of course, but on principle

(and for fear of Granny taking a heart attack if she found out), they never had anything to do with it. Dealing on the black market was a criminal offence, although everyone knew people who were getting away with it.

It was difficult too to keep cheery when there was so much bad news around. Closest to home had been the loss of Doctor Houston. None of them had quite got over that tragedy yet. Then poor Mrs McGregor's man had been killed. And as if that wasn't bad enough, Jimmy, one of her sons— a mere lad not long out of school—had been killed in a bombing attack on an airfield. He hadn't been a pilot or anything glamorous like that. All he'd ever wanted was to be a mechanic. Mrs McGregor said he'd just been happily working on the ground when a whole lot of bombs had rained down on the airfield. That's what she'd been told.

'Poor wee Jimmy,' Teresa said. 'It's just terrible. What can I say to poor Mrs McGregor? Her heart's broken.'

'I'm glad Malcy survived Dunkirk,' Wincey said, and meant it. 'It's a miracle anyone did, when you think of it.'

'Aye,' Erchie said, 'poor fella. His face got it, he said in the letter, an' him such a nice lookin' fella. Always so cheery.'

'Yes,' Teresa agreed, 'and with such bright twinkling eyes. I never could get angry with him, even when I knew about his gambling.'

'He told me before he left,' Wincey said, 'and I believe him, that he'd never gamble again.'

'It was a weakness he had,' Teresa said, 'but he was never a bad man. Charlotte always said he was good to her.'

Erchie examined the letter again. 'Maybe he'll no' be scarred. He seems to go on more about his shoulder an' his arm, but he makes it all sound as if it's more of a nuisance than anythin' else.'

'Have you replied to his letter yet?' Teresa asked Wincey.

'Yes, I wrote quite a long letter back giving him the news about Glasgow, as well as the family. I tried my best to keep it as cheerful as possible.'

'Good for you, dear. You'll let us know when you get any more word from him?'

'Yes, of course.'

It had not been as difficult a letter to write as Wincey had thought it might be. Once she'd got started, there seemed to be no stopping her. She'd described all the places in Springburn he knew, and told him everything that was going on. She gave him all the news about the factory—how they'd to work with the lights on day and night because they'd had to paint all the windows black, how Erchie was one of the few men left in the place. The others had either been called up or volunteered. It wasn't so easy nowadays to get or keep women workers either. Quite a few of the girls he would remember had joined the WRENS or the ATS or the WAAFs. Nevertheless the factory was still managing to keep going. She told him how she'd shared his letter with the Gourlays and that they sent him their love and best wishes, and how Teresa was remembering him in her prayers. She hoped she managed to make him smile or laugh at the some of the things Granny had said or done and finished her letter by urging him to take good care of himself and to write again if he could.

For a few seconds she hesitated about how she should sign the letter. She couldn't quite bring herself to write 'Love', so eventually she settled 'Kind regards, Wincey.'

His next letter caused some dismay among the Gourlays and with Wincey. It spoke about the increasing number and ferocity of aerial dogfights. He was obviously too near an airfield for comfort.

'It's all right,' he assured them. 'The RAF is knocking out dozens of Messerschmitts every day. I've lost count of the ones I've seen going down in flames. I can't see the Germans being able to mount an invasion now.'

It was good news in a way, but they still worried about Malcy's safety.

'Tell him in your next letter to go on bein' careful an' to look after himself, hen,' Erchie urged. Wincey, they all knew, had been better educated than them and could write a better letter. As a result, they'd elected her to write on behalf of them all. She spent quite a few evenings now bent over the kitchen table, her auburn hair flopping forward, a writing pad in front of her, chewing at her pen and thinking of what to write. Erchie and Teresa and Granny kept chipping in with 'Tell him this', or 'Remember to tell him that', and she did. It was the personal bits from herself that always proved difficult. She had always found it difficult to speak about her feelings, in fact, she seldom spoke about herself. Oh, it was all right to go into great detail about how she was running the factory, how she now visited her mother and father every weekend. She had not been able to tell Malcy about the reunion with her mother and father, but Teresa and Erchie had in the first letter that had been written. Now she could describe what they were like, but not her feelings towards them. She'd mentioned Robert Houston's death but nothing about how devastated she'd been, what regrets she'd had. She tried to shut it all out of her mind now. Life had to go on. Malcy was a survivor, but she was a survivor too.

She worked hard. That helped. She was lucky in having the love and support of the Gourlays, and her mother and father. She was glad that her mother and father had met Robert and liked him. Although she was a bit worried about her parents at the moment. Her mother was working longer and longer shifts as a VAD. Her father had more and more to do with the Home Guard. What spare time he had he was using to try to catch up with his writing. Recently, when she'd been having tea with a client in Copeland & Lye's restaurant, she'd seen her mother sitting at another table with a man with silvery grey hair. They were chatting and laughing together, oblivious of anyone else. Wincey decided not to approach her.

She'd told herself later that it could have been a perfectly innocent meeting. The man could have been an ex-patient or someone connected with her work. It made her feel uneasy all the same. She didn't like the thought of any trouble between her mother and father, especially if it meant her father getting hurt. She wondered if she should mention seeing her in Copeland's. That would give her mother a chance to explain, to say who the man was. She kept wondering, and doing nothing about it, until she saw her mother with the same man again. This time she was getting into his car.

Wincey decided to speak up then. It turned out the man was a doctor from the Royal. Her mother had laughed and said, 'Don't worry. It wasn't a clandestine meeting. We just happened to bump into one another and we were talking shop.'

Maybe it was just her suspicious nature, Wincey tried to tell herself. All the same, she couldn't help thinking that her mother had acquired a guarded look and she'd spoken too cheerily. Instinct told Wincey that something was wrong.

20

Just for the first second or two, Richard was stunned at the sight of well over a hundred planes with black crosses on their wings. Then he became very still and cool. He banked his Spitfire hard around until he was behind a twin-engined Messerschmitt 110. With the throttle fully open, he closed in and opened fire. The 110 flopped onto its back and went hurtling down, trailing smoke. Richard pulled up just in the nick of time as another ME 110 latched onto him. Flinging his plane around the sky in a series of desperate evasive manoeuvres, Richard suddenly saw the silhouette of another 110 filling his gunsight. He fired a long, withering burst that raked the German fighter from end to end. Smoke poured out of one engine, then flames. As it fell away and plunged down, a parachute blossomed and drifted out of sight.

A moment later the sky was empty and so were his magazines. He turned back towards the airfield, landed on the grass and parked his Spitfire away from the hangars. This was just as well because within twenty minutes, the hangars were bombed. He only stayed long enough for his ground crew to refuel his aircraft, put in a new oxygen bottle and more ammunition before he took off again. As the day wore on, Richard lost count of how many dogfights he had been involved in, how many of the squadron had 'gone west', and how many times he himself had cheated death.

By the end of the day, the runways and a couple of hangars had been damaged again, but it was nothing compared to what had happened at other airfields. One had recently been hit by a hundred bombers. The station HQ, the sick bay and three of the four hangars had been destroyed. A lot of people had been killed and many fighters destroyed on the ground.

Whenever they weren't in the air, Richard and the rest of the squadron tried to snatch some sleep, still wearing their clothes, including their flying jackets. They had to be ready to scramble at any minute, and ready to do it again, and again, and again. Despite his exhaustion, once Richard was up in the air he was completely alert. The exaltation rushed back as he wheeled and dived and fired. There was terror too, but it was all part of the excitement. He loved it. Sometimes, lying half asleep in his bunk, Richard would wonder if there was something wrong with him. Maybe he had already been at it for too long. Death and killing excited him. Even when he was with Davina now, he was restless to be back in the mess with the other pilots with their silly jokes and edgy remarks, and the way his stomach jumped when the tannoy clicked. The other young pilots, mostly from public schools like himself, were even more reckless than him. They got their excitement on the ground as well as in the air. Any time off was spent driving their Jags or Bentleys into London at breakneck speeds, bumping into obstacles, bouncing off and careering wildly onwards. Once in London, they had one hell of a time with women and booze before rampaging back to base again.

Any time off Richard had was spent with Davina. It was good to be with her, to hold her strong body and to make love to her. Afterwards, she would stroke his black hair and brows and trace her finger gently over his features. She'd say, 'How handsome you are, Richard.'

Jokingly he'd reply, 'I know,' and they'd both laugh.

He had less and less time off now, but he'd managed at least one letter to his mother and father, and one to his grandmother. He'd apologised for not writing more often, but said he was being kept rather busy at the moment. Understatement was becoming more and more the done thing. The last ten days of August had been very difficult. There just weren't enough fighters or pilots. Richard wondered whether they had enough left to last more than a few days. The Germans, on the other hand, seemed to have an unlimited supply of men and aircraft. Hundreds of bombers overwhelmed the Fleet Air Arm, damaged Coastal Command and the radar stations. Raid after huge raid swept over a wider and wider area. Fighters kept being diverted all over the place to meet the bombers and try to stop them. And as the battle intensified, men and machines were being lost at an unprecedented rate. It became so bad that even the WAAFs at the control centres started to be affected. They often had to listen to pilots crying out over the radio when they were hit. Men who, only hours before, had been chatting and joking with them, and who were now trapped in burning cockpits of doomed aircraft.

*   *   *

From September onwards, things began to change. London was now the bombers primary target. Richard had heard all about it from the American journalists who had been staying at one of the local pubs. Up till then, they had been fully occupied watching the spiralling vapour trails above the airfields, reporting on the dog fights, and predicting the outcome of the 'Battle of Britain'. Now, the journalists returned to the pub only to collect their belongings and to have a last few drinks. The next big story was in London. All was in chaos, they'd told Richard. The bombers were wreaking havoc throughout the city, causing large numbers of civilian casualties. Later he'd learned that many of the dead in London had to be buried in mass graves. In one of the worst incidents, more than two hundred people died as the result of a direct hit on a school in Agate Street.

Richard prayed that the bombing wouldn't escalate and extend to Scotland. He began to worry about his parents, his grandmother and his sister. He tried to banish any idea of Scotland getting hit. He had more than enough on his plate at the moment. Night after night, the bombers returned in force, each time widening their target area. On the ground, there was a shortage of anti-aircraft guns, and in the air the Blenheim and Beaufighter night-fighters were blundering around in the darkness with precious little success. Guns were hastily pulled out of the ports, factories and RAF bases they'd been protecting and rushed into London—but to little effect. From the top of hills miles outside the city, German planes could be seen each night dropping their marker flares, while tracers arced back up towards them, and searchlights lit up the sky in a last-ditch attempt to pick up the bombers. And every night, the bombs fell and the fires raged.

As London burned, Richard thought with a sinking heart of Glasgow's East End and all the tenements along the River Clyde. But there was nothing he could do about any of it. All he could do now was to get on with the job.

21

At first it had been perfectly innocent. She'd met him while
working in the Royal. She was still frightened to drive her car
in the dark and so he had begun giving her a lift. He lived in
the south side of Glasgow but insisted he didn't mind going
out of his way to drop her off in the West End. His name was
Donald Hamilton and he was a doctor at the Royal Infirmary.
He was older than her—quite fatherly she'd thought at first,
with his silver-grey hair and moustache.

She'd met him in one of the corridors. She'd been leaning
up against a wall, clutching at her white-aproned waist, grey-
faced and feeling sick. He'd stopped to ask if she was all right.
She'd blurted out, 'That poor man. There was surely no need
to be so rough.' She'd realised almost immediately that she
should have kept her mouth shut. She would not say another
word.

Doctor Hamilton, however, was determined to find out
exactly what she was talking about. Then, even though she
knew that it would mean she'd suffer hell from the nursing
sister involved when she found out, Virginia told him what

had upset her. She'd been holding the kidney dish for Sister by the bedside of a man suffering from VD. It had been a shock in the first place when the sister pulled the bedclothes away to reveal the man's enormous, grotesquely swollen testicles. Then with one vicious movement, the sister jerked the sticking plaster from the testicles. The man had cried out in pain. Virginia almost fainted. She was relieved when the ordeal of renewing the dressing was over and she could escape into the corridor.

Doctor Hamilton said gently, 'She wasn't really being cruel. She did the right thing. It would have been much worse, and only prolonged the agony if she'd tried to remove the plaster slowly.'

After a moment, Virginia said, 'Oh, I see.' She felt a bit of a fool. 'I'm sorry. I think tiredness must be affecting my judgement, or something. I've been up since the crack of dawn. I'm not usually as feeble as this.'

'You're not feeble, you're caring. A caring nurse is a good nurse. When are you off duty?'

'Now, actually.'

'So am I. Let me take you somewhere nice for a cup of tea—far away from the smell of illness and death and disinfectant.'

She had changed out of her blue cotton uniform dress, white apron and starched cap into her outdoor uniform, and had met him outside the Royal Infirmary. They had gone to Copeland & Lye's and drank tea and ate delicious cakes while listening to Copeland's orchestra playing. It was very soothing and relaxing and just what she needed. They talked easily and happily together. He told her of his home in Clarkston where he'd lived for many years with his late wife, Mary. She'd gone down south to visit an elderly relative to try to persuade her to move to Glasgow. There was so much danger in the coastal towns and villages now. This had been tragically proved when Mary and the old lady had both been killed in an air raid. He and Mary had no children, nor had either of them any living relatives left. That elderly aunt of Mary's had been the last.

'You live alone then?' Virginia said.

'Yes, I'm glad of my work. If I didn't have that, I think it might be a very lonely life.'

She knew what loneliness was and she too was glad of having her work to go to. She confided in him about Wincey and he was intrigued.

'Talk about truth being stranger than fiction?'

'Yes, I don't think I've really come to terms with it yet. So many years of worry and fear and uncertainty. Eventually the terrible grieving. Then the shock of her letter.'

'But it must be wonderful to have her back.'

Virginia sighed. 'The only thing is, she isn't properly back with me. I mean, she's living most of the time with the Gourlays. I only see her briefly at weekends. Any time she refers to the Gourlays' place, she calls it home.'

His hand covered hers. 'Well, it was her home for so many years. It will have become a habit to call it home. It's perfectly understandable. I'm sure she doesn't mean it as slight on you.'

'I suppose not. That's what I keep trying to tell myself.'

He was so kind and sympathetic and she needed somebody to talk to. They went on talking in the car and it was agreed that whenever possible, he would give her a lift home. They'd also have tea in Copeland's again, he promised. Their hours on duty did not always coincide, and there were times when he could not meet her, or take her home. More and more however, she looked forward to and enjoyed the times when he could. He was such a nice man—kind and attentive to his patients, and to her. Only when they were alone, of course. Hospital protocol frowned on the most innocent of familiarity between doctors and nurses, even in wartime. A nurse spoke when necessary to the staff nurse. The staff nurse communicated with the ward sister. The sister could speak to the matron or the doctor. The matron was top of the nursing pile and greatly feared by one and all, even by some of the doctors.

So every time Virginia met Doctor Hamilton outside the hospital, she'd hop into his car and they'd speed away like two naughty children. The idea made them laugh. She hadn't laughed for ages. After all, there was very little to laugh about these days.

Even listening to the wireless only added to the general feeling of doom and gloom. The latest news was that night after night, London was being bombed. There weren't enough public air-raid shelters and people fought to get into underground stations. At first the gates had been locked against them but eventually the authorities and the government were forced to give in after a large crowd of angry East Enders burst into the Savoy hotel demanding shelter. Now thousands of people trooped down into the bowels of the earth to sleep on draughty platforms.

Those who emerged from the shelters, or did not go down in the first place, stood and cheered on the Hurricanes and Spitfires as they tore into the German bombers. The onlookers cheered themselves hoarse as bomber after bomber plunged to the ground. One Spitfire pilot who had run out of ammunition deliberately crashed his plane into a German Dornier. As the two aircraft were sent spiralling to the ground, both pilots bailed out. The German pilot landed in the middle of an area that had recently suffered many casualties in the bombing. As he did so, a crowd of civilians came running from their houses with pokers and kitchen knives to attack him, forming a screaming melee around the dying man.

The bombers still came back every night, and not only to London. Now they were bombing Liverpool, Swansea, Hull, Southport, Bristol, Birmingham and many other cities, including Glasgow, although so far the raids on Glasgow had caused little damage and only a few casualties.

A tenement in the Scotstoun district had been hit. A bomb had dropped on Killermont golf course. Another bomb fell in George Square in the centre of Glasgow, and one hit HMS

Sussex, moored in Yorkhill Basin. Virginia had been more aware of the noise of the anti-aircraft guns than of the bombs at the time, and her life continued more or less as normal. Well, as normal as it could be in wartime.

She saw so little of Nicholas, and when she did see him, he was mostly in uniform, forever caught up with his Home Guard duties. Then there was the vegetable garden to attend to. He also took his turn fire watching. Nowadays, he hardly had any time even for his writing. Virginia herself was mostly in uniform and hardly ever in the house either, what with long working hours and queuing for food, and God knows what else. And now there was her relationship with Donald Hamilton. It had grown into a relationship. She hadn't meant it to happen. She didn't think he had either, but it had. He knew about Nicholas, and admired his writing. He'd remarked that he hadn't seen a new book of his in the shops for a while and she'd explained about all his other commitments.

'He still keeps his hand in, but he only manages a couple of hours in his writing room every now and then. There will be a new book coming out, but not for a few months yet. He had to get an extension of his deadline.'

Gradually it had come out that they had drifted apart.

'I'm not blaming Nicholas,' she said, not wanting to sound disloyal. 'It's my fault as much as his.'

'It's the war,' Donald said. 'It's affecting everyone's life in all sorts of ways.'

One evening, Donald phoned and invited her to dinner at his house in Clarkston. Nicholas was going to be out on Home Guard duty that evening. She said goodbye to him and he left dressed in his khaki uniform and tin helmet, and armed with his rifle. She hadn't been looking forward to spending the evening on her own so she gladly accepted Donald's dinner invitation.

'I'll take a taxi over,' she said.

'That would be best,' he agreed. 'I daren't leave the cooker. I'm not a very confident cook. You don't know what you're letting yourself in for.'

She wore a sheath dress in a soft blue material and little diamond earrings. Her hair was still an attractive golden brown, with very little grey. It was long and, for the evening, she wore it swept up. She began to feel flushed and as excited as a young girl as she set off for Clarkston. The taxi dropped her off at a villa on the main road. It was fronted by a rather unkempt looking garden. At the back of the house there was a much larger, secluded but equally wild and neglected garden lined with trees.

'I never get time to attend to the garden,' Donald explained, 'and it's impossible to find any gardeners nowadays.'

Virginia was surprised at how old-fashioned everything was inside. The walls were covered with dark brown embossed paper, up to a dado, with floral printed paper above. The patterned carpet looked faded and dusty. The furniture was heavy and of a Victorian or even earlier period. All of it was made of dark mahogany with a reddish tinge. There were button-backed chairs and an intricate floral arrangement displayed under a glass dome. The curtains were of brown chenille. A matching cover edged with long fringes was draped over the table in the dining room. Unfortunately, it reminded her of Mrs Cartwright's house.

'I'm sorry,' Donald said. 'I've been so long in the kitchen, I haven't had time to set the table through here.'

'Why don't we just eat in the kitchen,' Virginia suggested. 'It's so much homelier.'

'Well, if you're sure you don't mind.'

'Of course not.'

She followed him through to the kitchen which, to her relief, turned out to be brighter and more attractive than the rest of the house. It had cream walls and blue and cream linoleum tiles on the floor. She soon found out where dishes and cutlery and glasses were kept, and she set the table while he stirred a pot with great concentration. He had made liver savoury.

'Sorry it couldn't be fillet steak,' he said.

'Lucky you to find some liver,' Virginia told him. 'I haven't seen any in the shops for ages.'

'I've to thank my cleaning lady for queuing for it. The soup is made from vegetables out of her garden, but I did all the cooking myself.'

'It looks wonderful.'

He turned round for a second. 'And you look wonderful.'

After the meal they took their coffee through to the sitting room and settled next to each other on an uncomfortable horsehair sofa. By that time, she'd had quite a few glasses of wine. She blamed the wine for what happened afterwards but knew it was a weak excuse.

They had made love upstairs in the brass bedstead with its flounced valance. Across the foot of the bed was a chaise longue and the fireplace had polished copper scuttle and tongs, and a poker set on show within the fender.

Virginia felt as if she'd stepped back into another age. It was a peaceful feeling. In a way, her lovemaking with Donald was also peaceful. Certainly it wasn't a mad passionate encounter, as lovemaking with Nicholas had been at the beginning. Once she'd danced naked with Nicholas in the woods and they'd made passionate love on the soft mossy earth. Now Nicholas usually fell sound asleep as soon as he collapsed into bed each night. If she was on late shift, she did much the same thing once she arrived home.

This evening, with Donald, at least she was relaxed and happy.

22

'If Grandmother Cartwright knew what my mother's up to, all hell would be let loose.'

'You're not going to tell her, are you? Teresa's gentle face creased with worry.

'A doctor too!'

'How do you know that, dear?'

'Well, I told you I saw her with him a couple of times. Then on Saturday, I decided I'd meet her as she came off early shift, and take her out to lunch. I went into the Royal and there they were in reception, talking together. He was in his white coat, and with his stethoscope hanging round his neck. I recognised him right away.'

'But it needn't mean she's having an affair with him, Wincey. They could be just colleagues and friends. That's what she said when you spoke to her before, wasn't it?'

'Oh yes, that's what she said, all right.'

'Well then, dear.'

'But I saw how they were looking at each other, Teresa. They're having an affair, believe me.'

Teresa hesitated. 'It's really none of your business, Wincey. Although,' she added hastily, 'I know how you feel, dear.'

'It's my poor father I'm thinking about.' Wincey replied, 'He works very hard but Mother always seems so resentful, instead of having any sympathy or understanding.'

'That may be so, but all the same, you don't want to cause any trouble.' The words 'You've caused them enough trouble already' hung in the air, unsaid.

'Oh, I suppose you're right, Teresa, but I can't understand her doing this—after all they've been through, all that they've managed to overcome. Not to mention the opposition from the Cartwrights. And Father's so handsome and talented, isn't he? Whereas this man is just old. I can't understand it,' she repeated.

'But you won't say anything, will you, dear?'

'I suppose not. But Father's such a nice man. It makes me so angry. Guilty as well, because I have to watch Father innocently trusting Mother, never questioning her, while all the time I know what she's up to.'

'These things happen a lot nowadays. Everybody's life is upside down because of the war, and couples separated for ages, and all the temptations . . . '

'Mother and Father are not separated, but they will be—and for good—if she continues like this. I'd hate to see that happen. I want us to stay as a family now that we've found each other again.'

'I know, I know. Just try to be patient, dear. It'll probably all work out in the end. But it's for your mother to sort things out. Or your mother and father. Not you.'

'Oh, all right.'

Just then, Granny bawled from the front room. 'Are you two tryin' to send me to ma grave before ma time. It's like the bloody North Pole through here.'

'I'll get her,' Wincey said, and went through to fetch the old woman and her wheelchair.

'I thought you were enjoying yourself, Granny, watching

146

the world go by.'

'Feel they hands.' Granny lifted a couple of gnarled, shaky hands. Wincey took them in hers, gently rubbed them, and Granny said, 'Aye, it's well seen ye've been heatin' yersel'. Yer hands are like hot water bottles.'

Laughing, Wincey began pushing the wheelchair through to the kitchen and manoeuvred it as near to the fire as possible.

'There you are. You'll be as warm as toast in a minute or two.'

'Ah'm starvin' as well. An' ah see the table's no' even set. What have you two been bletherin' about aw this time?'

'I've just made a pot of tea,' Teresa soothed. 'That'll keep you going until Erchie gets in. There's a nice Skirly-Mirly.'

'No' that again. Tatties an' turnip wi' nae meat. What good is that to a workin' man, or to anybody for that matter.'

'We've used up all our meat ration, Granny. I'm not a magician, you know.'

'Ah suppose ma sweety coupons are aw done as well.'

'Yes, but I'll get your peppermints with mine. I haven't such a sweet tooth as you.'

Erchie had breezed into the room. 'Ma hasnae any teeth at aw, have ye, auld yin. But ye're a great souker, eh?'

'Aye, well, ye'll be auld yersel' wan day.'

Erchie laughed and rubbed his hands. 'Is that tea on the go, hen?'

'Yes dear.' Teresa poured him a cup and passed it over to him.

'Here's the paper, Ma.' He tugged a rolled up newspaper from his jacket pocket.

'Ye know ah cannae see right to read. Just tell me what's in it.'

Teresa groaned. 'Here we go again.'

'Ah dinnae make aw the bad news happen,' Granny protested. 'Ye cannae blame me for that.'

'I know, but I wish you didn't need to hear it every night.

147

It puts me off my tea—all these poor folk getting bombed. It's getting worse instead of better.'

'Aye, that's war for ye. Oor Malcy coppin' it'll be the next bit o' bad news.'

Teresa rolled her eyes and Wincey said, 'Malcy has suffered enough. They'll surely not put him into any more fighting.'

'Would ye listen to her,' Granny howled sarcastically. 'She's one that did come up the Clyde in a banana boat.'

Erchie lit up a half-smoked Woodbine. He inhaled with rare appreciation. He had to ration his smokes to a half at a time, they were so scarce now. 'Are ye gonnae write to him again tonight, hen?'

'Well, I hadn't planned on it, Erchie. I wrote a few days ago, remember.'

'Och, but the poor laddie's got nobody else, an' he's far from home. Ah'm sure it cheers him up to get aw the news from auld Glasgow.'

Wincey shrugged. 'I don't mind.'

And so after their meal, they all settled round the table again, Wincey with the notepad and pen.

Erchie said, 'Tell him no' to worry about the bombs up here. We're aw fine. It was nothin' like as bad as London. Mind an' tell him that.'

'Uh-huh.' Wincey tucked her hair behind her ears and began to write, reading out loud every now and again.

'Dear Malcy,
you remember the kitchen? Well, it's still the same. The
fire's crackling and sparkling in the grate. There's the
brass candlesticks and the black tea caddy with the
Japanese picture on it. Tea's rationed now, of course, so
the caddy's never as full as it used to be. But there's still
the same cream curtains over the hole in the wall bed, and
the matching valance hiding Granny's hurly bed
underneath it. And there's the same green linoleum on the
floor, and the rug in front of the fire that Granny had

made with lots of bits of coloured rags. At the moment we're all sitting round Teresa's scrubbed wooden table. Erchie is wearing his bunnet as usual, Teresa is in her floral, wrap-around pinny and checked slippers, and Granny is keeping cosy in her fawn crocheted shawl. We've tucked a tartan blanket around her knees because she got a bit chilled sitting through at the front room window. Erchie says not to worry about Glasgow being bombed. We've got the Home Guard very active here. There's even machine gun posts around the city. My father helps to man one. He does all sorts of things to help. He's making a great job of growing vegetables too and he often gives some to Teresa so that she can make her soup. He hasn't a very big garden so he even grows things on the earth covering the Anderson shelter. It's a great help getting the vegetables. Teresa says she'd never manage any soup without them. She sends you her love. Erchie says to tell you that Willie Henderson's joined the Navy and Benny McKay was turned down for the RAF and was terribly disappointed. His eyesight let him down so it's still the factory for him. He and Erchie are about the only men left there. Granny says she hopes you're behaving yourself. You'll have her to answer to when you come back if you're not. She still has her blether with old Mr McCluskey out in the close every day and she still gives his daughter cheek, which never fails to infuriate Miss McCluskey. Teresa says she'll give you a welcome home party when you come back, and she'll use up everyone's rations in one go, but nobody will mind. We'll all be so glad to see you come home safe and sound. We hope your injuries have healed all right. We're all well except for Granny's arthritis, which flares up worse every now and again, but as Erchie says, she's a tough old bird and she'll be belting out a song at your welcome home party, don't you worry. Florence and the twins send their love as well. The twins hope you'll always keep an eye out for Joe and Pete, and see that they're OK. They were so glad that you managed to keep together the way you did.

*They're looking forward to their own welcome home
party for Joe and Pete. They're keeping their houses
lovely for the boys coming home. They're sure Joe and
Pete will be prouder than ever of their nice homes. They
say they can't wait to hear what Joe and Pete think of
some of the improvements they've made and the lovely
velvet curtains they've hung in their front rooms—blue
velvet in Joe's house and gold in Pete's. The twins say
Joe and Pete'll just love these curtains when they see
them.'*

'I think that should do,' Wincey said to the others.

'Ye huvnae said much about yersel', hen.'

'Nothing much to tell, Erchie.'

Wincey signed the letter, folded it and put it into an
envelope.

'At least it'll keep him in touch,' Teresa said. 'I'm sure
Malcy will be glad of that. It's very good of you, dear.'

'Ye could have said more about Springburn,' Granny
complained. 'Ye never even mentioned the Sally Army band,
an' ye never telt him about Mrs McGregor's man, and wee
Jimmy McGregor getting killed.'

'For goodness sake, Granny, have a wee bit of sense,'
Teresa snapped.

'Ah cannae open ma mouth these days.' Granny chomped
her gums in agitation.

'Never mind, Granny,' Wincey said. 'I'll make you a cup
of tea.'

'Thanks, hen. Ah miss ye when ye go away at weekends.
Ye're the only one that's nice to me these days.'

Teresa rolled her eyes and Erchie said, 'Ye're a right auld
blether, Ma.'

Granny ignored him and asked Wincey, 'How's yer mammy
and daddy gettin' on, hen?'

'Fine, thanks, Granny.' Turning away, Wincey thought
sarcastically, 'Oh just fine.'

1941

23

'Is that another letter from Wincey?' Pete asked.

He passed it over for Pete to read. After a minute or two Pete groaned. 'Listen to this, Joe.' And he read out the bit about Euphemia and Bridget.

It was Joe's turn to groan. 'Fuckin' curtains. Can you beat it? What do I care about fuckin' curtains?'

Pete nodded in agreement. 'I don't know what to write to Bridget. I feel as if I haven't much in common with her any more.'

'I know what you mean,' Pete said gloomily.

Malcy replaced the letter in its envelope. 'Och, the girls don't mean any harm. They just don't know how things have changed for us. You'll be able to explain to them once you get back home.'

'The trouble is,' Joe said, 'I still love the silly wee midden.'

'How about you, Malcy?' Pete asked.

'What do you mean?'

'You and Wincey?'

Malcy looked astonished. 'Me and Wincey?' he echoed.

153

'That would be a turn up for the book. She always hated the sight of me.'

'Doesn't sound as if she hates you now. She's going to a lot more trouble keeping in touch with you than the twins are doing with us.'

'Well, I know, but . . . '

'But what?'

Malcy tried to laugh. 'You don't really think she might be interested? I mean, in *me*?'

'Are you daft, or something,' Joe said. 'Of course she's bloody interested. She's writing to you every other day, isn't she?'

'I know but . . . '

'Never mind your stupid buts, Malcy. Get in there man. She's one hell of a good catch.'

Such a thought had never occurred to Malcy before. Wincey of all people. He'd thought of her before right enough, and he remembered lots about her. He'd never imagined, however, anything like what he was trying to imagine now. He could accept that she had changed towards him. Even before he'd left Glasgow, she hadn't seemed too bitter. Hadn't seemed bitter at all, in fact. He reread all her letters and began to detect an increasing warmth in them. They certainly gave no indication of either bitterness or hatred.

Then he had an attack of anxiety and lack of self confidence. His face and scalp were scarred. He studied his reflection in the mirror. The doctor had assured him that it would heal in time and if he was lucky, it would only leave a faint mark. If he was lucky. Had he ever been that lucky? He tried to put Wincey out of his mind, but it wasn't easy because her letters kept on coming. In one of his letters he'd half jokingly referred to his scars and said that he now had a face that only a mother could love—and he hadn't even a mother. In her next letter, she said what did looks matter. It was the person that was inside that was important.

For the first time she signed her letter 'Love, Wincey'.

Previously she'd signed 'Sincerely, Wincey' or 'Kind Regards, Wincey'. He read the ending of her last letter over and over again. 'Love, Wincey'. 'Love, Wincey'. 'Love, Wincey' until it turned into 'Wincey love, Wincey love, oh Wincey love'.

The next time he wrote to her, he spoke of his longing to get back to Glasgow. But there was so much he wanted to tell her that he couldn't put in a letter. He tried to give her some hints about recent events in the south and why leave had been cancelled, but he learned from a subsequent letter from her that almost everything he wrote had been censored. Malcy reckoned such strict censorship wasn't really necessary. He no longer believed there was going to be an invasion, and by the look of things, Hitler had changed his tactics and was now trying to bomb the civilian population into submission. Even Glasgow was beginning to get it, albeit not as badly as London and elsewhere in England.

Malcy was becoming heartily sick of the whole business. He'd just missed being sent abroad again to fight. His shoulder and arm had not improved enough and he still had to wear a sling. He'd also caught a dose of flu. Poor old Joe and Pete had not been so lucky and were gone. He couldn't help wondering if he'd ever see them again. He hadn't relished the job of telling Wincey about that. The boys had been packed off so suddenly that they hadn't had the chance to write to the twins before they left.

Wincey had written back saying it hadn't been much of a Christmas and New Year for any of them. Teresa had made an eggless Christmas cake with carrots, of all things. He couldn't imagine it. She said shops were hiring out cardboard cakes, especially for weddings. They were decorated with chalk icing sugar and a real, much smaller cake was underneath the cardboard cover.

The twins were very worried about Joe and Pete and hadn't felt very festive. Granny had talked wistfully and in some detail about the family she'd lost, and about her dead husband. It was something she'd never done before and it worried them all. Wincey's letters were vivid and she portrayed Springburn Road and the Avenue and Wellfield Street and the 'Wellie' cinema so clearly that it brought a lump to his throat. Many's the time he'd sat in that flea pit of a picture house. There was sometimes an amateur variety show in the interval, and he and some of his pals used to boo and throw orange peel at the performers. Then there were the public baths in Kay Street and the Balgrayhill, leading to Springburn Park. He'd often fished for minnows in the pond there and collected them in a glass jam jar filled with water.

Now there was the Gourlays' house near the top of the Balgray. If he walked up there now, no doubt he'd see Granny wrapped in her fawn crocheted shawl, hunched forward, glasses balanced on the edge of her nose, peering out of the front room window. Or her wheelchair would be parked in the close beside her old pal, Mr McCluskey. He would gladly give a year's pay and more to be able to walk up that hill and into that close right now.

Malcy tried not to get depressed but the physical pain he was in didn't help. Still, he was lucky to have survived. He kept telling himself that. He managed to get a bit of time off and took the train into London. The journey seemed to take forever, as the train crawled cautiously along. In London, the devastation was terrible to witness and among the bombed buildings, notices had been stuck up reminding people that looting was punishable by death.

St Paul's Cathedral had miraculously survived undamaged amidst a sea of fire. Everything around it was bombed. The fires had been so bad that they were very close to becoming fire storms—raging infernos so strong that people could be sucked into them. Malcy tightened his stomach against flutters of panic at the thought of that ever happening in Glasgow.

He was tempted to tell Wincey about what he had seen in his next letter, but didn't want to frighten her. Although he couldn't help thinking she was not a lady who would be easily frightened. Not with that steady stare. He began to realise just

156

how much he admired her. Again he felt lucky. Without Wincey and the rest of the Gourlays, he would have had nothing, and no one, to go back to.

He'd thought he'd got used to that long ago. He was illegitimate, didn't know to this day who his father was, and when he'd been very young, his alcoholic mother had abandoned him. He'd been discovered stealing food from a grocer's shop and handed over to the police. They had taken him home only to find there was no one there. He'd been trying to survive on his own. From there he was taken to an orphanage. He ran away from there more times than he could remember. Eventually he'd got a job. He'd got digs. He was determined to make it, and dreamed of being wealthy. He was going to make something of his life, to show everyone who ever doubted him.

Now, showing them didn't matter any more. Everything had become very simple. He lived for the moment. Survival was the only thing that mattered. He needed to survive to get back to Glasgow. He needed to get back to Granny and Erchie and Teresa and Florence and the twins.

And Wincey.

24

The routine was now so familiar to Granny that she could have done it herself. She had come to enjoy it almost as much as the bewhiskered and bescarfed Mr McCluskey. First the old man got his pipe and his knife ready. He cleaned out the dead tobacco from the pipe and gave it a knock to loosen any remnants at the bottom. After that he took the plug of tobacco from the pouch and cut a slice off it. He rubbed the slice between his hands until it was all loose and small. Then he filled it very carefully into the pipe, making sure it was not too tight. After that he put the pipe in his mouth and gave it a suck to make sure air was coming through. Next he took a box of matches, sparked a match, applied it to the pipe and sucked contentedly. It made Granny feel contented too.

'Aye, ye like yer smoke, auld yin,' she said.

'Aye,' Mr McCluskey agreed.

After a while Granny said, 'See war, ah mind seein' at the pictures the Germans dive bombin' an' machine gunnin' folk in Spain. Do you?'

'Ah do. Ah mind the Daily Worker said it wis a rehearsal

for the bigger war tae come.'

'Aye,' Granny said, 'an' the Daily Worker wis right, wisn't it?'

Aye,' agreed Mr McCluskey.

Granny said, 'See if that siren goes again the night, come into oor lobby, Mr McCluskey. There wis about a dozen o' us the last time. Them frae upstairs came as well. We shut aw the lobby doors, ye see, so that nae glass or any o' that shrapnel stuff could come flyin' in. Tell yer lassie she'd be welcome as well. It's no' good to be on yer own at a time like that.'

'Ah'll tell her, but whether she'll come in or no' is another story. An' ah widnae like tae leave her.'

'Ah'll get Teresa to speak to her.'

'She's a nice lassie, your Teresa.'

'Aye.' Granny would like to have said—but didn't, 'No' like your lassie. That bitch wouldn't even let you into our house to enjoy yer smoke.'

'Don't you dare go into anyone's house and fill it with your filthy smoke, and give me a showing up,' she'd warned.

Granny was well wrapped up with a muffler wound round her neck and hanging down the front of her shawl. Although it had been a lovely spring day, a March wind was blowing through the close. Earlier Florence said the river was all shiny and beautiful when she'd looked out her window in Clydebank. Now the wind tugged at the rug protecting Granny's legs and ankles.

Mr McCluskey, despite his bunnet and muffler, must be feeling the chill because he had no rug or shawl wrapped around him. His jacket and trousers had worn pretty thin too, Granny noticed. It worried her. She knew only too well how your blood got thin when you were old and you were easily chilled. Poor old Mr McCluskey could catch his death of cold. The selfish bitch of a daughter of his never even got him to the barber's often enough—certainly not recently. His white hair was straggling down from his bunnet and his

159

moustache looked neglected as well. He wasn't in a wheelchair but he was a bit shaky on his feet and would need a helping hand or an arm to hang on to to get him down the road to the barber's.

'A bloody disgrace,' Granny had told Teresa. And Teresa had promised to ask the barber if he'd call up to see Mr McCluskey.

'Although,' Teresa added, 'dear knows what Miss McCluskey will say about me interfering, Granny.'

'Och, tell the barber to kid on that he just happened to be passin' the close. Warn him no' to let on that it was us that put him up to it.'

'Oh, all right. I'll try.'

She was a good lassie, right enough. She never thought twice about inviting everybody to shelter in their lobby if there was an air raid. There was a brick shelter in the back yard but it had no lights, no seats, no heating—nothing. It was a damp, dark horror of a place and nobody wanted to set foot in it. Especially Teresa, because dampness tended to go for her chest. Granny sat up all night in her wheelchair and tried to get a few minutes sleep when there was a raid on. Everyone else sat either on one of the chairs Teresa had brought from the kitchen, or they crouched on cushions on the floor. At first they had a bit of a blether—caught up with everyone's news. Then they had a singsong, more in an effort to drown the noise from outside than anything else. Eventually, fatigue overcame them and they just sat dozing, and listening to the racket, and trying not to feel afraid. Teresa always wanted to go through to the kitchen and make everyone a cup of tea but no one would let her in case a piece of shrapnel or a bullet got her. They'd heard of that happening to other folk. None of them were sure what was going on outside and causing the bedlam of noise.

In the morning when they emerged, there never seemed to be any bomb damage. At least not as far as they could see in Springburn. Erchie said it was the noise of anti-aircraft guns trying to shoot the bombers down. There were bombers right enough because the drone of them could be heard as loud and heavy as if they were only inches above the roof.

Next day, Granny would doze in her wheelchair by the fire, her head falling heavily down on her chest, her toothless mouth hanging open. Sometimes Teresa would say, 'You look awful uncomfortable like that, Granny. I'll bring out your hurly bed and you can have a proper sleep, even if it's just for a couple of hours.'

Granny hoped the siren wouldn't go again tonight. Mrs Faulds, a new neighbour in the top flat, was a terrible pessimist and last time she had maintained that tonight the sirens would go and it would be the worst raid ever.

'Oh,' Granny had said, 'has Hitler been in touch wi' ye then, hen?'

'It's the thirteenth,' Mrs Faulds said with a knowing look.

'Even if ye believe in that rubbish,' Granny said, 'it's supposed to be Friday the thirteenth that's unlucky. This is Thursday.'

'I've always believed that thirteen is an unlucky number.'

'Oh aye, an' what else do ye believe that could cheer us aw up?'

It was a mistake to have asked that, because Mrs Faulds launched into such a long list that Granny had eventually to interrupt.

'Aye, aye, we've got the message, hen. Now just gie yer tongue a rest.'

The siren did go however. Its eerie wail made all of their hearts sink in despair. It meant another apprehensive, sleepless night trying to be cheerful, trying to hide the fact that everyone felt worried.

To the surprise of all the Gourlays, old Mr McCluskey and Miss McCluskey returned with Teresa. Teresa had gone next door after the raid started to repeat her previous invitation to join the rest of the neighbours in the Gourlay lobby.

'It does sound rather worse tonight,' said Miss McCluskey,

keeping her head held high and her back stiff. Teresa offered two chairs for the McCluskeys to sit on. This meant Teresa had to make do with the floor.

'I told you,' Mrs Faulds cried out triumphantly. 'Didn't I tell you?'

'Aye, aw right,' Granny said, 'ye don't need to tell us again.'

It certainly did sound much worse.

'What a shame,' Teresa said, wrapping her woolly cardigan closer around her thin chest. 'After us having such a lovely time visiting the twins.'

It had been the turn of Euphemia to entertain her mother and sisters to a late afternoon tea. The twins and Florence had managed to get away early from work. This time Granny had gone with the twins because Erchie was busy in the factory and couldn't take any time off to look after her. Wincey had been working too. A factory was regarded as essential work, not like a department store, but Granny had been warned not to say this to the girls. Wincey had treated them to a taxi that took them all the way to Clydebank. It was even booked to call for them later to return them to Springburn. Teresa had been horrified at such expense and Granny had said, 'Folk'll be thinkin we're aw turned into bloody Tories an' capitalists noo!'

Nevertheless she allowed herself to be helped into the taxi and her wheelchair folded up to travel along with her. The journey was actually a real treat for Granny, although she'd never admit it.

Euphemia had a lovely spread waiting for them in her kitchen and Granny was duly impressed. She also greatly pleased the happy, sparkling eyed Euphemia by admiring the cream and brown kitchen with its splendid new gas cooker.

Bridget said, 'Mine is lovely as well, Granny. We could take you along after tea to see it. Both our toilets are out in the close, but there's a big cupboard in the hall and I'm saving up to get my cupboard turned into a toilet. Amn't I, Euphemia?'

Euphemia nodded enthusiastically, making her fat cheeks quiver and her curls bounce. An inside toilet converted from a cupboard was very impressive indeed.

'Fancy!' Granny said, not really believing it was possible but not wanting to burst her grand-daughter's bubble of happiness.

'I'm going to have it done too,' Euphemia informed them, her face even ruddier than usual with excitement.

'Are ye, hen? Good for you.'

Bridget said, 'We can't wait to hear what Joe and Pete will say when they see what we've done to make our houses so nice. They'll be over the moon, don't you think.'

'Oh aye,' Granny said, struggling to keep the sarcasm from her voice. 'They will that, hen.'

It had been a good outing all the same, Granny had to admit. The sandwiches, scones and cakes had been delicious. Indeed, they'd enjoyed the meal so much that they weren't able to eat their evening meal with Erchie and Wincey when they returned home. Teresa had written down Euphemia's recipe for carrot cake and eggless sponge and was planning to make them the next morning. Now she wondered if she'd have enough energy. Poor Erchie and Wincey were worse off though. At least she and Granny could have a rest the next day, but Erchie and Wincey had their work to go to.

'Maybe it won't last so long tonight,' she said to the crowd now crushed into the lobby, shoulder squeezed against shoulder and hip against hip.

'I told you.' Mrs Faulds sorrowfully shook her head. 'It'll be worse—much worse. It's a bright moonlight night. They'll see their way here no bother.'

Erchie said he was going to have a quick look outside and despite both Granny and Teresa's efforts in trying to dissuade him, he slipped out to the close. He seemed a long time in returning and Teresa was getting quite breathless with agitation. She had struggled to her feet and was about to leave the safety of the lobby as well. As she said, 'Erchie might be lying outside in the street injured and helpless.'

But just then he suddenly appeared again. His thin, beaky face had turned a sickly grey and his eyes, staring from under the peak of his bunnet, were wide and anxious.

'Whit's up, son?' Granny asked before Teresa could say anything.

'There's awfae big fires. The sky's red wi' them.'

'In Springburn?' Teresa cried out in alarm.

Erchie hesitated. He shook his head. 'One o' the wardens told me it's Clydebank.'

'Oh Erchie, the girls!'

25

Florence washed up and dried Euphemia's tea dishes and tidied them away in the kitchen press. Bridget carefully wiped around the sink and draining board. Euphemia brushed under the table. Granny was such a messy eater. Finally, Bridget packed away what food there was left into tins.

As soon as the kitchen was spick and span once more, Florence asked, 'What's on at the pictures?'

Euphemia picked up the paper and read out loud, 'Shirley Temple and Jack Oakey in *Young People* at the La Scala and the Regal. Gene Hersholt starring as the "pocket Ginger Rogers" at the Pavilion. *Maryland* is at the Bank cinema and *Daughter of the Tong* at the Palace. Anything there you fancy?'

Bridget made a face. 'I don't fancy *Daughter of the Tong*.'

'*Young People*, I think,' Euphemia said. She took a mirror out of her handbag and tweaked at the bunch of curls on her forehead. 'Shirley Temple has lovely curly hair. I wonder if it's natural.'

Florence said, 'Do we really want to go?'

'It's all right for you,' Euphemia said. 'You've got Eddie

to go home to. We're on our own. It's boring as well as lonely.'

'Well, there's nothing to stop you and Bridget going. I'd like to come but it's not fair on Eddie. We hardly see each other as it is, with us both working and him having to do such long hours. These days, the union has to go along with these awful hours, Eddie says. They need all the guns they can get, you see. Fancy Eddie making Sten guns. Him that used to make sewing machine cabinets!'

'Doesn't he usually work a few extra hours on a Thursday night?' Bridget asked.

'Dash, I forgot it was Thursday. I tell you what, I'll go home and see to his dinner. He nips across for something to eat to keep him going. After that, I'll go to the second house with you.'

'Fine, see you later then.'

Florence took out her compact, powdered her nose, smoothed a hand over her hair and then pulled on her new navy velour hat. Outside it had got a bit colder and she turned up the collar of her coat and quickened her step towards the Holy City. She always experienced a little thrill of pride and pleasure when she thought of the name—Holy City. Every time she saw the flat roofs too. Her colleagues had expressed surprise and curiosity when they came to visit her and saw the flat roofs and heard the name. She enjoyed explaining to them how the flat roofs were like those in Jerusalem. It was so unusual, so different. Not at all like your common or garden Glasgow tenements. Some people tried to tell her that apart from the flat roofs, the area was nothing like the real Holy City but she never paid any attention to them. They were just jealous.

She made a nice quick meal for Eddie because he hadn't much time. Then she cleared the table and washed up and swept the floor. She always swept the floor after every meal, although there was no need. Neither she nor Eddie were messy eaters, not like Granny.

166

Eddie said, 'Poor old Granny. You can't blame her, with her arthritis. She can't get a right grip of anything.' Eddie was such a thoughtful and understanding man, even about the house. He always wiped his feet on the doormat before coming in.

'I'm not angry with her or anything like that, dear,' Florence assured him. 'I'm terribly fond of Granny. I always have been, you know that.'

She told Eddie she was going to the pictures with the twins, in case he got back before her. After kissing him goodbye, she went to the window to give him a wave. She always did that, and he always turned and smiled. She sang under her breath as she went to meet her sisters, and then the three of them set off, arm in arm and giggling. It wasn't like Florence to be so unladylike but she felt quite reckless with happiness.

The picture house was packed and they settled down to enjoy the movie. After a while they heard the wail of the siren and the usual notice went up on the screen. 'There is an air raid in progress. Anyone wishing to leave the cinema should do so now.' No one moved. They were getting accustomed to the siren going and nothing happening. The picture continued but soon they began to hear alarming noises from outside. The noises became thunderous, then the screen went blank. A ripple of panic went through the audience. People got up and made for the exit.

Outside, white faced and trembling usherettes told everyone that bombs were dropping all over Clydebank and they would be taking their lives in their hands if they went outside. Some people retreated back into the hall to huddle under the balcony for safety.

Florence said, 'I've got to get home to Eddie.'

But neither she nor the twins moved when they saw and heard bombs screaming down. For a minute or two they were immobilised with shock and disbelief. It was such a terrifying and incredible scene. All around the sky was lit up by incendiaries, and raging fires quickly took hold, turning the blackness of the night into bright orange and scarlet.

'Oh my God,' Florence whispered. 'That must be Singer's timber yard. All that wood! I've got to go and make sure Eddie's safe at home.'

They all began to run, oblivious now of each other, just desperate to get back to what they believed was the safety of their homes. It was like running through a nightmare. After a few horrific minutes, Florence hardly knew where she was going any more. Every street was impassable at some point or another. It was difficult even to cross a road because tram lines had been torn up, and reared to the sky—distorted, grotesque iron sculptures.

On the ground rubble lay in heaps around deep bomb craters. Houses had been sliced in two and revealed—like open doll's houses—shelves with ornaments and books undisturbed, clocks and candlesticks on mantelpieces, and pictures hanging on walls. Other tenements had sunk into chaotic piles of concrete and rubble, from which muffled screams and faint cries for help could sometimes be heard. From the top flat of one blazing building came the eerie sounds of a piano. Florence thought it was somebody playing who had gone completely mad. Until a policeman said that it was the intense heat bursting the piano strings.

The policeman tried to stop Florence. He had a soot blackened face and his uniform jacket and trousers were grey with dust. A dense cloud of dust was billowing about the whole street.

'You can't go any further,' he said. 'There's unexploded bombs down there.'

'My husband,' Florence insisted. 'I have to get back to my husband.' And before the policeman had a chance to say or do anything else, she had sped away. She passed rescue workers struggling to extricate the living and the dead. There was the incessant drone of low flying aircraft, and she even saw one plane actually below the level of the flames machine gunning a number nine bus. She was forced to slow down because the ground beneath her feet was covered in a sea broken glass. There was an explosion some way in front of her and before her horrified eyes, she saw—by the light of the flames—dismembered bodies flying through the air. She had to stop to vomit.

Somehow, eventually, she found her way to Second Avenue in the Holy City. There she stopped, shock immobilising her for a few minutes. The buildings had been turned into gaunt, smoking skeletons. Windows were now black gaping holes. A few tattered curtains flapped from the holes. The flat concrete roofs had collapsed down through the houses. Only the tall rows of chimneys had mysteriously survived.

Florence began to stumble towards what had been her home. 'Eddie! Eddie!'

Wardens and rescue squad men caught her and held her back. One of them said, 'If he's in there, hen, we'll get him out. Don't worry. Just try and keep calm and stay out of our way.'

A tired looking nurse in a filthy and blood stained apron took hold of Florence's arm.

'I have to find Eddie,' Florence told her dazedly.

'They'll do their best. Just leave them be.'

'I want to help find him.'

'You're in no fit state,' the nurse said wearily. 'You're the one that's needing help.'

It was only then that Florence realised there was blood running down her face and staining her coat. She felt a sudden stabbing pain in her skull. She put a hand to her head.

'I've lost my new hat,' she wailed and began to weep brokenheartedly.

★　　　★　　　★

Euphemia and Bridget's plumpness prevented them from running for very long. They became so out of breath that they

169

had to stop. They stood scarlet-faced, gasping and choking.

'Euphemia,' Bridget shouted, suddenly too terrified to be without her.

'Over here,' Euphemia called and, sobbing with relief, Bridget picked her way across the road, skirting pockets of fire and twisted metal. Nearby, a tram car stood with its top deck half ripped off. Euphemia was crying too and the sisters clung together in distress. They didn't know whether to try to go on or stay where they were. The options were equally terrifying. Everywhere there were crowds of ARP men, policemen, rescue squads—all scrabbling about in the ruins of buildings, desperately searching for survivors. Some survivors were rescuing what they could of their belongings. Euphemia saw one woman handing out a tea trolley and chairs from a window to a man standing outside. Another man had a pillow and rose pink, gold and green satin quilts tied on his back. In the darkness he looked like the hunchback of Notre Dame.

Firemen were working in terrible conditions. The fire engines couldn't get near enough because of craters and debris, and fire hoses were damaged by being hauled over sharp glass and stones.

It had been discovered that there was no uniformity in hoses and hydrant couplings, and many of the fire brigades who had been brought in from outside Glasgow could not use their own hoses. Or they were unable to fix them to the fire hydrants. However, the Forth and Clyde canal was close to Singer's timber yard and to the sites of some of the other fires, so it was used a water supply instead.

The twins asked one of the firemen if there was a shelter nearby and the harassed and exhausted man said there was, but it had taken a direct hit and everybody inside had been killed.

'I want to go home, Euphemia,' Bridget wept.

'All right. Come on, we'll try.'

Hand in hand, they gingerly stepped forward. The ground shook under their feet as another bomb exploded. It quickened their pace until they were running, then gasping and choking, and having to stop again.

'We're nearly there,' Euphemia breathlessly tried to comfort a distraught Bridget. 'We're going to be all right. Don't worry.'

Starting and stopping, starting and stopping again, somehow they eventually reached home. They ran into the close, fumbled the key into the lock and got into safety. They wept with thankfulness.

'Thank God.' Bridget sank into a chair in the kitchen. 'What a ghastly nightmare. Just ghastly.'

'I know, but never in my worst nightmares . . . ' Words failed Euphemia. Eventually she managed, 'I'll make a cup of tea. I've never needed a cup more.'

'Me too,' Bridget said. 'I wish we'd never gone out in the first place. All these poor people. Did you see some of the ones they were bringing out? I'm sure most of them were dead.' She shuddered. 'And it's still going on out there— listen to it. Oh Euphemia, I'm frightened.'

'First thing tomorrow,' Euphemia said, 'we'll go to Mammy's. There's all this bombing here because of the shipyards and Singer's. We'll be safe at Mammy's, don't you worry.'

'I wish we could go now.'

'So do I, but I think we'll be safer to stay here for a wee while.'

Then, before they could even drink a comforting cup of tea, they discovered they were not safe at all.

1942-43

26

It had been a close-run thing, but the RAF had managed to stop the German campaign of bombing British cities. Now Germany had turned on the Soviet Union. They had invaded Russia along a one thousand eight hundred mile front. Italy and Romania had also declared war on the Soviet Union. With the entry of the Russians into the war, Britain had gained a powerful ally, and housewives now handed over their pots and pans to help build tanks for the Red Army. While the Russians stood firm against the might of Hitler's Panzers, the British navy escorted arctic convoys carrying vital supplies to Russia. Defying both the U-Boat wolf packs and the perils of the arctic ocean, the Merchant Navy performed feats of heroism that ensured Hitler would never win the war on the Eastern Front.

At long last, Richard began to get some leave. On his first leave since God knows when, he set off with Davina to visit his family. He made a point of going to his mother and father's first and they stayed at Kirklee Terrace for the first few days. For the next few days, they went to his grandmother's villa in Great Western Road. He was shocked to find that the villa had been damaged during one of the recent bombing raids on Glasgow. The top storey had been sliced off and workmen were repairing and reroofing the place. The rooms downstairs had been made habitable but the building now looked very odd and out of proportion. He was glad, although not surprised, that the old lady seemed untroubled by the whole thing. She had always been a strong character.

Apparently his father had wanted her to go and stay at Kirklee Terrace but she had refused. She wasn't at all pleased when Richard went to Kirklee Terrace to stay there for part of his leave, but for some time now he had been feeling guilty that in the past he had spent far too much time with his grandmother, and not nearly enough time with his parents.

It had been a pleasant and happy time as Davina got on so well with his parents and they obviously liked her. On the other hand, it was pretty awful to learn how badly Glasgow and Clydebank had suffered during the bombing raids. Wincey said that two of the Gourlay girls had been killed. Their homes in Dumbarton Road had suffered a direct hit. Another had survived but had lost her home and her husband.

He could see that Wincey had been deeply affected by the loss of the twins. She obviously thought of them as her sisters. But that was war. He had lost more than a few fellow pilots and friends. He had nearly had it himself when, after running out of ammunition, he had tried to ram a German bomber. It had been a mad thing to do but he would never forget that wild, reckless moment. It was the thrill of a lifetime.

A few months after that leave, he'd managed to get another break during which he'd gone with Davina to visit her parents. He was delighted and very impressed when he caught his first glimpse of her parents' house. It was called Castle Hill and he could see why. It wasn't so much a house as a castle—with towers and turrets, set high above a many tiered garden lined with birch and silver birch. There was a dignified silence about both the house and the garden. The green hills beyond

176

were turning purple in the dying light, giving the whole area a ghostly glow. The interior of the house was equally impressive, as he said to Davina, 'Crikey, you could get lost in here. So many corridors, stairways and rooms.'

'Oh, half the place is now taken over by the military. They're using it as a hospital. If you look out of the back windows, you'll see some of the men who are convalescing, sitting on the garden seats or walking about the grounds.' She laughed. 'You could easily get lost in the part we still have though. Or in the grounds, for that matter.'

Richard found the visit fascinating. It was like stepping back into a far distant past. Despite the fire crackling and sparking in the enormous stone fireplace in the hall, the place had a gloomy chill about it. Richard wasn't surprised that the heat didn't reach every corner when he saw the size of the hall and the wide dark stairway that led to innumerable corridors and other smaller stairways.

Davina enjoyed showing him around. 'The hospital part is completely cut off,' she explained, 'so feel free to just wander about.' He had no intentions of wandering about after the tour that Davina gave him. She obviously loved the house despite the shadowy gloom and the icy cold. It was beginning to send shivers creeping up his back. She'd been used to it all her life, he supposed, and she no longer noticed. But then she was used to working outside in all sorts of weather. He was proud of her and loved her, from her cheerful tanned face down to her sensible laced up shoes. Running around like a child again, she pulled him by the hand up many turreted stairs into tiny secret rooms where she'd hidden from her nanny if she'd been naughty. There she could peek out at what was going on in the garden below and on the private winding road beyond. Sometimes she'd watched the gardeners at work, or watched her mother sunning herself and enjoying tea brought out by one of the maids. Sometimes no one would be there and she would just sit with her chin resting on the window sill and admire the beautiful scenery.

'It is a wonderful place, isn't it, Richard? You love it too, don't you, darling?'

He assured her he did. It was certainly true to say that he was fascinated and impressed. What he refrained from saying was that he didn't much care for the dead animals' heads cluttering the walls in the hall. Nor did he greatly admire all the solemn paintings of ancestors in their heavy gilt frames crowding together and glowering down onto all the rooms in what he felt was a horribly intimidating and depressing manner. There was even one whole room devoted to stuffed animals, mostly birds, all covered in glass domes. He knew what he'd do if he ever got the run of the place—as no doubt he would one day. Davina was an only child and would eventually inherit everything. He would get rid of all the stuffed birds.

They had dinner by candlelight in the huge dining room at a long, heavily carved table. Three candelabra cast flickering light over the table. Another two sat on the sideboard. Even with all those candles, the room still seemed gloomy and oppressive. The meal was served very slowly by an ancient butler, who shuffled about as if he was half asleep.

The food turned out to be excellent. They either had a wizard of a cook, or somebody was taking advantage of the black market. The meals at his parents' house had been much more frugal. His mother had apologised for them, and spoken at length about rationing and how she was working such long hours, she hadn't time to stand in many queues. He assured her it was fine and so it was really, although he and Davina had fared better at his grandmother's. His grandmother had been saving up her sugar and tea ration and standing in queues all over the place so that she could do her best for him and Davina.

'Fancy the old girl standing in queues at her age,' he'd said to Davina. He'd felt guilty about it, but touched as well. He was fond of his grandmother; she'd always been good to him, although when he'd been younger and more selfish, he hadn't really appreciated how good she'd been.

178

That Glasgow visit had been a great success, and now the visit to Castle Hill was proving to be equally successful.

'Mother says you're extremely handsome, darling,' Davina told him. 'Tall, dark and handsome, that's you. I'm so glad they like you. And of course they're so full of admiration for how you won the Battle of Britain.'

Richard laughed at this. 'Me and quite a few others, Davina.'

After dinner, over port and cigars, he and Lord Clayton Smythe discussed the state of the war. The Pearl Harbour attack had brought America in. It meant that both Britain and America had now declared war on Japan. Japan had invaded Siam, Malaya and Singapore. Germany and Italy had declared war on America. Then the Americans declared war on them. Now Japan had attacked Burma. Total war had engulfed the world and there seemed no end in sight.

Lady Clayton Smythe, in conversation with her daughter, bemoaned the acute shortage of staff and the rationing of clothes. 'Silk stockings, as you know, are a thing of the past,' Lady Clayton Smythe told Davina. 'But what I feel the greatest blow to so many women—including myself—is the rationing of corsets and bras. They are essential to every woman, but especially as one gets older.' She sighed. 'Gravity sets in, my dear. One needs a little support.'

Davina wholeheartedly agreed. Her figure was far from sylph-like and she worried about not being able to replace the underclothes she had. She wouldn't have cared so much had it not been so important to remain attractive to Richard. A handsome RAF pilot could get any woman he wanted.

'Don't you know any place we could get any foundation garments,' she asked her mother hopefully.

Lady Clayton Smythe looked sadly apologetic. 'Darling, if I did, I'd be only too glad to tell you. But in any case, we probably don't have enough coupons. Oh, isn't this war such a nuisance at times!'

Richard said, 'What are you ladies looking so serious about?'

'Nothing, darling.' Davina managed a smile. 'Isn't it time

for the news?'

Her father leaned over and switched on the wireless. 'Although,' he said, 'that's not likely to cheer us up.'

'Oh, come now, sir,' Richard said. 'The Allies are doing very well, surely. All right, we lost Tobruk and Dieppe was an absolute shambles—I lost one or two very good friends there, and I had a few close calls myself. But we certainly gave the Jerries a hell of a beating at El Alamein.'

His father in law chuckled. 'Yes, good old Monty. I'll never forget what he said about Lord Mountbatten—a very gallant sailor, had three ships sunk under him . . . ' Then he paused. '*Three* ships! Doesn't know how to fight a battle.' Lord Clayton Smythe gave a hearty laugh. 'Obviously Montgomery does.'

'Yes indeed.'

Davina and her mother both smiled, but their thoughts were still on corsets and bras, and the difficulties caused by the lack of them.

But later that night when Davina and Richard were lying together in the four poster bed, Davina said, 'I hope you won't be involved in any more battles, darling. You've done more than your bit.'

'None of us are out of danger yet. There's still a lot to be done, Davina.'

His wife sighed and rolled over to entwine her arms around him. 'I wish I could keep you here for ever. This is where you belong—here with me in Castle Hill.'

He kissed her and held her close in a loving embrace, but he was thinking of friends who at this very moment would be soaring up into the clouds, far above the world, in a wonderful, lonely euphoria. That's where he belonged—with the lords of the sky.

27

'She was a fine woman,' Donald Hamilton said. 'Since the war started, she began doing a great deal of charity work too much, I used to tell her. She was in the WVS, you know.' His gaze dimmed, remembering. 'She looked very smart in her uniform. I was so proud of her.'

Virginia tried to look interested and sympathetic, but she felt cut off and isolated. Donald's heart and mind were obviously still with his late wife. He frequently talked about her. Her name was Mary and they'd known each other since childhood. Virginia had heard so much about Mary that she felt she knew her. Mary had been very house-proud and had spent a great deal of time before the war lovingly polishing the furniture and all the valuable ornaments. She'd had a cleaning woman who came in two or three times a week, but Mary would never allow the woman to touch either the furniture or the ornaments.

Virginia secretly thought that nearly everything in the house was old fashioned and ugly. She visited Donald regularly now and the place had begun to depress her. Donald's talk of his dead wife was beginning to have much the same effect. He hadn't been like this at the beginning of their relationship. He had been very thoughtful, and loving, and gentle. He still was loving and gentle, and she appreciated that. At the same time, however, she hungered for the passion she had revelled in so often with Nicholas in the part. Thoughtfulness and gentleness were all right in a friend, but not enough in a lover. At least not for her.

She was also beginning to feel that he was becoming thoughtless in imposing so many memories of Mary on her. In a way, she could understand how it had happened. He now felt comfortable with her, and he trusted her. It was no doubt a relief to open his heart and to talk about his life with Mary and the happiness they had shared. Mary had been his friend, his dear and sympathetic lifelong companion.

His grief at his loss was now being released. Virginia could see all this and she tried to be a silent and patient listener, but she was feeling sad and isolated. She began to wonder if it was her fate to feel like this. Was it something in herself? Did she create situations in which she always ended up with this sense of isolation? Yet still the hunger was there, burning forever inside her.

It occurred to her that the isolation is what Wincey might have felt when she was a child and living at Kirklee Terrace. The crowded Gourlay house and the close knit Gourlay family and their total acceptance of her must have been a welcome— indeed wonderful—change for the child.

Virginia suddenly felt truly grateful to the Gourlays. The seeds of jealousy that had begun to take root were firmly dug out and destroyed. Now, she asked herself, was she beginning to feel jealous of the dead Mary? She didn't think so. She felt sorry for Donald. It was terrible to have lost such a loving companion, and such a wonderful relationship. She felt sorry for the poor woman, having her life suddenly cut off in such dreadful circumstances. But things like that happened all too often nowadays. And as the war dragged on, each new tragedy

182

somehow seemed less shocking than the last, just part of the routine of everyday life.

The war was to blame for breaking apart so many things, and so many people's lives. She had such a longing for peace— perhaps that was part of the attraction Donald had for her at the beginning. She had felt some sort of peace with him. Even now, when he spoke about his wife, she would relax and her mind would lazily wander. She resolved to see more of the Gourlays and try to be more supportive to them, especially as they had suffered such a grievous loss. She was so lucky, when she thought of it. She was alive and well, thank God, and so were her husband, her son and her daughter.

There was hardly a family in the land that hadn't been affected by the war. Wincey had lost Robert Houston. It struck Virginia how strange it was that both she and Wincey had taken a doctor as a lover. Being a passionate woman herself, she took it for granted that Wincey and Robert must have been lovers.

She had always hated war, and now her hatred hardened to bitterness inside her. Recently a WVS woman had come to the door at Kirklee Terrace wanting her to agree to donate the iron railings at the end of the back garden to the war effort. Angrily she'd told the woman, 'I won't give as much as one nail to help kill another human being. There's been enough killing already.'

She felt sick of it all, so helpless and hopeless. She longed for the time before the war but it was like another world now. She wondered if that world would ever come again. Often now, her mind would wander far back to the days of her youth when she lived with her mother and father in their cramped tenement house. No hot water, no inside toilet (far less bathroom), no washing facilities except the communal wash house down in the back yard, where everybody had to wait for their turn to do their washing. Teresa Gourlay probably still had to do that even now.

Sometimes her mother had to take her turn at night, and

she didn't like to do her washing at night. There was no chance then of hanging it outside to be dried in the sun and wind. Virginia vividly remembered those nights in the wash house—guttering candles stuck in the neck of bottles along the window ledge casting mysterious shadows that flickered eerily in corners. Her mother would lift the lid of the brick boiler to check how the whites were doing, and steam would immediately fill the wash house. She remembered her mother's brightly flushed face shining with the sweat of heat and work. Her beautiful mother.

'I'm sorry,' Donald said, 'if I'm making you feel sad talking about Mary.'

'Oh no,' she assured him. 'I'm just tired, that's all.'

'I'm not surprised,' Donald said. 'We're so short staffed these days, it's not just ridiculous, it's downright dangerous.'

'I know.' Virginia shrugged. 'But what can we do, with everybody away at the war? And the air raids.' One way or another, it was always the war, the war, the bloody war.

'Another year gone, and it still doesn't look as if there's an end in sight,' Donald said.

She gazed at his familiar face. He looked exhausted. She realised with some shock that he was old. He was a tired old man. Unexpectedly, she experienced a flutter of panic. She felt guilty too. For some time now, she had realised that she did not love Donald. At least, not in the same way as she had loved Nicholas—and, she realised, still loved him. There was a passion and an intensity about Nicholas that was different from anyone else she had ever known. They still made love, although not nearly as often, and his passion never failed to awaken her. Thinking about it, she realised that the times in between making love with Nicholas had lengthened. It had now been a very long time since he had turned to her in bed and taken her in his arms.

Again she felt panic. This time it was more acute. She should have tried harder to talk to him, to confess how she felt. She should have made more of an effort to work out the

184

problems between them.

'It's time I went home,' she suddenly announced to Donald. 'I've so much to do before tomorrow's shift.'

'Yes, of course. I'll go and get the car out.'

'No, please, Donald. You look so tired. Just phone a taxi for me.'

'Are you sure?'

'Yes, definitely.'

He went out to the hall and she could hear him speaking to the taxi company. He returned to the room with her coat and hat. She pulled on her Red Cross cap and he helped her on with her navy uniform coat. Supposedly being at work was a useful cover for these clandestine meetings. So much deceit. They kissed goodnight and she thankfully left the gloomy old house and returned to Kirklee Terrace with its wide bright hall, cream speckled marble floor and the polished woodwork of the stairway. The kitchen was at the back of the hall and she was surprised when she entered it that Nicholas was lounging on one of the chairs by the kitchen table, nursing a glass of whisky. His long legs were stretched out in front of him. His dark eyes when he glanced up at her were slightly quizzical, slightly sarcastic. He didn't say anything and she felt frightened. He knows, she thought.

She forced herself to act calmly. She went over to the Aga and set a pot of potatoes to boil. 'Dinner won't be long. I've everything more or less prepared. What kind of day have you had? Did you get any writing done?'

'Not much. Richard phoned. He's been awarded a DFC.'

Her eyes brightened with astonishment and pride. 'A Distinguished Flying Cross! How wonderful! That'll make him so happy.'

'He deserves it too. He's a very brave young man.'

'Oh, I'm so happy for him, Nicholas.'

'I tried to reach you at the hospital.'

'Oh, when?'

'Hours ago. They said you'd left.'

'Oh, oh yes. I was going round the shops to see if there was anything. I stood in a couple of queues but no luck. Nothing left when it came to my turn. Have you told your mother about Richard yet?'

'Yes, she's immensely proud of him, but then of course she always has been.'

Maybe the whisky was just by way of celebration and that look in his eyes had simply been irritation at not having been able to share his news with her right away.

'I'm so sorry I wasn't in when he phoned. Was he speaking from Castle Hill? Can I reach him there if I phone just now?'

'No, it was just a quick call from his airfield, I think. He's off on some hush-hush operation. Something big is in the offing, I suspect. You'll just have to wait.'

She felt frightened again. This time it was about Richard. He had always been such a daring, adventurous boy, even at school. It was one thing, however, being reckless or daring on the rugby field or on a rock climbing expedition. She had worried about him then but he wasn't playing games any more. Now she felt ill with apprehension.

'I hope he'll be all right,' she managed. 'Oh, I wish I had been in when he phoned.' She'd never forgive herself if anything happened to Richard and she had missed the chance to speak to him one last time. And especially because she had been with a lover. It was too awful to think about.

'Well,' Nicholas said, 'you weren't.'

Again the suspicion that he knew returned. Oh God, she silently prayed as she blindly fussed about with more pots and pans, please keep my son safe. Please, oh please. She felt Nicholas's dark eyes boring into her back. She felt distracted. Forgive me, forgive me, she kept thinking.

28

Nicholas had been watching her, or having her watched. She knew, because he had caught her out again. This time, as it happened, she had gone to Donald's home to tell him as gently as she could that their affair was over. He had pleaded with her to think about it, not to make any hasty decisions.

'Take some time on your own,' he advised. 'Give yourself time away from me to think about it. Make sure it's the right decision, that it's what you really want, Virginia.'

Feeling sorry for him and not wanting to hurt him, she'd allowed him to hold her in his arms and tenderly kiss her. She really was very fond of him, but more as a kind of father figure. She had promised that she would at least give herself more time to think things through.

She'd arrived home to find Nicholas sitting waiting for her. She was struck more forcibly than ever by the difference in appearance between the two men. Donald's skin was paler, and his hair, eyebrows and moustache were silver. His muscles had begun to sag. Nicholas, on the other hand, still had a full head of black hair. His skin was tanned and his body was lean and fit.

This time she recognised the look in his eyes. She'd seen it directed at other people. It wasn't the same quizzical, sarcastic look as the last time. It was the concentrated, unblinking stare of the writer—darkly, deeply probing into a person's character and motivation. She resented such a look being directed at her.

'What's wrong with you?' she asked defensively. 'Why are you staring at me like that?'

'There's nothing wrong with me, Virginia.'

'Yes, there is, and I've known it for a while now. You've changed out of all recognition.' She felt angry and reckless. What had happened was as much his fault as hers. 'You're not the same person I used to know at all.' She struggled to calm down and be more reasonable. 'It's the war, I suppose,' she continued, echoing something that Donald had once said. 'It's changed everything and everybody.'

'I'm the same person that I always was, Virginia. There's never been anyone in my life but you. I have never been unfaithful to you.'

She felt sick with regret. Miserably she searched for words of explanation, justification, excuse or even denial, but before she could think of any words, he rose and said, 'I don't suppose you've noticed, far less cared, but my mother has been far from well. She's never been right since the bombing. I'm going to stay with her for a while so that I can keep an eye on her and try to arrange for some professional care. We'll talk later.'

She watched him go and, determined to retain some dignity and self respect, as well as show proper concern, she said, 'I hope your mother's health will improve and if there's anything I can do, just let me know.'

He didn't answer and left her feeling angry again. He knew perfectly well that she'd tried long ago to get on better terms with his mother. Originally she'd even tried to get close to her. It was his mother who had created the distance between them. All she'd ever had from his mother was hatred. Yet despite that, she'd continued to be pleasant and civilised to the old woman. She'd continued to welcome her at Kirklee Terrace. She was made far from welcome, however, at the ugly villa on Great Western Road. What did Nicholas imagine she could do in the circumstances? He must know perfectly well that his mother would never allow her to do anything.

At the same time she knew that she was dodging the real issue. She continued however to clutch at any straws of justification. Nicholas had been neglecting her and their marriage for years. Not in any material sense. He had always been a good and conscientious provider. It was his time and personal attention he had always been mean with. Well, not quite always. When she'd first known him, he'd been only too glad of her company and he'd treasured every moment of it. That's what he'd told her.

It was perfectly true what she'd said. He had changed. All right, it could be argued that everyone changes as they get older and have to cope with life's problems. Surely though they should have spent more time coping with them together. She'd been more than willing to do that but he had shut himself away in his writing room at every opportunity. Now it was the Home Guard and God knows what else.

The house acquired an oppressive silence after he'd gone. She roamed restlessly about, unable to settle. Eventually she forced herself to prepare some food for the next day's meals. Normally she was very well organised and planned most things in advance. Suddenly she thought, what was the point now? It seemed such a waste of time and effort to prepare meals just for herself.

Damn him, she thought, and wept with anger as much as grief. She'd never allowed any man—or woman for that matter—to get the better of her. Her father, she remembered, always said that she had a lot of spunk. He was right. She wasn't going to sit around feeling sorry for herself. She dried her eyes, put on her hat and coat and went out. Immediately, she was engulfed in the blackout and it was with some difficulty that she made her way to Springburn and the Gourlays' house on the Balgrayhill.

Teresa and Erchie and Granny were delighted to see her. Wincey said, 'Is there something wrong, Mother?'

'No, no, darling. I'm off duty tonight and I just thought I'd pay you all a visit.'

'Sit down, Virginia,' Teresa said. 'Make yourself at home. The kettle's already on the boil.'

It was then that Virginia noticed the soldier sitting opposite. He was a big, tough looking man with cropped hair and a scar down one side of his scalp and face. Wincey introduced him as Malcy McArthur, Charlotte's husband. Charlotte, Virginia remembered, was the Gourlay girl who'd died—not in the Blitz but long before that. Poor Teresa, losing three children. Granny was frail looking and bent and her fingers twitched constantly on her knees.

'He's on leave frae doon in England somewhere. That right, son?'

'Yes, Granny. I wish I didn't need to go back down there, I can tell you.'

Teresa said, 'Never mind, Malcy, the war won't last forever and then you'll be able to come back for good.'

'Aye,' Granny said, 'if he's still aw in one piece.'

'Ma!' 'Granny!' Erchie and Teresa cried out in unison.

The old woman paid not the slightest attention to either of them.

'He's had a few close shaves already, haven't ye, son?'

Malcy laughed. 'You could say that, Granny.'

Malcy had brought Erchie some Woodbines and Erchie gratefully lit one up and enjoyed a few puffs. 'By God, it's a wee while since ah've had a decent smoke. Ah'm fair enjoyin' these, son.'

Teresa made the tea. 'I'm so sorry I haven't a biscuit or a bit cake left in the house.'

'My fault,' Malcy said. 'There was a bit of a welcome do

190

for me here last night and all the rations were used up. It's a wonder there's any tea left.'

'Oh, that reminds me.' Virginia delved into her handbag and brought out a packet of digestives. She handed them over to Teresa. 'I get most of my food at the hospital so I've always something extra.'

'Oh thank you, dear.'

'Ma favourites.' Granny's face brightened with pleasure and anticipation. 'Ah love a digestive tae dip into ma tea.'

'How long are you here for, Malcy,' Virginia asked, as Teresa opened the packet of biscuits and put them onto a plate.

'They gave me a couple of weeks and it's been great to be back in Glasgow. I'd hoped to have been here before but I was in hospital for a while and what with one thing and another, I don't know what I would have done without Wincey's letters. They kept me going.'

He smiled so warmly over at Wincey that Virginia wondered if there was more than just letter writing going on between them. Wincey hadn't said anything and it was difficult to tell by looking at her. Virginia made a mental note to ask her the first chance she got.

'You'll have to forgive Florence for not coming through.' Teresa lowered her voice to a whisper. 'She's been staying here since . . . you know . . . '

'Yes.' Virginia's face screwed up with sympathy. 'Wincey told me. Poor Florence. It's just terrible.'

Teresa said. 'She goes to her bed awful early. She's not been well for a while. The doctor can't find anything wrong but she's got no energy. We don't know what to do for the best.'

'Poor Florence,' Virginia repeated helplessly. 'Tell her I asking for her, won't you.'

'I will, dear. How's your husband? Could he not come with you tonight?'

'No. Busy as usual with all his war efforts.'

'Bloody war,' the old woman growled.

'Granny!' Teresa cast an harassed, apologetic look in Virginia's direction. 'Sorry about Granny.'

'Don't you dare apologise for me, Teresa Gourlay. Ah'll curse this bloody war as much as ah like. It costs us dear enough.'

'Quite right, Granny,' Virginia agreed. 'I'm so sick of the whole business. I just hate it.'

'Are ye still workin' hard at the hospital, hen,' Erchie asked.

They chatted for a while and Virginia felt relaxed and was glad of their company. If it had been possible, she would have stayed all night. She dreaded going back to her empty house. However, the time came when she had to make a move and on finding that she hadn't brought her car, Wincey said, 'I'll drive you back, Mother. We can't have you hanging about waiting for trams at this time of night.'

In the car, Virginia said, 'Malcy seems a nice man.'

Wincey was concentrating on her driving and didn't respond. Virginia tried again.

'Are you . . . I mean, are you and Malcy . . . '

'We're just friends, Mother,' Wincey said.

'I'll see you at the weekend, as usual, I hope?' Virginia asked.

'Yes, of course.'

Wincey didn't come in with her but just waited and watched from the car until she got safely inside. Virginia stood motionless, her back to the door, listening to the car drive away, dreading moving further into loneliness. Eventually, her heels clicked across the hall as she went into the sitting room. There she drew the blackout curtain shut and switched on the light. She did the same in all the rooms, upstairs and downstairs, except the writing room. She didn't dare go in there. How still and silent the house was. Even when Nicholas had been shut away in his writing

192

room, the house had never felt like this.

She was devastated to realise how much she missed him—
and he'd only been away for a few hours. They'd occasionally
been apart before, but this was very different. This time he
might not come back.

29

Teresa was keeping going for Florence's sake. They all were. Even Granny, who was up at Springburn Park at the moment. Erchie had volunteered to take her to hear the Sally Band, her favourite. Florence sat at the room window most of every day, gazing out with blank eyes. Or she lay in bed all day. She couldn't work, couldn't do anything. Hardly ever even spoke.

'It would be so much better if she could get out to work,' Teresa whispered to Wincey in the kitchen. 'Being with all the other sales ladies in Copeland's would bring her out of herself, take her mind off things.'

'I would be perfectly willing to give her a job in the factory if necessary, Teresa, but . . . '

'I know. Poor Florence, you know what she's like. Yes, the factory would probably just make her feel worse. She was always so proud of being in Copeland's. Not that I think there's anything wrong with working in the factory, dear,' Teresa said hastily. 'And it's not that Florence ever meant any harm.'

'I know. I was only saying I'd do anything I could to help

her. But it's so difficult, isn't it?'

'I keep asking the doctor but all he seems to give her is pills and potions that make her more lethargic and sleepy than ever. She seems to have lost all hope, as well as energy.'

'I really do wish there was something I could do to help her. And you too, Teresa. You've had a worse loss than Florence. You've lost three children. Florence should try to think of you instead of thinking of herself so much. That would probably do her more good than anything.'

'If she would just get better, I'd be all right.'

'Time is supposed to heal but it's been over two years now, Teresa. There have been so many people who have suffered much worse than her. Look at that family who lost fourteen— or was it fifteen—from a baby of five months to a boy of nineteen years of age. Compared with them, Florence should think herself lucky.'

They hadn't noticed Florence come shuffling into the kitchen like an old woman. Her once glossy, well dressed hair was now straggling down over her face. Her eyes were dull and dark shadowed.

'I try to,' she said tearfully. 'I really do. It's just that I feel so tired all the time.'

'I know, dear.' Teresa ran to put an arm around her. 'We all understand that you're ill and we just wish we could help you get better. Isn't that right, Wincey?'

'Of course it is, Florence. I'm sorry if I sounded unsympathetic or unkind. I didn't mean to.'

Florence nodded. 'If I could just get back my energy, Wincey. I want to get back to work. I long to get back to work. But I'm so tired all the time. What's wrong with me, Mammy? Why can't the doctor help me?'

Teresa bit at her lip. 'Maybe if we tried to get another doctor. Asked for a second opinion, or something.'

'I could pay for private treatment,' Wincey said. 'And how about if you and Florence have a wee holiday somewhere, Teresa. Some sea air might help. How about somewhere up north? Money's no problem.'

'Well, it's very kind of you, dear, but there's so many other problems just now about travelling. There's these posters all over the place—Is your journey really necessary?—and all that.'

'Even if it meant going by taxi, Teresa, that would be all right by me. I could arrange it.'

'Oh, I don't know. Such an expense, dear,' Teresa said worriedly.

Florence widened her eyes. 'Maybe a holiday, right enough. Maybe that would make me better. If I could just get enough energy.'

Wincey said, 'Erchie and I could carry you out into the taxi if necessary, Florence. Or if I could arrange some time off, I'd drive you there myself. You don't need to worry about anything. All you need to do is leave everything to me.'

Tears blurred Florence's eyes. 'Thanks, Wincey. I'm so sorry for being such a nuisance.'

Wincey rushed over to give her a hug and a kiss. 'Don't be daft. You're not a nuisance. You're my dear sister.'

Florence clung to her. 'Am I?' she asked tremulously.

'Of course. Always have been. Now you sit over there beside the fire and have a nice cup of tea with me and your Mammy and we'll talk about where you'll go on your holiday. I've another idea as well. I've heard about a thing called homeopathic treatment. I think that'd be worth trying, if I can find a suitable doctor.'

'I've never heard of that, dear,' Teresa said, as she helped Florence over to a chair, then put the kettle on to boil. 'What kind of thing is it?'

'It was my mother that mentioned something about it. She'd read an article somewhere. I'll ask her if she knows any more when I see her this weekend.'

True to her word, that weekend Wincey asked her mother about homeopathy, and her mother showed her the article, and a pamphlet she'd found on the subject.

One of the principles of homeopathy, it said, was that because people varied in their response to an illness, the homeopath does not automatically present a specific remedy for a specific illness. He tries instead to determine the patient's temperament and so prescribe on an individual basis. Homeopathy provides remedies to assist the body's natural healing process, it said. It treats the patient, rather than the disease, and it treats like with like—the law of similars. It also acted on the belief that there were 'emotional diseases originating in the mind' which could be 'transferred in health of both mind and body by physical means'.

'I'm not sure what to make of it,' Virginia said, 'but it does sound interesting, doesn't it?'

'Yes, especially that bit about the emotional as well as the physical aspects of the person being used as a basis for diagnosis,' Wincey said. 'That's what Florence needs, I think. She's been emotionally shattered.'

Wincey watched her mother as she poured out a cup of tea and handed it to her. She looked tired and worried, instead of excited and happy as Wincey had expected her to be after getting the news of Richard's DFC.

'Are you all right, Mother?'

'Yes, of course, darling. A bit tired, that's all.'

'I thought you'd still be over the moon about Richard's DFC.'

'I'm so proud of him, of course. I told you, it's just that I can't stop worrying about him.'

Wincey smiled and tried to sound reassuring. 'Mother, he's got a special angel looking after him. Either that or he's got the luck of the devil. Look at all he's come through with hardly a scratch. He'll be all right. I'm sure of it.' And she was.

Her mother smiled in return. 'All right, I'll try not to worry.'

'Promise?'

'I promise.'

'Where's Father?'

'He's staying with Mrs Cartwright for a while. She's not been well. All that trouble with the house. She could have come here, but you know what she's like. Your father wants to make sure that she's being properly looked after. He's gone to keep an eye on her.'

Was it her imagination, Wincey thought, or had her mother's eyes become evasive. She was reminded about her mother's secret affair with the silver haired doctor and was for a moment tempted to confront her with the knowledge. She decided against it. What good would it do if she interfered?

'How is Teresa?' her mother asked. 'She doesn't look a physically strong woman but I do admire her spirit, after all she's been through. And Granny's.'

'Granny's looking awfully frail, don't you think? But as Erchie says, she's a tough old bird.'

'I must try to visit them more often, and they're always welcome to come here.'

Suddenly Virginia had an idea. 'Wincey, do you think it would help Florence to come and stay with me for a time? I could easily take a few weeks off. I've never had any proper leave since I started at the Royal.'

'Oh Mother!' Wincey was both astonished and touched. 'How good of you to even think of such a thing!'

'I mean it, darling. I think she'd enjoy it here. I could take her out to the Botanic Gardens and she could rest in the Kibble Palace. It's so lovely in there, and so warm.'

'Oh Mother!' Wincey repeated, this time in delight. 'She'd love it, I'm sure. I bet it would be just what she needs to perk her up. And I'll see about getting her some homeopathic treatment while she's here.'

'Well, if you're really serious about that, there was a hospital listed in that pamphlet I showed you. It's a big villa along Great Western Road. You could enquire about doctors there.'

'Wonderful!' Wincey felt really hopeful and excited now. 'I wonder if I should phone right away and tell Florence.' She forced herself to think calmly. 'No,' she said out loud to herself. 'Better to wait and tell her to her face. Anyway, you'll need time to arrange things at the Royal.'

'Of course, she might not want to come, Wincey. We shouldn't take anything for granted.'

'Oh, I'm sure she'll want to come, Mother. Trust me. I just know we'll be able to help her this way.'

'Well, I'll certainly do my best, darling, for your sake as much as for anyone else's.'

Wincey went over to her mother and hugged her. She wanted to say the words 'I love you' but no words would come.

But her mother seemed to understand. She nodded and smiled and said, 'Drink up your tea, darling. Everything's going to be all right.'

1944-45

30

Maloy was disappointed that he'd never had a minute with Wincey on her own. In the house there was always Florence or Teresa or Granny or Erchie, and all the neighbours coming in to say good luck. Then Wincey took Florence over to her mother's and stayed overnight with her to help get her settled in.

He'd called in to the factory, but even there in the short time he'd had, he'd been surrounded by people wanting to talk to him and wish him well. Even in Wincey's office he had no luck. She was with some man, talking business.

He gave up in the end. Anyway, he didn't just want a few minutes alone with her. He needed time to explain his feelings for her, and to try to find out exactly what she felt for him. He knew now without a doubt that he loved her.

Not in the same way that he had loved Charlotte. That would not have been possible. Wincey and Charlotte were two completely different people.

As the end of his leave drew near, he experienced a feeling of urgency that was almost panic. God knows when he'd see her again. He might never see her again. There were all sorts of rumours flying about amongst the men. It looked as if the final preparations were being made for an invasion. Not a German invasion this time, but an Allied one. He doubted if his luck would hold out through that.

On the last night of his leave, there was a crowd of well-wishers in the house and the next morning, the family all came to see him off at Central Station. They even managed to pack Granny into the taxi.

He shook Erchie's hand, he hugged and kissed Granny and Teresa. Then when he took Wincey into his arms, he just had time for an urgent, desperate, 'Oh Wincey, I'd so much I wanted to say to you.'

'Write to me,' she said.

The guard blew his whistle and they hustled him onto the train. He didn't want to go. If he'd been a child, he would have wept. He was weeping inside as he leaned from the window of the train and watched Wincey and the Gourlays gradually disappear.

He sank back into his seat and struggled to put them out of his mind. It was too painful to think of them. Instead he visualised what might lie ahead in the next few days and weeks.

★   ★   ★

All sorts of preparations were being made. Concrete blocks of various sizes had been transported to Selsey in Sussex, where they were fitted together. Nobody knew for certain what they were for. The rumour was that they were going to be towed across the Channel, where they would be used as piers, causeways and breakwaters. Other mysterious new devices were constantly appearing—like Flail tanks, fitted with rotating chains to destroy landmines. A vast armada of warships, aircraft, landing craft and transport ships was being assembled. There was going to be an invasion all right.

Finally, at 4am on the fifth of June, American and British soldiers, sailors and airmen got the command to go.

Malcy only just managed to appear calm on the outside. Inside, fear was rampaging through him. He remembered only too well the terrifying journey back from Dunkirk when he had waded up to his neck in the same water. Now here he was listening to the order, 'Lower the boats'. With a heavy splash, the door went down and seconds later he was in the water again.

Another soldier began to cry, and plead and cling to the deck. He was screaming that he couldn't move. Malcy and the others left him behind, the whine of bullets speeding them on. Suddenly there was a terrible explosion and Malcy felt himself losing consciousness. 'This is it,' he thought. But the next thing he knew, he had come to in the water. He could feel another soldier kicking and clutching at his legs, trying to make it to the surface but only succeeding in dragging Malcy down. Frantically Malcy kicked and struggled until he was free of the man. He shot to the surface and soon the body of the soldier who had been clutching at him floated by, its limbs still twitching.

Malcy sobbed at the horror unfolding all around him, but he had no choice—he had to move on if he was going to survive. Somehow, he struggled out of the water and joined the thousands of other men landing on the beaches. Now he could hear the incessant rattle of enemy machine guns, and his blood froze at the ghastly sight of countless bullets cutting a swathe through the men in front of him.

Mortar rounds were landing close by, exploding in a cacophony of ear-splitting noise. Landing craft were being sunk yards from the shore, and tanks were being hit by incoming shells almost as soon as they trundled onto the sand. Malcy could hear their crews screaming, trapped inside the burning vehicles. Men were being killed all around him, while in the water and on the beach the wounded were shouting for help. Malcy turned back to try and pull a soldier out of the shallows, but an officer bawled at him to leave the man and push on. They had no time. And so, without a backward glance, Malcy turned once more to face the storm of steel.

*   *   *

Wincey knew the sort of thing that Malcy had been wanting to say. She wasn't sure if she was ready to cope with that sort of intimacy, but she couldn't help herself from softening inside and thinking, 'Poor Malcy'. She didn't want anything bad to happen to him, of that she was certain. She wanted him to come back to Glasgow, safe and sound. In bed at night, she would think about him before drifting off to sleep. 'Poor Malcy,' she thought.

She kept seeing his gaunt, scarred face and close-cropped skull. His eyes now had a strangely haunted look. He had always had such a sturdy muscular body, but now it was painful to see the amount of weight he'd lost. 'Poor Malcy'. Thoughts of him and how he had suffered just wouldn't go away—no matter how hard she tried to banish them from her mind. Fortunately, her work helped to occupy her and tire her out, so that each night she could escape quickly and mercifully into sleep. She dreaded being vulnerable. She couldn't bear to suffer loss again, and be hurt again.

Wincey also occupied herself at weekends, helping her mother to attend to Florence. Whether it was the homeopathic medicine, or living at Kirklee Terrace, or perhaps a combination of both, Wincey didn't know. The happy fact was that Florence was getting better. There could be no doubt about that. They were at the stage now of taking her to the theatre or the cinema on Saturday nights. Her mother insisted that she could stay on at Kirklee Terrace as long as she liked. She was only too glad of the company, as Nicholas was still with Grandmother Cartwright in the house in Great Western Road. Wincey knew now that there was something seriously wrong

206

between her mother and father. After all, Grandmother Cartwright's house wasn't all that far away. He could have seen the old woman every day but still slept at Kirklee Terrace.

Wincey guessed he must have found out about the affair. Once, he had popped into Kirklee Terrace to see her and to say hello to Florence. He hadn't stayed long, however, and he had been noticeably cool to her mother. It was so sad, and she longed to say or do something that would bring them together again. But in this day and age, when so many dreadful things were happening, did an illicit love affair really matter all that much? Especially now, in the aftermath of D-Day, as Britain faced the new terror of Hitler's 'revenge weapons'.

These were the dreaded flying bombs—the V1 or 'Doodlebug', and the even more deadly rocket powered V2. The V1s could be heard coming, but then their engines cut out and there was fifteen seconds of ominous silence while they fell to the earth, where they exploded. They were very difficult to intercept—although a few brave fighter pilots did manage to shoot one or two down before they reached their targets. The V2s were much worse. These giant rockets flew much faster than the V1s. Travelling at supersonic speed they arrived without warning, causing so many casualties that people feared them more than anything.

Wincey hadn't heard from Malcy for months, which wasn't surprising. No doubt he'd taken part in the D-Day landings and would be fighting his way through France by now. Newspapers reported that the Allies had secured the beaches and were pushing ahead. Granny, Erchie, Teresa, Florence, Wincey and even her mother were all worried about Malcy.

Her mother said on one of her visits to Springburn, 'He didn't look fit enough to be going through all that again.'

'I know,' Teresa said. 'I'm really worried about him.'

'See war,' Granny muttered. 'It's bloody wicked. Ah'd put all them generals an' politicians in a field an' tell them to fight it out between themsel's an' leave ordinary lads like Malcy in peace.'

'If only,' Wincey said.

'Well, dear,' Teresa said, 'all we can do at the moment is to pray for all the lads to come home soon.'

'A Protestant or a Catholic prayer?' Granny asked sarcastically. Fond as she was of Teresa, she had never quite got over the fact that her Protestant son had married a 'Pape'. The house was full of 'Papish' ornaments and trinkets, and a picture of a mournful-looking Jesus hung above the kitchen bed.

'What difference does it make?' Teresa said. 'Every and any kind of prayer you like, as long as it helps.'

'Aye, well,' Granny grudgingly conceded.

By now Florence looked well enough to return to Springburn for good but she made it clear that she preferred to remain where she was.

'I hope you don't mind, Mother,' she said to Teresa. 'There's too many memories of Eddie here. It's been so good for me being in the West End. Virginia takes me to all sorts of interesting places, including the Art Galleries. And we had lunch in Copeland's. It takes my mind off everything. I can't bear to think about the past. I'd go mad if I was on my own, just thinking about it.'

'You'd never be on your own, dear,' Teresa said. 'There's always Granny and me here.'

'Please don't be angry with me, Mother. Please try to understand.'

Granny cast a sarcastic glance in Florence's direction. 'It's well seen ye're on the mend. Ye're gettin' more like yersel' every day. Whit happens, ah'd like tae know, when Virginia's oot workin'.'

'I have quite a lot of leave due to me,' Virginia explained before Florence could reply. 'In all the time I've been at the Royal, I've never taken one holiday. I've just taken it all at once now.'

'My word, ye must be well in.'

'Well, VAD is a voluntary service.'

'Whit dis yer man say about you keepin' a lodger?'

'Granny,' Teresa cried out. 'Mind your own business and don't be so cheeky. Have a piece of sponge cake. It'll be nice and soft for your gums.'

'Whit's in it?' Granny eyed the sponge suspiciously. 'No' any eggs, ah bet.'

'Dried eggs, Granny.'

'Dried eggs,' Granny howled in disbelief. 'What's up wi' the bloody hens now?'

'Nothing. They're from America.'

'America? They're no' bloody fresh then.'

'Do you mind if we say goodnight now, Virginia,' Florence suddenly announced. 'I get so quickly fatigued.'

'I should have noticed.' Virginia rose. 'Wincey, darling, could you drive us home?'

'Yes, of course.'

'Aye,' Granny said, 'oor Florence is on the mend, right enough.'

31

At first Virginia didn't mind Florence staying with her. She was glad her invitation had helped the girl. Florence's energy had returned and she was now trying to make herself useful, keeping busy, washing not just the breakfast, lunch, tea and dinner dishes every day, but dusting every ornament she could lay her hands on. She polished everything in sight as well, ignoring Virginia's pleas that she didn't need to do so much. She even polished the marble floor in the hall. Eventually, Virginia just let her get on with it, accepting that Florence was at her happiest being house-proud. There she was every day, glossy brown hair held firmly back in a bandeau, a crisp apron tied round her waist, searching out every speck of dirt or dust.

It was a bit pathetic in a way. It was also becoming very irritating. Virginia had never put much value on material things, nor did she like showing off. Florence was quite the opposite. On one occasion—admittedly with Virginia's permission—she had invited some of her former colleagues from Copeland's to afternoon tea. What a carry on that had been. It had taken every ounce of Virginia's patience to refrain from telling Florence not to be so ridiculous. How Florence had revelled in showing the girls around the house!

'This is the drawing room. Look at these pelmets and the way the curtains are draped. Satin, I think, or maybe heavy silk. The drawing room is where we always entertain guests. The sitting room downstairs is more for private family use. Isn't this a gorgeous bathroom? These bedrooms are so bright and modern, yet so cosy and comfy too. Feel the deep pile of that carpet. This staircase is so elegant, isn't it. And here's the sitting room I mentioned. Look at all the bookshelves. Of course, Nicholas is a writer, don't you know? These are some of his books. The kitchen is so well equipped too. One could eat here all the time if one wanted to, but there's also that elegant dining room. And here is Nicholas's writing room.'

Virginia had just caught her in time. 'No, we never go in there. That's Nicholas's private place.'

'Oh yes, of course, I forgot,' Florence said, leading her little group away across the hall again. 'Look at that marble floor. Isn't it so elegant?'

Virginia was embarrassed beyond words.

And Florence's company in no way made up for the lack of Nicholas's presence. On the contrary, once Florence no longer needed to be looked after, time hung heavy on Virginia's hands. She was glad to get back to work.

By that time, Florence was even cooking the meals. Virginia began to feel as if she had moved into another life. A Life that was gradually becoming a waking nightmare. Every day her true life, the only life she wanted—her life with Nicholas—was disappearing further and further into the past. She longed for him, ached for him, made love to him in her dreams over and over and over again.

To make the nightmare worse, the situation between Florence and herself was becoming more and more of a problem. Their roles had been reversed—Florence was trying to look after her now. 'Just you sit down and relax, Virginia,' she kept saying. 'Enjoy this drink while I put the finishing touches to dinner.'

Normally Virginia and Nicholas ate in the kitchen, but Florence now insisted on doing everything 'properly'. They sat at opposite ends of the long dining room table. Florence always wearing her best dress for dinner along with her pearl earrings and necklace.

'Isn't this lovely,' she would coo, 'just like in a film.' Everything had to be done properly. And while every day Florence grew stronger and happier, Virginia became more and more depressed.

'Virginia, you're looking tired, and no wonder. You're on your feet all day. Just you sit back and listen to the wireless now while I clear up.'

Eventually, in desperation, Virginia spoke to Matheson about the situation. And not just about the situation with Florence. She got everything off her chest. He knew that Nicholas was staying at his mother's place, but she'd originally told Matheson it was because Nicholas's mother was ill and needed him there.

'You what?' Matheson's voice raised incredulously.

'I had an affair with a doctor at the hospital and Nicholas found out.'

'Well,' Matheson said, 'I can only say I know just how Nicholas feels. You once did the same to me, remember.'

'Oh, James, that was different. I thought Nicholas was dead when I married you, and I'd been his lover long before I met you.'

'Are you still seeing this man?'

'Since I've been back at work, I've seen him, but not on his own. The affair's finished. It was a terrible mistake, James. I was just feeling so lonely and neglected.'

'I told you before what I think of that attitude. It's Nicholas I feel sorry for.'

She felt an unexpected surge of her old fighting spirit. 'Oh, that's right. Stick up for him as usual. I know I have my faults, James, but I can assure you Nicholas isn't as blameless as you always make him out to be. He's as much responsible for our break-up as I am.'

After a brief silence, Matheson said, 'Do you want him back?'

'Of course I want him back.'

'Well, don't just sit there talking to me about it. Go and talk to him. Get him back. And do something about that girl. I'm surprised at you letting her take you over so much. Why don't you tell her it's time she was back in Copeland & Lye's.'

'I'm exhausted most days when I get home from the Royal, and I'm glad of her help in the house. But she can be so irritating sometimes.'

She watched Matheson limping about the kitchen and putting two cups and saucers on the table. Recently he'd grown a moustache and beard, and it helped to disguise his twisted face. His hair was white, but thick and glossy, and he looked fitter than he'd done since he'd had his stroke. The fact that he was still teaching, she felt sure, had helped take his mind off his disability and keep him going.

He was right about what she should do about her marriage. After all, she'd fought for Nicholas before and won. If she was worth her salt, she should at least make an attempt to fight for him again. She determined to call at the Cartwright villa right away.

As soon as she'd had a cup of tea with Matheson, she set out to do just that. The builders had made a good job of reroofing the house; nevertheless it now had an odd, stunted, look. Virginia wondered if it would be Mrs Cartwright who came to the door. If so, she knew she would be lucky if the old woman allowed her in. She would have been milking the situation for all she was worth. Getting her son away from her former scullery maid was, after all, what Mrs Cartwright had always wanted.

Virginia realised that she could have waited until the

weekend, when Nicholas usually called in to see Wincey, but it was difficult trying to speak to him at any length, on his own, in those circumstances. Far better to face him and have it out with him right now.

She gave the bell a strong pull. It made an eerie jangle that seemed to echo all through the house.

Mrs Cartwright's house had always been gloomy, filled as it was with dark, Victorian furniture. An elderly woman in an apron made of coarse sacking material and carrying a pail of water in one hand opened the door.

'Oh,' she said. 'I was just coming out to scrub the front steps.'

'I'm Mrs Cartwright's daughter in law.'

'Oh, right. You'd better come in then. But she's having a wee rest just now.'

'Is Mr Nicholas Cartwright in?'

'Aye, I think so.'

Once inside the hall, Virginia caught sight of Nicholas emerging from the room she remembered as the Cartwright library. No doubt he was now using it as his writing room.

'Has something happened to Richard?' he asked anxiously.

'No, no, he's fine.'

'Or Wincey?'

'No, she's fine too. I just came to talk to you, Nicholas. We need to talk.'

'Come through to the drawing room.'

Following him through to a room across the other side of the hall, she couldn't help thinking, 'Oh, nothing's changed then. I mustn't interfere with your precious writing.'

With some difficulty, she controlled her feelings. This attitude had become at least part of the problem in their marriage. For years now, she had been jealous of Nicholas's writing. Or at least the time and priority he gave to it. It had become a downward spiral. And her resentful attitude had only made him withdraw more and more into his work.

'Drink?' He raised a questioning brow.

She nodded and sat down on one of the uncomfortable horse-hair chairs beside the fireplace. The empty grate was fronted by an ornate folding screen. The room had a fousty smell and felt as if neither a fire nor the sun had ever penetrated its chilly atmosphere.

'Thank you.'

She accepted the gin and tonic and took a few sips before breaking the silence. 'Nicholas, I don't want to excuse my behaviour. I'm sorry I was unfaithful to you. It was a terrible mistake. Rightly or wrongly—probably wrongly—I was feeling lonely and neglected. We hardly ever saw each other. You were always either shut away in your writing room, or out doing some sort of war work.'

'You were out working too.'

'I know. Most of the fault is mine. I admit that for years I've been jealous and resentful of the time you've spent at your writing. But I felt I didn't matter to you any more.'

'That's nonsense, Virginia.'

'Maybe, but that's what I felt. Think about it, Nicholas. Try to think honestly about the priority you gave to your work, and the time you shut yourself away from me.'

He hesitated. 'Maybe latterly.'

'Yes, and I was thinking that's probably been my fault too. The more angry and resentful I became, the more you shut yourself away. I'm so sorry, Nicholas. I'm so sorry for how everything's gone wrong between us and I bitterly regret my part in what's happened.' She struggled for calmness and composure. 'I keep remembering how happy we used to be at the beginning. Surely that makes it worth trying again.'

Suddenly, remembering it again, she burst into a flood of tears. 'Oh, Nicholas, please forgive me. I'm so miserable without you.'

He sighed, then came towards her, arms outstretched. 'What a couple of fools we've been. I'm as much at fault as you for everything that's happened.'

'Have you thought about me at all since you've been here?'

215

'Thought about you? Of course I've thought about you. I've thought about you all the time. I've just been too proud and stubborn, I suppose, to do what you've just done.'

He drew her towards the door. 'Come on, I want to show you something.'

To her surprise, he led her towards the library and then inside the room. A desk was scattered with books and papers. He picked up a sheet of paper and handed it to her. 'How do you think I got the inspiration for that? As you know, I haven't written poetry for years, but I wrote this after visiting Kirklee Terrace one weekend.'

It was a poem, headed *Creator* and she read:

I lived here, I had been in here.
And if my intuition is right,
I loved you long ago,
I had bought this book in the tiny antique shop
In the old town,
I was touching those yellow pages,
I was sensing fragrant flowers of wisdom.
I was drinking wine and water together with you,
I was watching the twilight,
I was sitting in a straw chair,
I was cradled on the waves in the ocean,
Somebody wanted me to miss this rough water for the rest
of my life . . .

I had felt this bitterness of wind in April,
I lived here, I had been in here.
And if I had been here,
One rainy day,
When everybody had forgotten I was here,
I will come again,
It would be the wonderful act of the Creator,
To repeat everything once more
Saying that nothing is wasted in this world,

And you will love me again,
And I would not complain about my destiny.

It brought home to her so vividly what a uniquely talented man he was.

'It's beautiful, Nicholas. Thank you for sharing it with me.'

Nicholas said, 'This is what we always used to do, remember? Share everything.'

She sighed. 'Yes, if only we could get back to the way we were in those days.'

'We could try,' he said. 'Maybe this is the first step.'

She gazed hopefully up at him. 'Does that mean you'll come back?'

'Yes, if you still want me.'

'More than anything else in the world, Nicholas. I'll give up my work if you like.'

'Not at all. Not unless you want to. But maybe it would help if we could both cut down on the hours we spend at work. And I include my writing in that. Now you get back home and leave me to break the news to Mother. It won't be easy. You know what she's like. I'll have to be very firm.'

He kissed her lightly on the cheek, grinned and said, 'I'm not going to kiss you properly just now, because I know within a few seconds we'd be rolling on the carpet. But look out lady, I've got a lot of passionate love making time to make up for.'

Virginia hadn't felt so happy and excited for years. She could have danced her way back to Kirklee Terrace. She almost had an orgasm at the thought of living with Nicholas again. But as soon as she stepped inside into the now immaculate hall, heavy with the pungent odour of Mansion polish, she remembered the other problem she had to tackle. This one might prove more difficult—in the sense that Florence's stay at Kirklee had become her buffer against her terrible loss. Maybe it was her only lifeline now.

217

How can I take it away from her, Virginia thought. Yet they couldn't go on as they were, especially with Nicholas returning.

As soon as Florence saw her, she rushed to put on the kettle. The kitchen used to have a homely feel about it, with herbs hanging from a beam on the ceiling, old cushions softening the seats of the wooden chairs, newspapers lying about, shopping lists pinned to the wall, and pictures of Wincey and Richard propped up in front of a cocoa tin. Now everything was bare and sterile. Even the photographs had been tucked neatly away in an album in the sitting room.

'You must be tired out, Virginia. Dinner won't be long but you can relax with a cup of tea now. On you go through to the sitting room. I'll bring it to you.'

'I'm fine,' Virginia assured her. 'I went to see my husband and I'm happy to say his mother is all right now and he's returning home this evening.'

'Oh, I'll set another place for dinner, then,' Florence said happily. 'I must give that table an extra polish to have everything nice for him.'

Virginia groaned inside. Florence meant well, but she was such a silly girl. Couldn't she even see that she and Nicholas needed to be alone together? What did either of them care about a table, polished or otherwise.

'I tell you what,' Virginia said. 'How about if you went to visit your mother and father this evening? You haven't seen them for a while, Florence. You mustn't neglect your own folks.'

'But your dinner,' Florence protested.

'I'll see to the dinner, Florence. I'd really like to do everything for Nicholas tonight. It's been such a long time since I've had the chance.'

'Oh well, if you're sure.' Florence sounded far from sure.

'Yes, definitely, Florence. Stay overnight. There's no need to struggle back through the blackout. Now please,' she raised

218

a hand, 'do as I say, Florence. I'm not going to take no for answer.'

Reluctantly, Florence agreed, and after she was gone, Virginia danced around the house forgetting, in her new found joy, that Florence would soon be back.

32

'Oh, I'm so glad,' Wincey told her mother and father. 'It's just so wonderful to see you both together and happy again.' It was also disturbing. There was such a strong sexual chemistry sparking between them. It was in the way they looked at one another and in the way they touched, and they were always touching. Wincey was genuinely glad that they were happy together but the strong sexual element forever sizzling in the air made her shrink into herself. One day she'd been coming into the sitting room and had seen her mother sitting loose limbed on a chair. Her father was leaning over the back of it and sliding his hand down the inside of her mother's blouse to cup her breast. Her mother's eyes were closed, her face uptilted in ecstasy. Wincey had drawn back unseen and stood in the hall for a few minutes in something akin to distress and fear. She was reminded how she had only loved Robert Houston with words, never with actions. She felt like weeping, desperately wanting to love and be loved, but unable and afraid to break through the protective barrier she'd built around herself.

Later Virginia managed a whispered few words with Wincey while Florence was through in the kitchen fetching the tea trolley.

'Darling, what am I going to do about Florence? I don't want to hurt her or anything, and I appreciate what a wonderful help she is in the house, but she has got rather carried away, don't you think?'

'It's your own fault, you should never have allowed her to go this far, Mother.'

Virginia sighed. 'I know. I know.'

'Your mother was only trying to help the girl,' Nicholas said. 'I've offered to have a word with her, but she won't hear of it.'

'Let me handle it then,' Wincey said. 'Florence and I are like sisters. I know her better than anybody.'

Just then Florence came bright eyed and smiling into the room, the trolley bumping and chinkling before her. She had discarded her bandeau and apron and changed into her best afternoon dress of cinnamon coloured wool. She was wearing a little string of pearls and her hair was brushed smooth and curled neatly in at the ends. She looked flushed and extremely pretty.

'Tea everyone?'

'I'll pour.' Virginia moved forward.

'No, no, I can manage,' Florence said. 'Sit down and relax, Virginia.'

Wincey felt the air immediately become tense, but obviously Florence was unaware of it. She was very ladylike in the way she poured out the tea and handed china teacups and tiny cakes around.

'A new recipe,' she informed everyone as she settled down with her teacup and raised pinky. 'Dried eggs, of course, but I find it very good. And some porridge oats, would you believe. Do have another one, Nicholas. They're very small, I know, but they look so dainty, don't they. Appearance is important, I always think. In food as well as in everything else.

221

I just refuse to do as everyone else is doing now and make a coat out of army blankets or a dress out of curtain material. I'd rather go on wearing my old, good quality garments. Purchased in Copeland's, you know.'

'I was just saying to Mother,' Wincey told Florence, 'that she and Father should treat themselves to an evening out tonight to celebrate. They could have a meal somewhere and then go to the pictures.'

'But I've got dinner all planned. It's vegetable soup, spam and salad and uncooked chocolate cake,' Florence protested.

'Sounds great. I'll stay and have dinner with you and we can have a long talk like old times.'

'Good idea,' Nicholas said, lifting his newspaper. 'Let's see what's on.'

Virginia smiled over at Florence. 'Your mother would be pleased to see you the other night. And Erchie and Granny.'

'Yes, although poor Granny is getting very frail.'

'Wonderful spirit though.'

'Oh yes. I have to laugh at her at times.'

'I must pay her a visit soon, Florence. Next week I'm on late shift but I could drop in one afternoon, perhaps.'

'No, no, Virginia. That would be too tiring for you. Better they come here for morning coffee, or lunch perhaps. That way I could organise everything and save you any bother.'

'It's no bother going to visit friends, Florence. I enjoy it.'

Wincey could see that her mother was struggling to be patient. 'Why don't you go and get ready, Mother?'

'Yes.'

Nicholas rose too. 'And I'll see about booking a table.'

'We should do this more often,' Nicholas told Virginia, taking her into his arms the moment they reached the bedroom.

Virginia smiled. 'We do it all the time.'

Nicholas tutted at her in mock reproof. 'Treat ourselves to a meal out and a show at least once a week, I mean.'

'Don't tell me it's because I need a rest or it's too tiring for me to make a meal here or I'll scream.'

Nicholas laughed and rubbed his face into the curve of her neck. 'You're very patient with her, darling. I just hope Wincey can get through to her and she gets the message.'

'It's not that I don't appreciate her help, especially now when there's no Mrs Rogers.'

'Forget about Florence. Get yourself out of that uniform and into something really glamorous. We're going to forget about everything except enjoying ourselves—and each other—tonight.'

She clung to him and as they kissed, he danced her slowly round the room, as they'd once danced naked in the woods when they were young.

*   *   *

'That was a lovely meal, Florence. I really enjoyed it. You must give Teresa the recipe for that chocolate cake. I bet Granny would appreciate it.'

'I'll write it down for you and you can give it to Mother.'

'I don't think you realise, Florence, how much they're missing you. It was so terrible for Teresa losing the twins, and then you.'

'She hasn't lost me.'

'It feels like that. They hardly ever see you. I wouldn't see you either if I wasn't coming here every weekend.'

Florence looked uneasy. 'Well, I'll try to get over to Springburn more often.'

'I think the best idea would be if you shared yourself between here and the family. After all, that's what I do.'

'What do you mean?'

'I think you should help your mother and father by living there with them, but every morning come over here to help my mother and father from Monday to Friday, say from ten o'clock until two. Then I'd take over here as usual at weekends. It would make Teresa and Erchie and Granny so happy, Florence, and you know my mother feels terribly guilty about taking you away from them for so long. It's your own family who really need you now, Florence.'

An anxious, unhappy look appeared in Florence's eyes. 'Am I really making Virginia unhappy? She's been so good to me and I was just . . . I was just trying . . . '

'I know, Florence.' Wincey hastened to put a comforting arm around Florence's shoulders. 'And she's so grateful for all the help you've given her. And she wouldn't want to lose you. But she wouldn't have to if you agree to what I've suggested. That way everyone would be happy.'

After a few seconds, Florence nodded to herself. Then she gazed round at Wincey and said, 'Do you think I'll be all right?'

In her eyes, Wincey could see the shadow of grief—or the fear of grief—that had never after all gone away. Florence, it occurred to Wincey, had been frantically busying herself in order to avoid thinking about the loss of her home, and her Eddie. Wincey suddenly realised that she had been doing the same to cope with the grief of losing Robert Houston.

'Of course you will. You'll have the family, and me, to look after, as well as everybody here, every day. But it won't be all work and no play.' Wincey smiled and gave Florence's shoulders a squeeze. 'We can go out for a meal and to the pictures as well, you know.'

Florence managed a smile in return. 'I was missing Mammy and Daddy right enough. And awful old Granny.'

'You don't mind if she's cheeky to you then?' Wincey said.

'She is awful cheeky to me but I'm used to it. No, I'm very fond of her really.'

'That's settled then. Will you tell my mother, or shall I?'

'No, I'll tell her, Wincey. Or we both can when she comes back this evening. I always have a hot drink ready for her if she's been out at night.'

'Right, that's what we'll do then.'

After a moment, Florence said, 'I was just thinking. Something ought to be done to that house in Springburn. It needs a proper clean out for a start. And I don't suppose anything in the house has ever been polished.'

Wincey had a sudden terrible vision of Florence struggling to polish Granny's wheelchair.

'Well, you'll have your own room, Florence, and I'm sure you'll have it looking a picture in no time.'

By Sunday evening, everything had been arranged and agreed to and Florence returned to Springburn and the Balgrayhill with Wincey.

'I'll see you tomorrow at ten,' Florence assured Virginia and Nicholas.

'I'll look forward to that,' Virginia said. 'Although you won't see much of Nicholas. We mustn't disturb him at his work.'

'Except when I clean out his room. Or take him his morning coffee.'

'No!' both Nicholas and Virginia cried out in unison, and Virginia added, 'Nicholas has so many papers and books lying around and only he knows where to lay his hands on them. He sees to his own room, Florence. It only gets a good clean out when he's safely finished writing his novel. No one must interrupt him, not even with a cup of coffee. It's a strict rule. He takes a flask and sandwiches in with him. The same applies to lunchtime.'

'Well,' Nicholas said, 'I think I could relax the lunchtime rule if I started a bit earlier in the morning.' He winked in Virginia's direction. 'I'd hate to miss Florence's cooking.'

Once they were out on the Terrace, Wincey and Florence turned and waved. Virginia and Nicholas waved back. Wincey had never seen them look so happy. She linked arms with Florence as they walked towards her car.

'It's going to be all right,' she said. 'Everything's going to be all right.'

She tried to believe it, but the war still cast its shadow over them all. The whole country was war weary. They continued to put on a show of keeping their spirits up but the pretence was wearing a bit thin. It was all very well for the government to plaster pictures all over the place of happy smiling mothers sealing vegetables and fruit in jars, and a happy smiling child saying, 'We'll have lots to eat this winter, won't we, Mother?' And big letters underneath the picture saying' Grow your own, can your own.'

But as Erchie said, 'Most folk here live in tenements with no gardens. So where are we supposed to get the vegetables an' fruit? Where do we even get the bloody cans?'

There was a big pig bin out in the back yard beside the brick shelter, into which they were supposed to put all their so-called waste food for the pigs to eat.

'What waste?' Granny asked. 'We eat it aw oorsels.'

'Aye,' Erchie agreed. 'Anythin' out there'd just give the rats a treat.'

They couldn't even get away for a wee holiday any more. 'Is your journey really necessary?' the posters kept demanding. Petrol rationing, even if you could get your ration, made holiday travel impossible. Trains were so uncomfortable and slow that no one travelled on them unless they had to. 'Go by Shank's pony,' another poster urged.

'When's it aw gonnae end?' Granny asked. 'Ah'm fed up. Ah cannae even get a decent bit o' sponge cake any mair.'

Christmas and New Year and other times that they had once celebrated came and went. They were not worth celebrating any more. But the worst thing about the war, and the thing that was seldom spoken of—in the Gourlay house at least—was the terrible loss of life. The loss of their friends and neighbours was bad enough. The spectres of first Doctor Houston, then poor Eddie and young Bridget and Euphemia continued to haunt them.

Now they were anxious about Joe and Pete and Malcy. 'Write to Malcy again hen,' Erchie said to Wincey, 'an' ask him if he's heard anythin' about Joe an' Pete.'

She had written several letters recently and received no reply. She was secretly beginning to feel panicky. She kept remembering Malcy when he'd had his last leave. He wasn't at all like the jack-the-lad character he'd once been. No longer was he the laughing, twinkling eyed man who had the gift of the gab and a great way with the girls. His gaze was serious. He was a tough and seasoned army man who'd seen too much death and suffering, and who'd been longing to reach out for some love and happiness again.

In her heart she had known that—and she'd denied him it. Just as she'd denied loving Robert as she should have, and as he deserved to be loved. Poor Malcy, she thought, and prayed that wherever he was, he was safe and well. She got out her pen and notepad and began another letter.

This time, instead of beginning 'Dear Malcy', she wrote 'My dear Malcy' and she ended the letter with 'All my love'. She doubted if she could ever address him in person in such affectionate terms but it might be a step in the right direction. She hoped so.

33

Now Malcy really knew what heart sick meant. He was sick to his very heart at what he'd seen in Buchenwald and Belsen. It was completely beyond him to understand how human beings could do to fellow human beings what the Germans had done to the inmates of these camps. Were the Germans human, he began to wonder. It was difficult to believe after the terrible scenes he had witnessed. It was equally difficult to comprehend that the crowds of ghostly, skeletal figures he had seen wandering around the camps were the lucky ones. At least they'd survived. Unlike so many others, who had died horrible deaths at the hands of Nazi doctors who had performed hideous experiments on them. Malcy could only guess at how many people had been tortured or starved to death, or met their terrible end in the gas chambers. Perhaps no one would ever really know.

For the rest of his life, he would never forget these sad remnants of humanity. Never, never, would he forget what the Germans were capable of. Or indeed any nationality. The Americans had dropped an atom bomb on Hiroshima and the pilot, looking down from a height of thirty three thousand feet, said afterwards that in two minutes, the surface was nothing but blackness, boiling like a barrel of tar. Where before there had been a city with distinctive houses, buildings, now you couldn't see anything.

And what was the target? Ordinary men, women and children. Young typists in offices, old people sitting at home, nurses in hospitals, mothers out shopping, babies in prams— everybody going about their ordinary, everyday business. All in the boiling tar barrel. And the Americans are on our side for God sake, Malcy thought.

Then three days later, they dropped another bomb on Nagasaki. Why? Nobody could yet figure it out. Malcy was unable to figure it out. How could human beings be like this to one another? War brought out so much cruelty and evil in so many people, of all sides and all nationalities. He had killed, hadn't he? And he'd seen a decent young man—Andy, his name was—who normally would never have hurt a fly, machine gun a dozen German soldiers in one go. And these Germans had been giving themselves up, walking towards Andy with their hands above their heads. But Andy had seen some of his best mates blown sky high in a boat bombed by a German Stuka.

And so it went on. The whole sickening business. What could be normal any more? Even knowing the war was over didn't help much. He'd known it was the beginning of the end when Berlin had fallen to the Red Army. Then in May the war in Europe finally came to an end. Now, the war with Japan was over. It was all over, so they said. But it wasn't all over in his head. Or, he suspected, in the minds of many other servicemen. He'd learned Joe and Pete had been prisoners of war. The Red Cross had passed on postcards from them. They'd been captured by the Japanese and used as slave labour, building a railway where men had died like flies—one for every sleeper that was laid. He didn't think he could bear it if Joe and Pete had died after all they'd come through

229

together. But he knew he'd have to bear it, just as he'd had to bear everything else.

Then he'd been shipped back to England and he heard that Joe and Pete were back in Britain as well. He found out that they were in hospital in the south of England. His relief was enormous and the hospital was the first place he made for when he landed. He'd spend all his leave with them, if need be.

And there they were—nearly as emaciated as the people he'd seen in the German concentration camps. But at least they were alive. That was the main thing. They were even up and about, although still wearing pyjamas and dressing gowns. There they were, grinning all over their gaunt faces.

'Well,' Joe cried out, 'you're a fuckin' sight for sore eyes!' They shook hands and then Malcy thought, To hell, and hugged the pair of them. He didn't say anything about them losing their wives. The Red Cross had already been in touch with them and let them know what had happened. They'd realise that he felt for them, and one day perhaps they would talk about it. At the moment, they were just grateful for being reunited.

They told Malcy they weren't allowed out yet, and were only allowed out of bed for a few hours every day. 'They're trying to build our strength up, so they say,' Pete explained.

'I'll find a place to stay locally,' Malcy told them, 'and come in and keep you company every day.'

'Don't be bloody daft,' Joe said. 'Away you go home and enjoy your leave. We'll have a right get together when we get back.'

'I don't mind waiting here for you,' Malcy said.

'Go home now, Malcy. The Gourlays, especially Wincey, will be desperate to see you.'

'They'll want to see you as well, don't forget. They want you both to stay with them, at least until you get fixed up.'

'We know that. But you get up there as quick as you can, mate, and best of luck to you.'

230

'All right, I'll go, but not right this minute.' He settled down on a bedside chair and they slumped onto the beds. Malcy offered them a cigarette and after lighting up, he said, 'How did you hear the war had ended?'

Joe said, 'We'd been working as usual. Then the guard told us to rest before we began the march back to the camp. On the march, we passed another crowd of men and this big, bearded guy with a shovel over his shoulder shouted out to us, "They've had it".'

'Then,' Pete said, 'when we got back to the camp, the commandant told us that the war was over. We heard later that he'd been hanged.'

Joe took up the story again. 'But the next thing that happened was a great bulky guy in a fancy American uniform arrived. He must have thought he was a bit of a comic. Everyone crowded around him and asked him to tell us all the news. He said Charlie Chaplin was the father of Joan Barry's kid. It wasn't until much later that we found out about the atomic bombs.'

They talked until a nurse came and told Malcy that his time was up.

'See you in the Boundary Bar,' Malcy said as he left.

Joe and Pete gave him a thumbs up sign and another big grin and Joe shouted out, 'You get stuck in there with Wincey.'

Malcy had sometimes thought of Wincey but not often now. He had to cope with so many other more vivid and more immediate images filling his mind. He supposed that what he still wanted was to get home to Glasgow to try to pick up some of the threads of normal, ordinary life. Although he wasn't sure what that was any more.

He wasn't even sure if he wanted to make his home with the Gourlays. They had insisted, via Wincey's letters, that that was what he must do. He didn't know what to do about anything any more, except perhaps to be on his own to try to sort himself out.

Maybe he could rent or buy a place of his own. However,

he wrote to Wincey and told her when he would be arriving in Glasgow. He almost dreaded the reunion in his home city—and to think he'd once longed to be back among all the people he knew there.

Now, they seemed as if they were from a different world. Only fellow servicemen like Pete and Joe belonged to his world. Only they knew what it was like. He had moments of near panic when he decided not to go back at all. He'd stay in London. There were plenty of clubs and places for servicemen there. He tried to pull himself together. To chicken out of this last ordeal would do no one any good, especially himself. He'd faced the war. Now he'd have to face the peace.

He bought his ticket to Glasgow and boarded the train. That wasn't easy for different reasons, but mainly because he was so loaded down by his kit bag that he could hardly manoeuvre himself through the door. Finally, he had to sling it onto the train before clambering on himself.

He sat in a corner by the window, smoking and trying to prepare himself for what was to come. They'd probably meet him at the Central Station. Teresa and Erchie and Wincey. Or maybe Wincey would decide she couldn't take time away from her factory.

Thinking of the factory made him remember Charlotte. Yet even she had become not only a ghost from the past, but someone from another world. Had he ever belonged to that world?

He felt as if he was on his way to meet a crowd of strangers. He kept trying to brace himself. He wished he could have stayed in the hospital, been allocated a bed next to Joe and Pete. Maybe he didn't look as ill as they did and in need of rest and treatment, but he felt as if he did. That's what he secretly longed for. He was so tired. Perhaps it was his exhaustion that was distancing him from everything. He just sat there, hunched in the corner smoking one cigarette after another and listening to the rhythm of the train and allowing it to rock him into a mindless trance.

For a while at least, it gave him a blessed respite from waking dreams of men being blown to bits; drowning men clutching at his legs; men screaming for help; men, women and children crawling towards him from the concentration camps; men, women and children burning.

He became conscious eventually of the train's rhythm slowing down. Opening his eyes he saw the first sign of Glasgow—the shining silver of the River Clyde. Frantically he struggled not to weep.

34

They all waited excitedly on the platform—Teresa, Erchie, Florence, Wincey and Granny. Granny's specs had slid to the end of her nose and she was wearing a bashed black felt hat, a long coat of the same colour and a tartan blanket tucked round her legs.

Wincey stood on tiptoe and cried out, 'There he is,' and waved. Then she said, 'Go and help him, Erchie. Look, he's loaded down.'

Erchie was already running towards the carriage door. The rest of the family hurried as quickly as they could behind, bumping Granny's wheelchair and jostling her about in the process. She clung grimly on, but didn't complain.

'Welcome home, son,' Erchie took hold of Malcy's kitbag after giving him an awkward hug. They all hugged him and echoed that cry of 'Welcome home, Malcy'.

Malcy gave a half smile. He looked confused. He allowed himself to be led away, his gear stuffed into the boot of Wincey's car and himself pushed into the front seat beside Wincey. She drove very confidently, laughing and chatting with Teresa and Florence who were in the back seat. Erchie and Granny were following on in a taxi. Malcy tried to respond to some of the questions that were fired at him until Wincey said, 'Give him a break. He's tired. He's probably been travelling for days.'

He gazed out of the window at places he'd come to believe he'd never see again. His eyes strayed up to the ornate facade of the Central Hotel. They didn't build them like that nowadays. There was Hope Street with its equally beautiful Victorian architecture. And St Vincent Street and Renfield Street. Street after beautiful street, everything seemed intact and just the same as it had always been. It was as if the war had never happened.

Then there were the high black tenements of Springburn Road. There was the Avenue on the right with Wellfield Street branching off it. The Wellie picture house would probably still be there. Further along Springburn Road now, there was the Balgrayhill rearing up in front of them. He cringed as he saw the banner stretching across the top of the street with huge letters emblazoned on it, 'Welcome home, Malcy.' There was another one draped across the close, and flags and balloons floated at windows.

He managed a smile and a wave to the neighbours standing around the close and greeting him with shouts of 'Glad to see you, son' and 'Have a great party'.

Oh God, he thought, a party! The smile stuck to his face and he waved back as if he hadn't a care in the world. Inside the house was all decorated with paper chains and balloons. Somebody helped him off with his heavy khaki greatcoat and shoved a drink into his hand.

Soon Erchie and Granny joined them, followed by a crowd of neighbours, until the kitchen was packed and the rag rug became rumpled against the fender. The table was cluttered with glasses and bottles. People were perched on the draining board at the side of the sink and on the high bed in the recess. Teresa had a struggle to get the press door open to fetch out

235

more glasses. The noise of chattering voices and laughter bounced off walls and ceiling.

The only thing for it, Malcy supposed, was to get drunk. Even getting drunk, however, proved difficult but at least it helped him to loosen up a bit and become more talkative. He assured everyone that Pete and Joe were all right, and would soon be home too. He warned however that they had suffered a lot and were very thin and undernourished. They needed to stay in hospital and have their strength built up before they'd be fit enough to travel.

'Ye've lost a pound or two o' flesh yersel, Malcy,' somebody said.

'Poor laddies,' Granny kept muttering. 'Poor laddies.'

Florence told him that there had been lots of marvellous celebrations on VE Day and VJ Day and all the neighbours agreed. There were shouts of 'Marvellous', 'Smashing', 'Magic'. Florence assured Malcy it was especially good fun on VE Day. Her eyes rolled with pleasure, remembering.

'You should have seen the mass of people crushing into George Square, Malcy. Chock a block, it was.'

There were cries of 'Like sardines we were'. Then one woman added, 'Ah said tae wan man, if we get any closer, we'll huv tae get married.'

'It's a wonder no one was seriously hurt in the crush,' Florence said. 'But we managed to dance all the same, didn't we, Wincey? Everyone was dancing like mad. What a laugh it was.' Florence giggled. 'Men we'd never set eyes on in our lives kissing and hugging us. What a scream it was, wasn't it, Wincey? A real scream.'

'Ah bet them wernae the kind o' screams Malcy's been used to,' Granny muttered. She was very bent and shaky nowadays, and spoke as much to herself as to anyone else.

'Granny, for goodness sake, this is supposed to be a happy occasion. Don't you go spoiling it.'

'Ah cannae open ma mooth these days,' Granny muttered into her chest. 'Ye'll be auld yersel' wan day.'

Malcy went over and took the old woman's hands in his. 'You're quite right, Granny. But I suppose I've got to try and forget all that now.'

'Aye, well, ah just hope ye'll be able to, son.' After a minute's thoughtful silence, she added, 'But maybe it's no' good to forget aw thegither.'

'I know what you mean, Granny.'

'Ah'm no' talkin' about bloody useless stone monuments an' paper poppies, mind.'

'I know.'

'Aw these names frae the First War on aw them stone monuments. Every town an' village has them. Now they'll be carvin' other ones for another million or mair poor laddies. What good is that tae their wives an' mothers? Folk like Mrs McGregor doon Springburn Road. Her man an' her poor wee Jimmy.'

'For God sake, Ma!' It was Erchie's turn to protest. 'This isnae the time or the place. We're tryin' tae gie Malcy a cheery homecomin'.'

'Aye, well, ah'm glad tae see ye're back aw in wan piece, son. Ah am that.'

'Thanks, Granny.'

They put records on the gramophone. *It's a grand night for singing*, and *I've got a lovely bunch of coconuts* and *Don't fence me in*. They belted them all out until Granny complained, 'Where's aw the good auld Scots songs.'

So they launched into Scots songs, including the favourite, *I belong to Glasgow, dear old Glasgow town*.

Everyone joined in, including old Mr McCluskey and his daughter, Miss McCluskey. She, by force of circumstances including war work, had mellowed somewhat. It turned out that she had quite a sweet singing voice. The house was packed and the party went on well into the early hours. Granny fell asleep in her chair despite the racket. Her head sunk forward into her chest, her mouth puttering with snores. There was a lot of talk about rationing, which was still going

237

on, and the difficulty folk coming back from the war were having in getting a place to live. But mostly the talk was about scarcity of food and other items. Theirs had been a different war from Malcy's.

At last people began to say goodnight. They shook hands with Malcy again, and told him again how glad they were to see him. Before they left, of course, they all joined hands to sing *Auld Lang Syne*. He appreciated their warmth and friendliness, although he was so exhausted that he was glad to see them go. Refusing a cup of tea from Teresa, he collapsed into bed and oblivion. He hadn't even the energy to get undressed.

Next morning, he was thankful that, unlike most of the tenements in Springburn, this house had a bathroom. He couldn't remember the last time he was able to relax in a warm bath. Through in the kitchen, Granny, Erchie, Florence and Teresa were at breakfast. Wincey was nowhere to be seen.

Teresa said, 'I was going to give you your breakfast in bed, Malcy. I thought you needed a long lie.'

'This is late for me.'

Florence said, 'Did you know I'm housekeeper for the Cartwrights of Kirklee Terrace now, Malcy?'

Granny said, 'She means she dusts an' polishes an' makes whit she calls their lunch.'

'I start at ten,' Florence pressed on with determined cheerfulness. 'And it's time I was away. Wincey says she's taking the afternoon off, so she'll be seeing you then too. She'll be back earlier than me though, in time for lunch. Then this evening, we've all to visit Kirklee Terrace as guests of the Cartwrights. We can call them Virginia and Nicholas, of course, because we're family in a way. Wait until you see that lovely house, Malcy. You'll be so impressed.'

Malcy tried to look impressed.

Erchie rose. 'Wincey wanted me to stay off as well today but somebody needs to be there to keep an eye on things.

Ah'll see you the night, Malcy. OK?'

'Right, fine,' Malcy said.

After Erchie and Florence left, and Teresa was washing up the breakfast dishes, and Granny had nodded off, Malcy announced that he was going out for a walk.

'A good idea, Malcy. You relax and enjoy yourself, son.'

He needed to be alone to think. It was as if he was convalescing from an illness. He felt not only that everyone around him was a stranger, but he was a stranger to himself. He clumped along Springburn Road in his big army boots, occasionally catching a glimpse of his reflection in a shop window. He saw a big, rough looking man with a scarred face and shaved head showing under his khaki bonnet. That wasn't the man who used to swagger whistling along Springburn Road, winking at all the pretty girls. So many years ago.

He wandered away up to the park and sat on a bench, staring ahead at nothing in particular. It was only when the cold began to seep into his bones that he made a move. As soon as he entered the close, Teresa had the door open and was rushing out to meet him.

'Malcy, I was worried sick about you and Granny's been watching for you at the window for ages.'

'Sorry, I seem to have lost track of the time. I was just wandering about.'

'Come on through, son. You need to get yourself in front of the fire. You look blue with the cold.'

'Where's Granny now?'

'Here she comes. Wincey's pushing her through.'

'Whit dae ye think ye're playin' at. Ye nearly had me freezin' tae death.'

'Sorry, Granny. I don't know where the time went.'

'Whit a bloody daft thing tae say. Get oot o' ma road. Ah'll have tae get a cup o' tea tae thaw me oot.'

Teresa had already started to pour out tea for everybody. 'I've only made scrambled eggs on toast tonight, Malcy, because I'm sure we'll get lots to eat at Virginia's later on.'

'Oh yes,' Florence said. 'I offered to prepare supper in advance but Virginia wouldn't hear of it. But rest assured she'll do us proud. And wait till you see the house, Malcy. You'll be . . . '

'Yes, yes, dear, we know,' Teresa interrupted. 'Now all sit round the table and have your tea. I'll help Granny.'

'Did Virginia tell you that Richard is coming home soon,' Wincey asked.

Florence ate a dainty mouthful of scrambled eggs before replying. 'I believe she did mention it.'

'And his wife of course. I thought he'd end up living in Castle Hill, but apparently it has been taken over by the National Trust,' Wincey said. 'His mother and father in law are now living in a cottage in the grounds. Castle Hill got to be too much for them to cope with in their old age. I'm not surprised. What a size of a place it was.'

'Will Richard and his wife be living at Kirklee Terrace, do you think?' Florence asked.

'No. With old Mrs Cartwright.'

Florence said, 'I think she must have spent all her money making that place of hers habitable again, but it still looks awful. And it must be terribly cramped inside. The bedrooms were upstairs and they're all gone now. I don't think Richard and his wife will stay there for long.'

Wincey shrugged. 'I suppose he'll have to find a job and a place of his own eventually. It'll be changed days for Richard, I'm afraid.'

'Especially,' Florence went on, 'when she's not a pleasant character. The old woman, I mean. I know she's your grandmother, Wincey, but I'm sorry, I just don't like her.'

Wincey shrugged again. 'I can't say I'm all that keen on her myself.'

'Now, now, girls,' Teresa said. 'She's an old woman and she's had to suffer being bombed.'

'Well, actually Mother, she was a couple of miles away at her bridge club meeting when the bomb dropped.'

Teresa wasn't listening. She was gazing worriedly at Malcy, her fingers tucking and twisting at her floral, wraparound apron. 'Eat up, son. You've hardly touched your eggs. Oh, there's Erchie. I was so worried about you that he went out to look . . . Well, not especially to look for you,' she hastily corrected herself. 'He had to go out for his paper, you see.'

Erchie's small, skinny figure breezed into the kitchen and waved his paper at Granny. 'Plenty tae read tae ye the night, Ma. Hello there, Malcy. Had a nice day, son?'

'Yes, fine thanks, Erchie.'

'Do you not like scrambled eggs?' Teresa said worriedly. 'I can easily make you something else. Just say the word, son.'

'No, it's great, Teresa. I just don't seem to have much of an appetite these days.'

'No wonder you've lost so much weight, Malcy. You're a big man. You need to eat. Now how about some baked beans. I could quite easily . . . '

Suddenly Granny bawled, 'For God sake, Teresa, will ye shut up an' leave the man in peace.'

Teresa's pale face acquired two pink blotches. 'I was just trying to help.'

'And I appreciate it, Teresa,' Malcy assured her. 'I really do. I feel so lucky you've all accepted me as family like this. Where would I be, what would I do without all of you.'

'Och!' Teresa went over to give him a hug, her old slippers scuffing across the linoleum. 'You'll always have a home here, Malcy. You'll always be one of the family.'

Granny had nearly dropped off again but she suddenly roused herself. 'Aye, that's right, son. Now forget about the bloody eggs. It's jist that dried stuff anyway. Jist think yersel' lucky it wisnae spam. See aw that Yankee junk.'

'Granny, it's wicked, talking like that,' Teresa scolded. 'It was very kind of the Americans to help us out with all that food, and spam's really tasty. So is dried egg. Everybody thinks so.'

'Ye cannae have it poached or boiled, and spam cannae

hold a candle tae a pork chop or a plate o' good steak mince.'

'But if we hadn't had things like spam and dried egg, we'd have had next to nothing, Granny. I know because I'm the one who's had to trail around all the shops looking for a bite to eat. I'm the one who's had to wait in mile long queues for hours on end.'

They were at it again. Food and rationing and shortages. It was all they seemed to talk about. Malcy sat staring at his plate, allowing the conversation to wash over him, as he drifted further and further away.

35

Kirklee Terrace was an elegant cul de sac separated from Great Western Road by a sloping green bank that in spring was covered in crocuses, then daffodils. It had been designed by the architect C. Wilson in 1845. Overlooking Great Western Road at the front, the Cartwright house also had excellent views of the Botanic Gardens.

Florence gave Malcy a running commentary on the house as they travelled in Wincey's car. 'There's a gorgeous entrance hall,' Florence enthused, 'with a marble floor—a marble floor, would you believe. Downstairs there's the kitchen and the dining room and sitting room and a study that Nicholas calls his writing room. A grand staircase leads up to the bedrooms and the bathroom. There's a drawing room upstairs as well. Wait till you see that drawing room, Malcy.'

'All right, Florence,' Wincey said. 'Just let him wait, will you.'

She swung the car off Great Western Road at the junction of Kirklee Road, then sharp right onto Kirklee Terrace. A golden carpet of autumn leaves crackled under their feet as they walked from the car towards the front door.

'Of course, in the old days,' Florence said, 'there would have been a maid to open the door. But it's impossible to get staff since the war. Everyone has to do more or less everything themselves.'

'Aboot time tae,' Granny said. Erchie had helped her from the taxi which had followed Wincey's car. 'Spoiled, lazy sods! They lived the life o' Riley an' tried tae make oot they were superior tae the likes o' us. They gave folks like us absolute hell an' we were supposed tae believe we were the inferior ones. Well, no' me. Ah believe it's the other way roon.'

Teresa rolled her eyes. 'Well, not any more, Granny. At least the war has evened all that out.'

'Ah aye said you came up the Clyde in a banana boat.'

Just then the door opened and Virginia welcomed them in.

'An' dinnae think they're aw like her,' Granny persisted. 'She came frae a Gorbals slum, an' used tae work as a scullery maid.'

'Granny!' Teresa looked distraught. 'I'm black affronted, Virginia. She was going on about class, you see, but I'm sure she didn't mean any offence.'

Virginia laughed. 'Don't worry. I'm not ashamed of my background.'

'Ah should think no',' Granny said, ignoring Teresa's furious glare.

'Come away in.'

'See what I mean about the hall, Malcy.' Florence, head tipped proudly back, gazed around in a kind of ecstasy. She was dressed for the part in her best hat with its winged birds and draped veil.

'Will somebody shut her up?' Granny said. 'Ah'm fed up wi' her witterin' on aboot this bloody hoose.'

Virginia laughed and led them into the sitting room.

'We could carry Granny up to the drawing room,' Florence said, easing off her hat. 'We could all go up there.'

Wincey said, 'Florence, will you never learn. We've come

to visit my mother and father.'

Florence withdrew into a silent huff. They all knew however that this would not last. One of the unfortunate things about Florence was she never remained offended or silent for long.

Nicholas rose to greet them and, as Florence had told Malcy more than once, he was a very handsome man indeed. 'And a genius as well, Malcy. An absolute genius.' Florence had always had a dramatic imagination and a talent for exaggeration.

'No, Florence,' Wincey said. 'Not a genius.'

'But he's won literary awards, and he's made a fortune.'

'He's a good writer, and he makes a good living, but he's not a genius and he doesn't make a fortune.'

'Fancy you denigrating your own father!'

'I'm not denigrating him. I'm only telling the truth. He'd say exactly what I've said about himself.'

'He's so modest too, Malcy. Just wait till you meet him.'

The two men shook hands and after warmly welcoming Malcy, Nicholas turned to Granny. 'And how are you, Granny?'

'Fine, son. An' how's yersel?'

'Well, I'm glad to say I've a lot more time now. I'm no longer with the Home Guard. I've still to see to my strip of back garden though.'

Teresa nodded. 'Yes, it looks as if food's going to be scarce for a long time yet. Only the other day I waited for hours in the biggest queue I've ever seen. I stood there . . . ' Teresa was off on her favourite theme.

Malcy allowed his mind to drift. He wondered how Joe and Pete were. He now hoped that they would be kept down south for as long as possible. He couldn't see them fitting very easily into civilian life here. If he felt a stranger in Glasgow, how much worse would Joe and Pete feel after all they'd been through. He suspected that it would take them years to get over their experiences, no matter where they were. Maybe they never would.

It suddenly occurred to Malcy that maybe he wouldn't

either. But he knew he had to make the effort. He took a deep breath and attempted to join in the conversation, or at least to look interested. A couple of times he caught Wincey's eye. He remembered that straight, deep, determined look. His heart became heavy again. He didn't know what to think about Wincey any more. He was fond of her, had been for some time now. How could he not be when she'd been so kind and loyal and supportive in writing to him so often?

She still looked the same, with her fringed red hair and delicate sprinkling of freckles. That strong steady gaze was certainly the same as he remembered it. She was some girl. He'd always thought so. Later she came over and sat beside him. The others were through in the kitchen sampling the food and drink that Virginia had set out ready.

'A buffet supper,' Florence had explained. 'One just helps oneself.'

He had just put a spoonful or two of potato salad on his plate, lifted a glass of wine and returned to the sitting room. Wincey had been the first to follow him through.

'We never get a chance to talk on our own,' Wincey said. 'How about me taking you out tomorrow to, say, the Central Hotel for supper. They have a nice lounge there where we can relax with a drink after the meal and talk as long as we like.'

After a second or two's hesitation, Malcy said, 'Yes, all right.' The truth was he just wanted to be on his own. He needed time to at least try to free his mind from the horrors still milling around in it. Dead men on land and sea still returned in his nightmares to haunt him, along with the living dead of the concentration camps. It was too soon to get back to normal. He didn't know how to do it. The next day, however, there was no getting out of the date with Wincey. Everyone colluded with it.

'Come on now, son.' Teresa encouraged. 'It's what you need, to get out more. Wincey'll take you a wee drive around Glasgow and it'll make you feel really at home again.'

'Aye,' Erchie said. 'Ah bet many a time ye've dreamt about

the dear green place.'

He supposed he had.

'Away ye go, the pair o' ye,' Granny said. 'Enjoy yersels.'

They didn't speak in the car and Malcy was grateful for the silence. She drove round George Square and he was as impressed as he always had been with the magnificent architecture of the City Chambers. They passed Hutcheson Hall with its clock and steeple and the City and Courts building, with its twenty nine bays along one side. The Robert Adam Trade House he knew well. All the buildings in Virginia Street too. Malcy remembered the tales he had heard as a schoolboy—of how this part of the city had been developed as a result of the tobacco trade with America. In Royal Exchange Square there was a magnificent building that had once been a mansion of one of the tobacco lords.

Familiarity brought a trickle of pleasure moving slowly through his veins, relaxing him. Everything he saw reminded him of some distant memory, some bit of folklore about his beloved city. They passed the point where Argyle Street was bridged by the Central Station. With a smile of recognition on his face, he recalled how that part of the street was known as the 'Heilanman's Umbrella'—because at one time it had been a meeting place for Highlanders on wet days.

The elaborate Victorian ironwork of the entrance to the Central Station signalled the end of their journey. They parked the car and went up the steps into the Central Hotel.

Malcy and Wincey strolled in together, still in complete silence. Eventually she said, 'Do you fancy a drink before dinner?'

'Fine by me.'

They went upstairs to a lounge with a bar and settled in a quiet corner with their drinks.

Another silence, then she said, 'Are you glad I wrote to you while you were away?'

He stared at her in surprise. 'Of course. Your letters meant a lot to me.'

'Did they?'

'Yes, they did.'

'I'm glad,' she said. 'I think we got to know each other a lot better through them, don't you?'

'Yes,' he said, remembering the letters now, and how their tone and contents gradually grew warmer, more intimate.

'For me it was a release, in a way,' she said. 'It's funny how much easier it is to express yourself in writing than it is face to face.'

'You're doing all right,' he said with a smile.

To her it was only the ghost of the cheeky grin she remembered from so long ago but she said, 'You're still the same.'

'No,' he said. 'I'm not the same person I was, Wincey.'

She nodded, then fixed him with one of her serious, concentrated stares.

'And I'm not the same woman that I was.' She tucked a stray lock of her auburn hair behind an ear. 'I've been thinking . . . ' Her stare clung earnestly to him as she went on. 'How about if you booked us a room here for tonight. That way we could have a chance to find out more about the new Malcy and the new Wincey.'

He studied her in silence for a minute or two. Then he half laughed and shook his head at her.

'Wincey!'

'Don't you dare turn such a good offer down,' she said.

His smile returned again, still faint and ghostly, but a smile all the same. 'I know the war has had an effect on me, Wincey, but it's not made me that daft.'

'Fine then.' She raised her glass. 'Cheers!'

He shook his head again and helplessly repeated, 'Wincey!'

But as he raised his glass to hers, he began to feel better.

THE GLASGOW BELLE

As the great age of canal building comes to Glasgow, powerful men are willing to risk everything on this new venture, gambling vast fortunes on its success. Meanwhile, in the city slums, the age-old struggle for survival continues unchanged. On the banks of the canal, a wild and beautiful young girl is rescued from a life of poverty and abuse thanks to the kindness of the old Earl of Kirklee. Isla Henderson had always dreamed of becoming a Lady, and when she goes to live at Kirklee Castle as one of the family, it seems as if all her dreams have come true. Evoking all the wealth and squalor of 18th century Glasgow, *The Glasgow Belle* is a powerful tale of rivalry and ambition, bitter hatred and enduring love.

'The stylish work of this born storyteller is a cut above the rest'
EVENING TIMES

THE CLYDESIDERS

In the summer of 1914, as the storm clouds of war begin to gather over Europe, life in Glasgow goes on as normal—for the rich in their elegant mansions, and for the poor in filthy, overcrowded tenements. Up at Hilltop House, Virginia Watson is a kitchen maid whose life is an endless round of hardship and drudgery. Back in the Gorbals, her family are fighting a losing battle against bad housing, hunger and disease. Everything changes for Virginia after a chance meeting with Nicholas Cartwright, a wealthy and dashing young army officer—but their illicit romance, defying all the conventions of the time, has hardly begun when war breaks out and Nicholas leaves to face the horrors of the Western Front. A powerful tale of love and loss, *The Clydesiders* is also a brilliant portrayal of Glasgow during the First World War.

THE BREADMAKERS SAGA

The Breadmakers Saga is the epic trilogy of a Glasgow working-class community living through the dark days of the Depression and the Second World War. The lives and loves of the people of Clydend are vividly and absorbingly depicted—people like Catriona, a young woman trying to cope with an overbearing husband; the baker Baldy Fowler and his tragic wife; Alec Jackson, the philandering insurance salesman; and a host of other characters who face up to the ordinary challenges of life and the extraordinary challenges of war with honesty, optimism and hope. Available for the first time in one volume.

'Mrs Davis catches the time with honest-to-goodness certainty'
THE GUARDIAN

THE DARK SIDE OF PLEASURE

A powerful story of passion and tragedy set in early Victorian Glasgow, *The Dark Side of Pleasure* chronicles the rise and fall of two families—the wealthy and respectable Camerons, and the Gunnets, desperate people who will do anything to escape the poverty of the slums. Alfred Cameron, the owner of a prosperous coaching firm, his wife Felicity and their beautiful daughter Augusta enjoy a life of privilege and luxury, surrounded by servants and the trappings of success. But the family firm is in danger—threatened by the encroaching railways, and undermined from within by Luther Gunnet, a ruthlessly ambitious man who will do anything to raise his family from the slums.

LIGHT AND DARK

Set in Edinburgh and West Lothian at the end of the Victorian era, *Light and Dark* is the powerful story of the Blackwood family—Lorianna, a beautiful young woman, married at sixteen to a considerably older man; Gavin, her austere and sanctimonious husband; and Clementina, their wild and wayward daughter who grows up rebelling against everything her parents stand for. The Blackwoods appear to live an affluent and normal family life in their impressive mansion, but things are not quite what they seem, and the whole family are about to be engulfed in a dreadful tragedy that will overshadow the rest of their lives.

'Passionate, steamy and a tear-jerker of the first order'
GLASGOW HERALD